"The sexiest and edgiest of the Bodyguards books yet. You'll feel like you're right in the thick of the conflict."

—*Writers Unlimited*

"An intense escape from cold weather and winter doldrums."

—*Fresh Fiction*

"Spectacular. . . . Gerard's best book yet! A masterpiece of tight scenes, excellent dialogue, steamy sex, and heart-stopping adventure. You'll be thinking of this one long after it's finished."

—*Romance Readers Connection*

"Moves fast and is both a tightly-woven thriller and a beautiful, sexy romance. . . . Outstanding series."

—*Reader to Reader*

"Fantastic story . . . heart-pounding action."

—*Romance Divas*

"Fast-moving story, which has suspense and sexual tension moving in parallel. Characters are extremely well drawn. . . . First-time readers will no doubt start seeking Gerard's prior books in the Bodyguard series, which in reality is one of the greatest tributes to an author. This one is strongly recommended."

—*The Romance Reader*

TO THE LIMIT

"A super action-packed investigative thriller."

—BarnesandNoble.com

"Gerard has done an excellent job capturing the same blend of action and lust that powered her first book in this series, *To the Edge*. Though reading the books in order is a plus, this is one tale that can stand on its own. The characters are riveting, the action fast-paced, and the storyline superbly created. This is a great tale that lets you appreciate the slower pace of your own life while reveling in the adventures of the heroine."

—*Fresh Fiction*

"A real page-turner with wonderful chemistry between our two main characters . . . readers will be drawn into the story."

—*Romance Designs*

"This second book in Gerard's 'The Bodyguard' series is even better than the first, *To the Edge* . . . taut, suspenseful . . . filled with action, sizzling sex scenes, and fascinating settings and situations."

—*Romance Readers Connection*

"Engaging . . . as always the action keeps rolling along, the interaction and dialogue is swift and cutting, and the romance is oh so satisfying to witness. Kudos for Cindy; she's done it again. A definite keeper!"

—*A Romance Review*

"Edgy, exciting, and sexy with two fabulous lead characters and a cleverly done mystery. This story doesn't just sizzle, it blazes."

—*Romance Reader at Heart*

TO THE EDGE

"Edgy and intense, this tale of romance, danger, and past regrets is a keeper."

—*Romantic Times*

"A tense, sexy story filled with danger . . . romantic suspense at its best."

—Kay Hooper, *New York Times* bestselling author

"Heart-thumping thrills, sleek sensuality, and unforgettable characters. I have one word for Nolan Garrett. Yum!"

—Vicki Lewis Thompson, *New York Times* bestselling author of *Nerds Like It Hot*

UNDER THE
WIRE

BOOK FIVE IN THE BODYGUARDS SERIES

CINDY GERARD

St. Martin's Paperbacks

This is a work of fiction. All of the characters, organizations and events portrayed in this novel are either products of the author's imagination or are used fictitiously.

UNDER THE WIRE

Copyright © 2006 by Cindy Gerard.
Excerpt from *Into the Dark* copyright © 2006 by Cindy Gerard.

ISBN: 0-312-98104-X
EAN: 9780312-98104-4

Printed in the United States of America

St. Martin's Paperbacks edition / December 2006

St. Martin's Paperbacks are published by St. Martin's Press, 175 Fifth Avenue, New York, NY 10010.

10 9 8 7 6 5 4 3 2 1

As always, this book is dedicated to the brave men and women of the U.S. military who defend, on a daily basis, all that we hold dear.

Also to my sisters in the trenches—you know who you are. May you always meet your deadlines, always make the lists, and always know that I answer to "friend."

AUTHOR'S NOTE

I had a wonderful time researching this book. Some of my sources include *Sri Lanka*, Edition 2, Bradt Travel Guide, written by Royston Ellis; *Sri Lanka*, 9th edition, Lonely Planet Publications, written by Richard Plunkett and Brigitte Ellemor; *Insight Compact Guide: Sri Lanka*, written by Martina Meithig; and the Lonely Planet *Sinhala Phrasebook*, 2nd edition, written by Swarna Pragnaratne.

Through reading these wonderful books and consulting various maps, I fell in love with Sri Lanka, its beauty, its cultural diversity, and its stunning and varied topography, which ranges from the diamond blue waters of the coastal cities, to the arid region of the north, to the lush and exotic beauty of the rain forests. It is my fondest hope to someday visit this amazing place. Just as it is my hope that the people of Sri Lanka may someday see total peace between the Sinhalese and the Tamil.

For the sake of the story and in an attempt to showcase Sri Lanka's incredible beauty, I took many liberties with location and geography. The same can be said for the portions of the book set in Nicaragua. Many places are real. Many, however, have been fabricated to enhance and entertain but were drawn from various areas of the country and do actually exist—only NOT where I put them. I take full responsibility for those calculated errors.

Special thanks to:

SSG Ian Trammell, USAREC, my go-to guy for all big things that go boom.

Mark Pfeiffer from the Weapons Info news group for his generous and expert assistance in pinpointing appropriate weaponry.

Gail Barrett, for her generosity of time with my Spanish translations, and the always resourceful KOD-CNN loop for putting me in touch with Gail, who consulted her friends Kuni Takebe of Spain and Margarita Unger of Colombia.

Sgt. George Sanchez—my Nicaragua connection and stand-up soldier.

And last but not least, Tommy—for putting up with deadline dilemmas and settling for frozen pizza too many times while I finished this book.

PART I

Nicaragua, in the midst of the Contra revolution against the communist Sandinista government, seventeen years ago

CHAPTER 1

Manny Ortega awoke from a dead sleep. Fully alert. All senses vibrating with awareness.

The sharp crack of breaking wood splintered the night silence like a gunshot. A blinding light pierced his eyes like a needle and glinted off the barrel of a Simonov carbine locked dead center on his chest.

Four Sandinista soldiers towered over his rumpled bed. Their faces were hard. Their weapons, ranging from the SKS to an AK-47 and a pair of Tokarev pistols, were drawn. The emblems on their uniforms identified them as members of Gen. Jorge Poveda's death squad.

Dios.

Trouble didn't get any deeper than this.

Yet Manny's first thought was to protect his lover. He reached for her, but Lily was gone. He was alone in the bed that smelled of sleep and sex and the scent of her. The tangled sheets beside him and under his palm were as cool as the night breeze drifting in through the open window. Relief that Lily was safe registered peripherally as a hard boot hit him midthigh.

"Levántate, perro traicionero, o te matamos ahí mismo." *Get up, traitorous dog, or we will kill you where you lie.*

Manny shifted from shock to self-preservation mode. He raised his hands, smiled, and did what he did best: lied through his teeth.

"¿Traidor? Amigos, tienen al hombre equivocado. Soy uno de ustedes." *Traitor? Friends, you've got the wrong man. I'm one of you.*

He nodded toward their uniforms—the same uniform he wore, although his reasons for wearing it were much different from theirs. "Soy Manolo Ortega. El teniente Ortega." *I am Manolo Ortega. Lieutenant Ortega.*

"Sabemos quién eres, marrano contra. Y también lo sabe el general. Porque su puta americana, ella también abrió las piernas para tu placer, ¿eh? Y tú le dices todo." *We know who you are, Contra pig. So does the general. Because his American whore, she spread her legs for you, too, eh? And you tell her everything.*

Pain exploded through his head as the butt of the SKS slammed into his temple. He fought both dizzying nausea and the blinding effect of the blow as they dragged him from the bed, then ordered him to pull on his pants. Blood ran down his face and into his eyes as they shoved him, barefoot and shirtless, at gunpoint from his sister's third-floor apartment, where he'd spent the last week with Lily.

His American whore . . . you tell her everything . . .

The soldier's words hit Manny full in the face as he stumbled down the stairs.

Poveda's whore? Lily?

Manny didn't want to believe it. But they could only be talking of Lily Campora of the diamond black eyes and beautiful smile.

No torture the tyrannical general could inflict now that he knew Manny was a spy for the freedom fighters could be as painful as thinking Lily might have betrayed him.

He didn't want to believe it. And yet . . . she was gone. As if she had known Poveda's men were coming for him.

Betrayed.

He had been betrayed.

He'd been a fool.

And now he was a dead man.

His eyes burned from the blood and the sting of anger. He could not bear to think that the woman he loved could have turned him in. But why else—*how* else—would Poveda have found a reason to send his thugs and brand Manny a traitor? The things he had told Lily in the dark of night, naked and spent, he had told no one else. So what other explanation could there be?

He could not think of that now. If he wanted to live, he could not think of *her* now. He had to figure out how to get out of this. Then he would deal with Lily Campora.

Anger rolled over his heartbreak. Resolve kicked him into survival mode. Talking himself free was not an option. Poveda's soldiers did not want to hear anything he had to say. He was on his way to prison—if he made it that far.

The Managua streets were midnight dark and as deserted as a ghost town when they hauled him roughly to an open military jeep, then took off down the pocked and cracked pavement.

The rope cut into his wrists where they'd tied his hands behind his back. Already he could feel the loss of circulation in his fingers. The business end of the SKS was still aimed at his heart.

And he was running out of time.

He glanced at the soldier riding shotgun in the front seat. Recognized him, though he'd never met him. Garcia. Poveda's hatchet man. Specialized, it was said, in using a stiletto. Garcia also had a penchant for employing electricity to make his victims talk. He particularly enjoyed using it on freedom fighters.

Manny didn't recognize the driver or, in the seat at Manny's side, the young corporal with the SKS. He watched Manny like a hawk, his eyes narrowed and intent on Manny's face.

Well trained, Manny thought. *Always watch a man's eyes. They are telegraphs to his thoughts.* For that reason, Manny kept his eyes as blank as white paper.

The jeep rumbled past the airport on the outskirts of the city, then turned off Carrtera Norte and onto a back road; he didn't let on that he'd figured out where they were taking him. He'd heard of the torture camps deep in the jungles. And he knew of no one who survived them—which was why he could not let the soldiers take him that far.

Miles and maybe an hour went by. The city grew distant. Up ahead he saw the glimmer of moonlight bouncing off water and realized they were approaching the Rio Tipitapa Bridge.

He didn't so much as glance ahead or to the side.

He sat. He waited. Hunched over as if still dazed from the blow to his head and resigned to his fate. They would soon find out he was far from it.

The city lights were a memory as the jeep hit a slight incline leading to the narrow stone bridge he had known was coming up. Manny counted to five, then made his move.

With a sharp kick at his guard's chest, Manny dislodged the SKS long enough to sway the barrel up and away from him. The rifle discharged wildly into the air; the fire flash shot from the end of the barrel like mini volcanic eruptions as he stood and leaped from the moving vehicle.

He landed on the pavement with a bone-jarring jolt, then rolled like a square wooden wheel. His shoulder and hip screamed in pain, but he forced himself to his feet to the serrated screech of squealing brakes and guttural shouts.

He didn't wait to see if the soldiers had drawn on him. Off balance with his hands tied, he vaulted to the stone rail of the bridge. Without a backward glance and swallowing back his fear of heights, he launched himself toward the muddy Tipitapa, flowing fifteen feet below.

The night exploded in a hail of gunfire just before he hit the surface of the rapidly running river. The current sucked him under. He shot toward the riverbed like a bullet, found the silty bottom with his feet, and, praying he had the lung power, pushed off.

His lungs burned. His throat ached. But finally, he surfaced. On a gasping breath, he shook the water from his eyes. Then for the first time since Poveda's men had shattered his sleep and his illusions about Lily, he found something to smile about. The swift-running current had already carried him fifty yards downriver. This far from the bridge, there was no way the soldiers could spot him in the inky black night.

It was the rainy season, *gracias a Dios,* or he'd more than likely have broken both ankles landing in two feet of water instead of fifteen. His smile was short-lived. The current sucked him down again in a vortex of speed and suffocating darkness. Without the use of his arms, the river rolled him like a deadhead—a waterlogged stump— spinning him out of control. The harder he fought, the deeper the river took him.

Holding his breath, battling unconsciousness, he forced himself to relax, to sink to the bottom again, then pushed off with a prayer. For the second time, he broke the surface with a gasp, coughing mud-clogged water and sucking air. He was a good hundred yards downriver now. The jungle had thickened like a gray-green fog, closing in on the meandering path that years of spring and summer floods had cut into the bank as the Tipitapa flowed toward Lago de Nicaragua a hundred miles downstream.

It wasn't until his third trip down that he figured out what to do. The only way to fight the current and gravity was to go with it. When he surfaced the next time, he spread his legs and, using them as rudders, rode the river.

With concentrated effort, he let himself be a log instead of fighting the fact that he was one. Logs float. So he floated. Coughing and spitting and gasping for air. Sometimes on his back. Sometimes on his belly. However the river wanted him. But always with an eye toward the shore, searching for an opportunity to beach himself. But the night was dark; it was difficult to see, and staying afloat took most of his concentration.

He didn't know how long he drifted that way. Long enough that his strength had faded. And he suspected he knew the reason why.

Besides the bump and gash on his head from the rifle blow, one of the soldiers had gotten lucky. As Manny was free-falling off the bridge, he'd felt the round connect with his shoulder. Felt the slice, felt the burn.

And now he felt the effect of the blood loss.

Light-headedness. Fatigue. And for the first time, disorientation.

A wave of darkness hit him and he sank under again. He battled the urge to struggle. Slowly let himself drift to the surface and grabbed the breath he desperately

needed. He fought for his life. Fought the chills that
overtook him in the depths of this hot summer night.
Made himself stay relaxed so he wouldn't sink like a
stone again.

And then he was combating something that snagged
at his legs. Grabbed at his feet.

Panic hit before understanding, and with it an adrenaline spike that revived him. The Tipitapa was home to
any number of night stalkers—including the only fresh-
water sharks in the world. And if the bull sharks didn't
get him, there was a good chance a bushmaster would.
He'd never tangled with a pit viper but knew that one
venomous bite from the monster snake could kill a man
in minutes. He prayed to God he wouldn't have to fight
the snake now. It was a battle he could never win.

He kicked for his life and managed only to become
more entangled. And that's when it hit him. Brush. He'd
hit a patch of brush. Which could mean a downed tree.

Which meant shoreline.

Tree branches, not a shark or a snake, had latched on
to his pant legs and ended his free float down the river.

He was saved. And yet this saving grace could be the
death of him as the current and the brush sucked him under one more time.

One more time, Manny surfaced, his lungs screaming
for oxygen, his head pounding from the pressure. He had
to figure out a way to break free, yet use the tree to keep
him from floating away or sucking him under again.
Each time he'd gone down, it had become harder to come
up. He strongly suspected he had very few resurrections
left in him.

Drawing on the last of his reservoir of strength, he
dug deep and threw a leg over what felt like a stout arm

of the tree. The serrated rip of tearing fabric blended with the sounds of the rushing river and his panting breath. When he felt a connection, he clamped his thighs together like a vise and heaved his weight into righting himself.

He fell face-first on the log, teetered like a tightrope walker as his St. Christopher medal clinked softly against it. Chest heaving, he used his chin, his shoulders, his forehead; he levered himself upright. The river waked around his hips, strong and determined to knock him from his perch.

But he hung on.

Gasping for breath. Fighting the pain that screamed through his arm and head. Pain that kept him clinging to consciousness. And conviction.

No way was he going back into that spin cycle. This, he understood, was his last chance. If he fell back into the river, he was done for and Poveda would have won. That fact, above all, kept Manny going.

He shook his head. The deluge of pain cleared the cobwebs. Battling for balance, he straddled the tree trunk and fought to orient himself to his position. The night was dark, but a sliver of moonlight skimmed the rippling water. Beyond, he could make out the riverbank. See the roots of the downed madrono tree that held him, the base of its trunk disappearing into the water some thirty feet away.

Thirty feet that separated him from drowning.

On a bracing breath, he leaned back, just far enough so he could reach the tree with his hands and gain a measure of balance. Now, if he could only *feel* his hands.

Inch by cautious inch, he pushed forward, his eyes on

the bank, his mind blank of anything but reaching his goal. He didn't think of the pain. He didn't think about falling. He didn't think about the clammy night air that cooled his bare, wet skin and made him shiver. Didn't think about the dizzying rush of water beneath him or the light-headedness that made him nauseous.

Most of all, he didn't think about Lily. To think of her would make him weak. To think of her betrayal would make him want to die.

So he pressed forward at a snail's pace. It felt like years. A century passed as mosquitoes bit him incessantly and night creatures slithered along the surface and brushed against his bare feet.

Finally, his toes touched mud.

Gracias a Dios.

Relief ran as deep as the night. He was utterly exhausted, barely conscious. Muscle memory and guts propelled him as he threw his leg over the log—and sank up to his chest in thick, muddy water and muck.

He sucked in a wheezing breath when the cool water rushed over the inside of his thighs that had been scraped raw from grating across the madrono bark. His arm throbbed and burned like someone had nailed him with a branding iron. His head pounded.

He had no feeling in his hands. No conception of time as he half-stumbled, half-crawled his way out of the water. Digging with his chin, his shoulders . . . knees, toes, whatever it took . . . he worked his way up the steep, muddy bank.

Where he collapsed on the ground. Facedown. Covered in muck. The religious medal hanging from his neck slapped him in the face when he dropped.

Darkness sucked him under like the river. He passed out cold—passed out deep. And alone with his tormented body and mind, he dreamed fitful dreams of Lily.

Of the first time he'd seen her beautiful, treacherous face.

CHAPTER 2

Lily needed air. And she needed it now. Even more, she needed to get out of this crowd.

It wasn't proper. It wasn't politically correct, but Lily Campora couldn't take another second of the oh-so-polite, oh-so-porous posturing of the thirty or so guests milling about inside Gen. Jorge Poveda's garishly opulent home.

She no longer cared that she represented her Doctors Without Borders medical team stationed here in Managua. It no longer mattered that her attendance at this sham of a celebration was the equivalent of a mandate issued by the grandiose military leader of Nicaragua's communist Sandinista regime. She could no longer tolerate the boorish general's subtle but aggressive attempts to seduce her.

She abhorred Poveda, despised all he stood for, and if she didn't get away from him soon she was going to do or say something she'd regret. Something that, in this war-torn country, could place her and her DWB team in a volatile and dangerous situation.

So she left. Slipped silently out the double French doors and onto the terrace where she could be alone in the humid Central American night.

Alone to think. Alone to grieve over news she'd barely had time to absorb. To deal with the guilt that had been carving on her conscience all evening like a rusty knife.

Kara Kaiser was dead.

Lily still couldn't believe it.

The night was warm and sultry. The soft breeze was scented of the bougainvillea-draped terrace and of sea salt from the southernmost waters of the North Pacific. Yet a chill cut to the bone when she thought back to the horrible news she'd received only minutes before she'd had to leave for this grueling dinner party.

Kara was dead.

A tear fell—the first Lily had let herself shed—as she stood at the ornately crafted concrete rail surrounding the stone terrace. She stared without seeing at the lush tropical gardens beyond and thought back to the moment this afternoon when Dr. Russell Davis, her DWB team's head surgeon, had come to the tent she had shared with Kara at the clinic compound.

One look at his eyes and Lily had known something terrible had happened. The strain on Russ's face foreshadowed news that could only be grim.

"What? What's wrong?"

He'd sat down on Lily's cot; his legs had just sort of folded, like the weight he carried was too much to bear.

A terrified trepidation had filled Lily's chest as she waited for Russ to gather himself.

"We lost Kara," he finally said, looking weary and old for someone so vibrant and young.

No soft soap. No buffer to ease the way.

We lost Kara.

"Oh God."

Russ had buried his head in his hands. "They were evacuating an injured child from Jinotega to Managua. The pilot radioed that he was experiencing engine trouble. That was at noon. We didn't hear anything more until a few minutes ago. A search party found the bird.

"Jesus, Lily." Tears had misted the generally unflappable doctor's eyes when he looked up at her. "No one survived the crash."

Lily's heart had stopped. So had her world. Kara Kaiser, like Lily, was one of six nurses on the team who had worked side by side in the fetid, draining heat for the past six months. Because Lily had drawn the short straw and gotten herself delegated to represent the team at this damn gathering tonight, Kara had taken Lily's run in the chopper today.

Muffled laughter bled outside to the terrace. Lily touched trembling fingertips to her lips, wishing she were anywhere but here. Each month, the pompous general bestowed platitudes and long-winded speeches, and personally decorated "heroes" for the benefit of the invited press. Each month, one of the DWB team members dutifully attended at Poveda's request. Playing his nasty game lessened the chances of their visas being arbitrarily revoked, which would force the team to leave before their work with the mudslide victims of Nicaragua was done.

Before their work was done.

Kara's work was done.

Kara's life was over.

Tears trickled down Lily's face. Why had this happened? Why was there so much suffering—not just here but all over the world? And why, at twenty-eight, did Lily feel like an old and used-up soul?

She should have been dead, not Kara, who was barely twenty-two and wide-eyed, her spirit not yet sullied by the grim reality of life.

Guilt, crushing and relentless, weighed like lead.

Grief, absolute and consuming, suffocated her.

And heaped over it all was the resounding awareness of her own mortality. Like Kara's, Lily's life could be over in a heartbeat. And what would Lily have to show for it? A bad, childless marriage that had ended over a year ago after lasting five years too long. A career where she saw more pain and suffering than the bandages she regularly applied could heal. An existence void of anything but work.

God, she was tired. She braced the flat of her palms on the terrace rail. Regret, for a life that had begun with so much promise but had digressed to one tragic scene of poverty, disease and despair after another, drained her of what spirit she had left.

She felt empty. Empty and wholly, achingly alone.

"Senorita."

Startled, she looked over her shoulder. A young soldier approached her, his smile tentative as if he were afraid she might run.

She thought about it. About running, not necessarily from him, but from her life. The weight of it. The pain of it. The recurrent cycle of sameness.

But then she looked into his eyes. And it struck her. Here was something different. Here was someone different.

"It is a beautiful night, yes?" he asked in a wonderfully accented English that, combined with his equally beautiful presence, both intrigued and anchored her where she stood.

"Yes," she agreed. "Beautiful."

Before barely an hour passed, and against everything Lily stood for, she agreed to much, much more.

———

Her name was Lily. Lily Campora. Stunning. Beautiful. American. And before the night was over, Manny was determined to make her smile for him . . . perhaps even more than smile.

All evening, as he'd endured Gen. Poveda's "celebration" dinner, Manny had been waiting for his chance to be alone with her. When he saw her slip quietly outside of Poveda's grandiose and palatial house, Manny waited a few minutes, then followed her out to the secluded terrace.

As she had when he'd first set eyes on her, she took his breath away.

"Senorita." He approached her tentatively, afraid she might be startled when he walked up behind her. "It is a beautiful night, yes?"

Her head came up. She sniffed delicately and wiped the back of her hand over her cheek before glancing over her shoulder at him. "Beautiful," she agreed, and looked away.

Then she walked away. Not far. Only a few steps down the terrace railing where pink and white bougainvillea twined and clung. Still, it was far enough to let Manny know she did not welcome company.

The gesture was small deterrent for a man on a mission. Even before he had found her out here alone with the weight of tears glimmering on lashes as dark and thick as the heavy fall of black hair tumbling down her back, he'd recognized the sorrow and despair etched in her eyes. Eyes the color of a midnight sky and set in the most extraordinary face—a face that had mesmerized him through each of the five dinner courses.

Hers was an angel's face—porcelain skin, delicate brows, Cupid's-bow lips that had rarely tipped into a smile all evening. Even then those smiles had been forced. Yes, she had an angel's face. So appropriate, because Manny knew that she was an angel. An angel of mercy who was being honored tonight for her service with her American DWB medical team. Just as he was being honored by the Sandinista government for his bravery as a soldier.

The bitterness he felt over that dubious honor and the hatred he felt for Poveda and all he stood for were overshadowed in this moment by his concern for the beautiful American.

So he ignored her subtle attempt to get rid of him. He'd waited all night for a chance to get her alone. He was going to take full advantage. "It is too beautiful a night to spend alone and unhappy, would you agree?"

She was quiet for a time, then turned to face him with a look that relayed controlled patience. "You're very kind—"

"But," he preempted, knowing she was about to launch another dismissal, "you would much prefer it if I left you alone."

She tilted her head, studied him with more tolerance than interest, then reluctantly glanced at the emblem on his uniform. "Lieutenant, is it?"

He bowed, clicked his heels together in an exaggerated show of military élan. "At your disposal, Senorita Campora."

To the tilt of her head she added a slight narrowing of her eyes. "You know my name."

"I made it a point to, yes."

Her back stiffened marginally. "I'm afraid you have me at a disadvantage."

"Oh no, senorita, it is I who am at a disadvantage. Your beauty has . . . how do you say in English?" He frowned, then flashed his most guileless grin. "Ah . . . it comes to me. Your beauty has left me without speech."

One corner of her beautiful mouth tipped up into an almost smile. She found him amusing—perhaps even ridiculous. That was fine. He would take her smiles however he could get them.

"Speechless?" She shook her head. "That's a hard sell, Lieutenant, considering you haven't stopped talking since you walked out here."

"This is true," he admitted, smiling with her. He lifted a hand, a show of agreement. "Maybe my words, they were not so right. My English sometimes . . . is not so good." His English was fine, but pretending otherwise better suited his purpose tonight. "Maybe 'senseless' is the term I am searching for."

Another slow, soft smile had Manny's heart swelling—along with another body part that had been on the verge of response since he first saw her.

"Tell me," she continued, her interest piqued even though he could see that she was hesitant to allow herself this small curiosity. "How does one so young become such an accomplished flirt? And a lieutenant to boot."

"Flirt?" He pressed a hand to his chest, feigning innocence and shock, then negating both with a self-deprecating grin. "But no. I only meant to make you smile. Tears on such a beautiful woman . . . no. It is not right. And I am not so young as you might think," he assured her with a slight bow. "Manolo Ortega. And I'm very pleased to finally meet you."

Again, she was tentative, but he knew he held her interest when she allowed herself another question. "Finally?"

"It has been an eternity since I first saw you at the far end of the table at dinner."

She shook her head with a "give me a break" roll of her expressive eyes. "Let's amend that to 'very accomplished flirt.' "

Manny took a chance and walked closer; he leaned an elbow on the concrete rail, plucked a flower from a bougainvillea vine, and grinned up at her. "You misinterpret my intentions."

"Do I?"

He touched the pink petals of the flower to her bare shoulder, let it trail slowly down her arm, then drop away when she stiffened. "It is just that you are so sad. And now, no matter how hard I try to make you happy, for some reason you don't feel you deserve to be. And that knowledge hurts my heart."

He offered her the flower.

Her eyes softened, misted over, before she accepted his gift. "Okay. So maybe you're not so young after all."

Her tears weren't the only giveaway. The quiet regret in her words also told him that he'd been right. She was desperately unhappy—which made him more resolved than ever to make her forget that pain.

And yes, he would make her forget, because about one thing she was correct. He was an accomplished flirt. He was also a very determined man.

"So, Lily, what should we do with you, do you think?"

She was still guarded, but she turned to face him again, leaning a slim hip against the terrace rail. "We?"

"But yes. In my experience," he said, intrigued by the play of moonlight over her ivory skin and by the lovely curve where her neck met her shoulder, "two make things so much better than one, alone. Especially on a night like this. For instance, have you even noticed the stars?"

She breathed in the flower, glanced guiltily at the sky, then back at him. "Actually . . . no."

"Well then, you see? It was meant to be. What you do not appreciate by yourself, I can help you enjoy. Now you must look again. Up, up," he insisted when he was met with an impatient sigh. "I will point out what you have missed out here on your own."

If for no other reason than to placate him, she tipped her head back.

"Amazing, is it not?"

She gave a reluctant nod. "Yes. It's quite beautiful."

"Do you have skies like this in America, Lily? Ink black and glittering with brilliant prisms of light?"

"We do, yes," she said after a moment, then made an admission that seemed to surprise her. "But it's been a long time since I've taken time to stargaze."

"Too long, I am thinking."

She startled when he pushed away from the rail and moved in close behind her.

"Much too long. A woman as lovely as you should always have stars in her eyes.

"Look there," he said when he sensed she was about to put some distance between them. "Do you see the one directly above? The one that shines blue?"

When she appeared to be searching and not finding, he took her hand in his, lifted it skyward, and pointed due west. "Just there. Do you see it now?"

Her skin beneath his fingers was as petal soft as the flower. Summer warm. Her scent, this close, was fresh and clean and undeniably woman. And the tension that he sensed tighten her slight body made a transition from uncertainty to awareness. Awareness that he was only too pleased to awaken.

Yes, she was still resistant, but she was aware of his intentions to seduce her—he'd made no bones about that. Aware that she was more open to the idea of pleasure, just for herself, than she might have thought.

"I . . . I'm not certain."

Manny was. He was certain they were no longer talking about stars. What she was uncertain about was the sexual tension arcing between. A tension that had shifted to something profound the moment he'd touched her.

And he was certain that before this night was over, not only would the beautiful Lily smile for him, but she would also undress for him. Open her lovely legs for him, take pleasure from him in the most intimate way that a man could pleasure a woman, and she would forget all about her pain.

"There," he whispered, pressing his cheek to hers and with his hand at her throat tipping her head ever so slightly upward. "Just there . . . do you see it now?"

Nuzzling her hair aside, he touched his lips to the pulse that jumped wildly at her throat. When she didn't resist, he slid one hand around her small waist, folded the hand that was holding hers in and against her body.

He held her that way for long moments. Letting her get used to the feel of him. To the idea of succumbing to the allure of the undeniable sexual spark arcing between them.

The notion of acting on such an attraction to a stranger was foreign to a woman like her. He understood that. Just like he understood the moment she decided to surrender.

Her head fell back against his shoulder. A shuddering breath eddied out; beneath the modest neckline of her black dress her generous breasts rose and fell; the tight little beads of her nipples pressing against raw silk spoke of her arousal.

And yet she resisted. "I . . . I should go back . . . inside."

Poor Lily. It seemed she was programmed to resist, yet he took heart when she didn't move away from him.

In a voice as soft as the night breeze, he challenged her. "Do you always do what you should do? Have you ever, even once, considered doing something that only makes you happy?"

She didn't answer. But her body, heated now and trembling, told him everything he needed to know.

"What will make you happy, Lily?" he whispered against her ear. "Because that is all I want for you. You are a woman, I think, who deserves to be happy. And yet, you are so sad."

The breath she emitted was more need than denial, a heartbreaking sound that moved him deeply. With the slowest of caresses, he slid his hand from her waist to her belly, drew her back against his hips so she could feel the length and thickness of his erection pressing against her.

"I could make you think of nothing but me."

She pushed out a strained laugh and shivered in his arms. "Do I honestly look like a woman who would allow a stranger to seduce me?"

Ah. One last attempt to fight it.

"But no." He nuzzled along her neck and fed that little fire he wanted to stoke to an inferno. "And that is why you are so special. And why you look like a woman who needs to be seduced."

She trembled when he kissed her jaw, let her head fall

to the side, and allowed him to explore her throat with his mouth.

"I . . . this . . . my God." Her breath caught when he rocked his hips against hers. "What am I doing?"

"You are doing what comes natural, yes? You are responding like a woman. You are thinking of us." He lowered his voice to a raspy whisper. "Together. With my mouth here." He filled his palm with the generous weight of one breast.

"And here." Relentless, he slid his other hand with slow, hot friction down her belly to brush his fingers across her mound. "Just think of my mouth here, Lily."

She groaned and covered his hand with hers—initially, he thought she meant to push it away. Instead, she pressed him closer. He went rock hard.

"Come with me. I will make you forget everything but the moment."

She sucked in her breath on a gasp when he made another pass of his fingers across that place he was dying to taste.

"I don't know you. I must be crazy to even . . . to even think of going with you."

"Crazy? But no, *mi amor.* Lonely. You are but lonely. And hurting. Very badly, I think. Let me make it better."

And at this moment there was nothing Manny wanted more than to hear her lusty sighs of pleasure, smooth those lines of pain on her tragically beautiful face.

He turned her toward him, drew her against him until they meshed, belly to belly, breast to chest. She searched his eyes. Her breath feathered out, shallow and thready, telling him that her arousal was at a level that mirrored his. And yet she wavered.

"Pobrecita." *Poor little thing.* He folded her gently into

his arms then. Eased her cheek against his chest and held her. "Is it really so hard to do something just for yourself?" Ever so slowly, her arms wound around his waist.

"Casual sex . . . it's never been my strong suit. You must think . . . you must think that I'm foolish to be so skittish."

He drew back and framed her face in his palms, forcing her to look at him. "What I think is that you're beautiful. That this is a big step for you. And can you honestly believe that what I want from you is casual?"

Even he was surprised to realize there was nothing casual about it. He was a sexual being, yes. He was young. His blood ran hot. But the life he led did not allow for lasting love. Yet something . . . something about this woman intrigued him. Something he had yet to comprehend. He only knew he couldn't let her go. Not yet.

"How can it be anything but casual? You don't know me, either." Tears glistened again as she searched his face with those depthless black eyes.

He brushed silky hair away from her temples with his thumbs. "You are so wrong, Lily. I knew you the moment I saw you. I know you are gentle and kind and that your spirit does not break easily. Yet, tonight you cry."

Because he couldn't resist any longer, he lowered his mouth and kissed her. A gentle touch. An endless taste of this lush, amazing woman. A delicious beginning to what he was certain would be a very important event in his life.

Her lips were unbearably soft, achingly tentative, and tasted of both her sweetness and her tears. With great reluctance, he lifted his head, laced his fingers at her nape, and caressed her jaw with his thumbs. "So you see, I do know you, beautiful Lily. And it is important, I think, for you to know me, too.

"Come," he murmured between kisses. "Come with me."

His own heart beat as wildly as hers as he watched her face and waited.

For an eternity.

Maybe longer.

Until she finally smiled for him and with that small gesture of trust, agreed to let him take her anywhere he wanted to go.

CHAPTER 3

She was out of her mind. Over-the-top, certifiably insane, Lily thought as she allowed the seductive young Lieutenant Ortega to tuck her under his broad shoulder and steer her back inside the general's house. She stood mute as a post as the lieutenant convinced a darkly scowling Poveda that she was feeling ill and that Manolo would see her safely back to her quarters across the city.

At least that's what she thought the Latino soldier was saying. Though her Spanish had improved since she'd arrived in Managua five months ago, she still had some difficulty grasping the rapid-fire conversations between the locals. Had special difficulty tonight given that she was still reeling over the most instantaneous and arousing physical response she'd ever had to a man.

She followed enough of this particular conversation, however, to understand that in addition to being an accomplished flirt, Manolo Ortega was a skilled liar and an impressive negotiator. Poveda appeared suspicious, even angry—which could prove dangerous—but since it would be bad form to deny an ill woman's request to leave early, the general eventually relented.

Yes, the young soldier was a skilled manipulator, she thought again as she walked toward the front door beside him. And a practiced seducer of women—as were many of the men she'd encountered during her limited stay way, way south of the border.

So why haven't you let any of the others talk you into bed? Why this man?

Because, she admitted reluctantly, tonight she was more needy and more vulnerable than she'd realized. Because this man was outrageously attractive. And because his words were seductive and convincing. At least they had been in the moment. She'd needed to hear them. Needed to hear that she deserved to feel something other than lost and alone. And she so wanted to believe that something could make her forget about her empty life for a little while.

She brushed the bougainvillea blossom over her cheek and glanced up at him, at his bold, dark profile, his exotic good looks, and thought, *Why not?* She'd been a good girl all of her life. Good daughter. Good wife.

And what had it gotten her? She was a disappointment to her parents, who considered her nursing degree a failure because they had wanted her to be a doctor. She was divorced. A disappointment to herself—and apparently to the man whose interpretation of "forsaking all others" only applied if he didn't get caught.

Maybe Manolo Ortega was offering her exactly what she needed. Despite all of his insistence that this wouldn't be casual, that he *knew* her, knew who she was, and wanted something more with her, she suffered no illusions.

He was offering her nothing more than a no-strings, no-strain night of intimacy. A wild night with a virile younger man, a hot Latin lover.

But more than even that, he didn't know that he was offering relief from the real world that seemed to be closing in with grief. For Kara. For Lily's own life that had once been long on dreams but now seemed seeped in despair.

With his hand riding the small of her back, she let him walk her out the door toward an armed soldier who opened a tall, ornately scrolled iron gate and let them out of the fenced-in grounds.

"My sister has an apartment only a short walk from here." Manolo pulled Lily close to his side as they descended stone steps to street level. "She's out of the city on business and invited me to stay while I'm on leave."

If Lily was going to back out, now was the time to tell him that her moment of insanity had passed. That her brain had re-engaged and that one-night stands with young, sexy strangers were back on her "don't even think about it" list.

Yet she kept on walking. With the moon shining down, the warm, masculine scent of this impossibly gorgeous man holding her close against his side, the strong hand wrapped around her ribs hovering tantalizingly close to her breast, she kept on walking. Remembering the commanding presence of that hand on her breast, the touch of his fingers against that part of her that said yes a hundred times to every one time she'd tried to muster up a no.

How long *had* it been since she'd let a man touch her this way? A year? Longer? God, she couldn't even remember.

And how sad was that?

His kisses make me feel alive.

Alive. Yes. Lily needed to feel alive.

Because Kara was dead.

Lily stopped abruptly as guilt slapped her in the face. She stared at the sidewalk, then up at him.

He frowned, more concerned than curious. "Lily. There is that sad look again. The one I cannot bear to see."

"I'm sorry. I thought I could do this."

He touched a hand to her face. "So, so hard on yourself. What sin, sweet Lily, do you think you have committed that you cannot allow yourself one night of pleasure?"

A consuming ache filled her chest. "It's so easy for you, isn't it? Sex. Seduction. Living for the moment."

He looked charmingly perplexed. "But of course it is easy. It is natural, yes? God gave us this gift . . . for man to pleasure woman. For woman to pleasure man. The only sin is in denial. In not accepting His generosity."

The ache intensified, sweet and deep and knotted in yearning, and she waffled again. *Good Lord*. Why couldn't she just embrace what seemed so easy for him to accept? Quit being a wimp.

"It does not have to be so complicated," he said gently, making her weaken again in the face of the earnest guile in his dark eyes.

"Lily." He whispered her name in that way he had of breaking it into two words and making it sound as if he adored each one. Adored *her*. "Do not complicate things, *mi amor*. It is so simple. Just come. Come with me. You will see. I will show you how easy love can be."

He kissed her again then. In the middle of the street, with traffic going by, he kissed her, his amazing, skilled mouth manipulating her into a pliant longing to stop questioning this gift and make it hers.

Overcome suddenly by a helpless loneliness and a raw disillusion that weighed like lead, Lily gave up.

She accepted that if this seductive creature had approached her any other night, any other time, any other place, she'd have smiled at his bold daring, told him he was a beautiful man, and sent him on his way. But the wound of Kara's death was too fresh. The guilt that it hadn't been Lily was too raw. And the fatigue and sometimes heartbreak that accompanied her profession was all too weighty. The ambitious and boorish advances of Jorge Poveda added insult to the pain she was feeling—while Manny Ortega offered a beautiful, irresistible star to light a sky shrouded by the darkest of clouds.

She allowed herself the luxury, then, of getting lost in his smoldering kisses and burning black eyes. Let herself sink into his sexy, slashing smile that said he would make things better—at least for a little while.

A little while was all she needed.

Just a little respite.

Just a little release.

And acknowledgment that she was still a woman . . . with a woman's needs . . . a woman desperate for affirmation that she was vital and desirable and alive.

———

Manny undressed her slowly. It was the part he relished most. Watching her dark eyes shift from anxiety to anticipation. From anticipation to bold, achy need. From need to insatiable hunger. And his Lily—she had been hungry for a very long time. It showed in her gaze as she watched him. Resounded in her sighs when he but barely touched her.

Hungry. Yes. She was very hungry.

He would feed her. But first, he would feast. His eyes. His senses. His mouth.

She trembled as they stood beside the bed in a softly lit room that smelled of the sandalwood candle he had lit and of the woman whose skin he could not wait to expose inch by ivory inch.

"Your skin is amazing." Standing behind her, he lowered the zipper of her dress, and the creamy width of her back was revealed to him.

He pressed a kiss there along her spine, just between her shoulder blades, then ran his tongue up to her nape, humming his pleasure while he drew the dress off her shoulders and let it fall in a rustle of silk to the floor.

He kissed her neck, long, lingering kisses, and steeped himself in her scent. Slowly, he unhooked the back clasp of her black bra. Slower still, he lowered the satin straps down her arms, then filled his palms with the warm, luxurious weight of her bare breasts.

"*Mi amor,* I do not know how long I can wait to be inside you," he whispered, then turned her around so he could see her. "Beautiful. Heavy and full." Her nipples hardened as she watched him caress her.

Ah, yes. His Lily was starving. He wanted her ravenous. Greedy. And wonderfully impatient as she stepped out of her dress and stood before him only in black panties and slim high heels that made her legs look a mile long.

Watching her eyes, he unbuttoned his uniform jacket and tossed it aside. His shirt followed; then he sat down on the bed and drew her between his thighs. Her lovely breasts were at mouth level. With his hands gripping her waist, he drew her toward him. Savoring every moment, he bussed his nose around her velvety soft areola, absorbing the feel, the scent, the heat of her, and loving her response. Her soft sighs. Her slight trembling. Her wildly erratic heart rate. The unsteady cadence of her breath.

"You like that, *mi amor*?" he murmured when she lifted her hands to his shoulders and arched against his mouth. "Yes, I think you like that very much." He smiled against her breast and finally took her nipple with his mouth. Growling low in his throat, he opened wide, then laved and licked and sucked until the small hands gripping his shoulders clutched like talons and her sigh became a whimper.

On a low groan, he drew her deep inside his mouth and experienced her like he wanted to. With his own hunger and greed unchecked. With nipping teeth and questing tongue. He molded her in his mouth, taking as much pleasure as he gave, and fought the urge to tumble her back onto the bed and plow into her with all the finesse of a bull.

He made himself hold off. Lily was very fragile this night. She needed care. She needed special attention. He gave her both until he felt her knees buckle.

With a pleased chuckle, he gripped her by the waist. Turning at his hip, he laid her sideways across the bed. Then he stood and, very aware of her dark eyes watching him, stripped off the rest of his clothes.

"See what you do to me, darling Lily?"

She lifted a hand to touch and stroke his jutting erection. Again he smiled, but it was with great cost that he pulled away from her soft, inquisitive hand.

"Soon enough," he promised, and eased down to his knees by the bed. "There will be time for that soon enough," he repeated, and, gripping her slim calf, lifted her leg and removed first her left heel, then her right.

"Right now," he caressed her foot, lightly bit her calf, "I have something else in mind for you. And for me."

He watched her eyes go dark as he reached for her panties and slipped them down her hips. She hiked up on her elbows so she could see what he was doing. Her expression was one of shock and excitement as he brought the scrap of black lace to his face, inhaled deeply of her intoxicating woman scent and her arousal.

"Sexy woman." He breathed deep one last time, then tossed the panties to the floor.

"Will you open for me, Lily?" He covered her thighs with his hands, caressed. "Will you let me see you? Taste you? Make you come with my mouth?"

He'd shocked her again. And excited her. Her eyes were so expressive and so telling of her thoughts. Even before she opened her thighs, he'd known she would let him. And even before he draped her legs over his shoulders and gently parted her lips so he could see her lovely pink sex, he'd known she would shiver in anticipation and desire.

He skimmed his lips along her inner thigh where her skin was velvet soft and damp. "Do not look away. I want to see your eyes when I taste you. Give me that, Lily, and I will give you everything."

Her eyes were already glazed over as he lowered his mouth and kissed her there, where she was wet and hot and swollen. She jerked when he made the first sweep of his tongue, sucked in her breath on a gasp when he delved deeper, then, to his great pleasure, dissolved into a quivering mass of raw desire when he held her open with his fingers and gave her clitoris special attention. Tender nips. Slow licks. Lush, long kisses.

She collapsed back on the bed with a low, keening

moan when he sucked her. He closed his eyes and indulged. In the heady taste of her languor, the liquid flow of her quick-trigger release, the indefinable taste of a woman well beyond the edge of control.

Such need. Such honest abandon. Her response amazed him, humbled him, and took him to a place he'd never been with a woman. Now, as when he'd first seen her, she touched him in ways he didn't fully understand. Of only one thing was he certain: He could pleasure Lily Campora forever if she'd let him.

Long moments later, when she'd dissolved into a tangle of limp limbs, he crawled up the bed and covered her, sheathed himself inside her tight, giving heat. Pleasure, profound and pure, rushed through his body. He whispered her name, sank in and out of her . . . again and again and again, dragging her with him into oblivion.

And as he spilled himself inside her, drowned himself in her essence, the notion crossed his mind that forever with Lily might not be long enough.

———

Lily was naked, in a bed with a stranger, in a room bathed in moonlight and the soft glow of a flickering candle.

With great effort, she opened her eyes. A soft whisper feathered across her ear.

"You are awake, sweet Lily."

Oh yeah. She was awake. Awake and aware and wasted on the most incredible sex of her life. And despite the lingering flush of back-to-back liquid, electric orgasms, she was having huge second thoughts about the reckless decision that had led her to this bed.

She glanced up at her lover's questioning eyes. And

melted. Oh my. This man could be addictive. This darkly
handsome and very naked man lying beside her, who had
hiked himself up on an elbow and was frowning with
concern.

"You are all right, *mi amor*?"

She touched her hand to her head. "Apparently. I
thought the top of my head might have blown off, but it
seems all is well."

He chuckled and pressed a kiss to her bare shoulder.
The big hand that lay across her abdomen began a sensu-
ous kneading. "You make a joke. That makes me smile.
You are in a better place now, yes?"

She turned her head, looked at his slumberous black
eyes, his kiss-swollen lips, and wondered if there was a
more beautiful man anywhere on earth.

She mentally shook herself. *A better place,* he'd said.
That was debatable. She'd forgotten about Kara for a
while, yes. He'd seen to that. Lord, had he seen to that.
But a better place?

Her heart and her morality hit her a good one in the
chest. This had been a mistake. A huge, huge mistake.

"I'd better go." She sat up.

A gentle but firm tug on her arm brought her to her
back again. Dark brows knit together over eyes still filled
with concern. "Go? Lily, no. You want to go? You want to
leave this bed and my arms when we have barely gotten
to know each other? *¿Por qué?*"

He was hurt. She let out a deep breath, stared at the
ceiling, avoiding the Latin black eyes that could easily
suck her right back into the most lovely delights she'd
ever experienced.

Ever.

"This was . . . it was wonderful, Manolo—"

"No, no, no. You must call me Manny, *mi amor*. And yes, it was wonderful. But it is only the beginning for us. You will see."

It took every ounce of her resolve to shake her head. "Look. I really need to g—"

She sucked in her breath on a gasp as his big hand slid to her inner thigh, stroked, and sent a tingling shock of arousal along every erogenous zone in her body. It seemed that all he had to do was touch her and she went up in flames.

"Need . . . to . . ." she tried again as blunt-tipped fingers trailed enticingly along her hip point, waylaying her best intentions.

"Need . . . to . . . go," she finally managed in a voice made faint by his expert distractions and by the wild knocking of her heart.

"It should be against the law," he whispered, ignoring her and lowering his head to her breast, "for a body like yours to ever be covered by clothing."

Another feeble protest died on her lips when his amazing mouth opened over her nipple.

"A woman like you," he continued between eating, biting kisses and long, lush strokes of his tongue, "was made to be pleasured. Your body is so beautiful, Liliana."

He lifted his head, studied her glistening nipple as if it were a work of art, then turned to watch her face as he covered her mound with his palm and slipped a finger inside her.

She bit back a moan when he found her wet again and swollen.

"Yes, you need to be pleasured. Pleasured by me." His eyes grew dark, his voice gruff. "I could so easily fall in love with you, Lily."

Love, she thought fleetingly, was not on the table—or, in this case, the bed. Love, emotional love, was an illusion she was no longer certain she believed in.

But love, physical and fine, the way Manolo Ortega interpreted it, was something else. He could make her a believer.

She should go.

Instead, she closed her eyes, caught her breath on a gasp as sensations rose and built, and fed on the amazing manipulations of his mouth and fingers.

She arched sensuously, opened her legs wider. This couldn't be real. This couldn't be her. It was someone else naked in bed with this extraordinary lover whose deep, seductive voice rode the rhythm of words spoken in both English and Spanish. In either language, they were as thrilling as his touch.

"Tell me you do not want to leave me," he urged as he rolled to his back and brought her with him. He lifted her, fit himself to her opening, and, gripping her hips, slowly slid her down until he filled her, full and deep.

She sighed his name when he started moving inside her. Sweet friction. Amazing heat. Sensation spiked, scattered, and doubled back in on her, purging her of coherent thought. All her senses were tuned to that incredible place where their blood flowed the hottest, where he was the hardest and she . . . she was lost.

She felt her eyes roll back in her head, braced her palms on his broad, smooth chest, and rode him thrust for thrust, aching for release yet never wanting this exquisite pleasure to end.

She came with a breath-claiming burst of the most incredible force. It saturated her sensitive nerve endings, imploded through her body in a series of arching, electric shocks, pulsing through pleasure points she'd never known existed. Clenching her inner muscles, she clung to the rush, crying a little . . . dying a little . . . to hold on, to hold off . . . wishing it would never end as he pumped one last time and held her hips tight to his.

She thought she heard him swear—both in English and in Spanish—but the ringing in her ears muffled the words as she collapsed onto his chest, utterly destroyed.

He wrapped his arms around her, pressed his face into her neck, and together they drifted down, hearts hammering, breath ragged, stamina drained.

"Tell me you do not want to leave me, *querida*," he whispered urgently into her hair.

"I don't want to leave you," she murmured, obedient, acquiescent, wholly and totally giving up the fight.

———

Lily didn't leave him. Not for a moment during the next forty-eight hours. Manny had been given a week of leave, so she put in for a long overdue weekend off herself. For two days and two nights, they only left the bed long enough to eat—sometimes not even then—to shower, and to shop for food to sustain them.

When she had to go to work at the clinic on Monday, she couldn't get back to the apartment soon enough after her workday ended. She was, in a word, enthralled, no matter that she'd been determined not to be.

Manny Ortega, Lily quickly learned, was the most sensual, giving man she had ever encountered. He was also one of the most beautiful.

Poster perfect handsome, she thought Monday night, watching him sleep. She lay awake in bed beside him not wanting to wake him but unable to resist fingering the St. Christopher medal he wore around his neck.

Last night she'd told him how gorgeous he was.

He'd just grinned his sexy grin and taken it in stride. "As my momma says, my face, it will not break plates."

No. His face would not break plates, Lily thought, grinning over his refreshing lack of modesty. Hearts, yes. But not plates.

Even in sleep, everything about him was dazzling. She resisted the urge to run her fingers through his glossy black hair, full-bodied and lush; she loved touching it, playing with it. Although he kept it short—not military short but neat and well groomed—she suspected it would curl or at the very least wave if he let it grow. His skin was an amazing butter caramel color, as if he had a perpetual tan. Against her pale, prone-to-sunburn coloring, his skin tone was exotic and dark.

And it didn't end there. She was fascinated by every physical aspect of her lover—maybe more so because she wouldn't allow herself to become emotionally attached. Something she'd promised herself she would not do that very first night they'd spent together.

Beside her his body was hard and hot. He had the conditioning of an athlete, all taut muscle and sinewy lines beneath the skin that she so loved to touch. His chest was satin smooth, free of hair; his shoulders were broad, his waist and hips narrow, and the arms that held her in the night muscular and strong. Here and there were the marks of a soldier . . . narrow scars, thick scars that said he was all man. All warrior.

He was both a demanding and inventive lover and yet so sensitive to her needs . . . and to her pain. Earlier tonight, when she'd returned to the apartment from a memorial service for Kara, he'd taken one look at Lily's face and then he'd taken care of her.

He'd drawn her a bath, undressed her, and settled her into a warm tub of bubbles. After she'd soaked and cried, then cried some more, he'd wrapped her in a towel, dried her tenderly, brushed her hair, and taken her to bed.

Where he'd held her while she told him about Kara. Would have done nothing *but* hold her if she hadn't turned to him in the night and begged him to make love to her.

In his arms, she'd found everything. Everything she needed. For how long, she didn't know. She only knew that right now, what she had was enough.

CHAPTER 4

Sunlight filtered in through a long window as Lily sat at the table in Manny's sister's small kitchen the next morning, sipping strong, rich coffee and enjoying the sight of a naked and semiaroused man cooking her breakfast.

"How did you get like this?"

Unabashedly free of inhibitions, he glanced over a broad shoulder and grinned at her. "How did I get naked? I believe that was your doing, Liliana."

So it was. After all they had done together, she still blushed.

"Evolved," she said, picking up a slice of mango that he'd set out for them. "How did you get so evolved? I mean, in your culture . . . men are very macho, right?"

He laughed and expanded his chest. "Muy macho, sí."

She laughed, too, glad she hadn't offended him. "What I mean is, a man here takes care of his woman, but not in the kitchen."

"Yes, *chica bonita,* we take care of our women. My mother and my sister, they love me. They fuss over me. But they cannot cook. So in self-defense, I learn. From my father," he added with a wink.

He hadn't talked much about his family. Lily found

herself asking him now. "What does your father do?"

"He is an engineer."

"Really? What does he engineer?"

Manny set a plate heaped with fried plantains and eggs dripping with cheese in front of her. "Bridges. Commissioned by the Sandinista pigs. Bridges which I make certain are blown to bits."

He sat down across from her as if he hadn't just dropped a grenade big enough to blow her out of the kitchen.

"Excuse me?"

He glanced up at her, then away. "You should eat, Liliana. Before it goes cold."

"*Sandinista pigs?*" she repeated his words with building dread. "Manny? *You're* Sandinista. You wear the uniform."

It was an issue she had tried not to let bother her. He was just a man trying to make a living, and here, in Nicaragua, the army was often the best way to do that. For some, it was the only way. She understood. It was a means to an end. But she also understood that the Sandinista government was often cruel and oppressive to the general populace.

"Manny?" she pressed when he remained silent.

Finally, he relented. He leaned back, propped the heels of his palms on the table, and met her eyes. "Things are not always as they seem, *mi amor.*"

She sat back in her chair as the implication of what he *hadn't* said took root. Her pulse rate ratcheted up several beats. "You're not really Sandinista?" She held her breath.

He shrugged, forked a mouthful of eggs into his mouth, chewed thoughtfully, and seemed to come to a decision.

"No, Lily. I am not one of them—even though I share the same last name with President Ortega, I do not claim him as a relative."

Whatever relief Lily felt over knowing that Manny wasn't committed to Ortega and Poveda and his army of thugs was outweighed by concern. Nicaragua was a place of danger, intrigue, and civil war. And the man sitting before her, looking as if he didn't have a care in the world, was caught up in the middle of it.

"If you're not Sandinista . . . that leaves only one thing."

When he didn't dispute her, she felt her entire body go stiff with alarm. He was a freedom fighter. And that meant he was a spy against the government.

Oh God. While many in the world felt the Contra effort was the work of terrorists, her time in Nicaragua had shown her otherwise. The Contras were more than guerrillas attempting to overthrow a harsh and cruel regime. They truly were freedom fighters and they had the heart and the backing of not only the United States, who helped finance their fight, but also the silent majority of the people they were fighting to free.

And Manny was one of them.

Which meant he put his life on the line every hour of every day.

"Do not look so worried," he said, working on his breakfast as if he didn't have a care in the world.

Lily pushed out a humorless laugh. He'd infiltrated the communist army to obtain intelligence. That placed him in grave danger if anyone in the Sandinista camp were to find out.

"Worried? Why would I be worried? It's not like what you're doing is dangerous or foolhardy or—"

He reached across the table, covered her hand with his. Only then did she realize she was shaking.

So much for not getting emotionally involved.

"Not foolhardy, Lily. Necessary. You see the way our people are treated by the government? You of all people see the poverty and sickness and despair, yes? A fool would let it continue. I cannot."

She turned her palm up and linked her fingers tightly with his. "But Poveda . . . he's ruthless with those he considers traitors."

"Poveda is ruthless with all." Manny squeezed her hand, then resumed eating. "Now eat. You will need your strength for what I have in mind for you today, woman."

He was smiling, teasing, trying to steer her away from the truth of his perilous existence. But she had to know.

"How long? How long have you been . . ." She let the thought dangle, afraid to say it out loud.

"A spy?" He shrugged. "I joined the army at sixteen."

Lily lowered her head to her palm. "You were just a boy." A boy who had gone to war and become a man under fire. It was a way of life here. One she would never understand.

"Lily," he said gently. "It is the way. It is not—how do you say it? A big deal."

"The local newspapers are filled with notices every day about the fate of Contra rebels who dared fight the regime. They're tortured, hung, beheaded—all without trial. Sometimes people just . . . disappear and are never heard from again."

She pleaded with her eyes. "You can't minimize this. It is a *very* big deal."

He expelled a deep breath, sat back from the table, and evidently felt the need to explain. "It is not like in

America here. Here, we grow up as all boys do, yes. With a need to fight. But here, boys do not fight for sport. Not for fun or to show who is the most macho. We fight to protect. We fight to get back what the Sandinistas have taken from us. My father—he is a principled man. He made certain I saw the way of things."

"He encouraged you to fight?"

"With the Sandinistas in control you either become . . . how do you say it . . . immune? Yes. You become immune and ignore the suffering or you become a man. You turn your head when your family is robbed of their dignity and possessions or you fight."

He lifted a shoulder in a negligent shrug. "I choose to fight. It is still my choice."

"But that choice stole your childhood."

His eyes grew dark. "Poveda and his kind took care of that."

She looked away.

"I was a Boy Scout. Does that help?"

She pushed out a humorless laugh at his attempt to lighten the mood. "Something tells me that for you, Scouts wasn't a club where you got to go on weekend campouts."

Again he shrugged, as if it were of no consequence. "Yes, that is true. The Scouts were a means to an end. I learn survival there. I learn to make the knots that my life would someday depend on, to forage for food and water in the jungle that would one day keep me alive.

"And I learn that I like to meet the challenge of the jungle and know I can survive nights in the rain, days in the heat, even a fall from a cliff because my knot held."

She dragged the hair back from her face, expelled a heavy breath. "And did you learn how to be a spy there, too?"

Regardless that she was being sarcastic, a certain pride tinged his smile. "Yes, *mi amor.* I learned cunning and skill. When I joined the Sandinista army I was ready to do what was asked of me. If it means intercepting tactical information and feeding it to guerrillas, then that is what I do. I fight them by becoming one of them."

And he could die, she thought as a heavy sadness weighed on her heart. This beautiful young man whom she did not dare fall in love with could die tomorrow. Or next week. Or next year.

Her team would leave Nicaragua in less than a month and she would never see him again. Never know what happened to him. Never know so many things about him.

She could not fall in love.

And yet her heart melted every time she looked at him.

She was in so much trouble here.

"Come, Liliana. No more talk of fighting."

He held out his hand. She rose and rounded the table. With his dark eyes watchful, he opened her robe, pushed it off her shoulders, and let it fall to the floor. As naked as he, she straddled his lap. Offered him her breast, let her head fall back as he took her in his mouth with a swift and greedy possession.

Then she gave. Everything he'd given her, she gave back.

And knew it would never be enough.

———

"I've never met anyone like you," Lily whispered into the dark later that night.

Naked as the day she was born, she lay stretched out over the length of an equally naked Manny.

"That is a good thing, yes?" His voice was heavy with sleep, and yet that smug satisfaction she'd grown to love colored his words.

"Yes, Manolo." Grinning, she lifted her head, crossed her hands on his chest, and rested her chin there. "That is a very good thing."

A big, caressing hand slid over her bare hip. Drowsy and content, she hooked her pinkie around the chain that held his St. Christopher medal.

"So . . . these men who were once in your life—they were stupid? Lousy lovers? Unappreciative of the most amazing woman in the world?"

Deliriously sated, she grinned at him. "All of the above."

He made a sound of disgust. "American men. They are fools." He filled his palms with her buttocks and squeezed possessively. "My good luck.

"What?" he asked when she continued to watch him. "What are you thinking about so hard?"

"I don't know. It's just these past few days . . . you've made me realize some things," she began, hoping she could get this out right.

"That you love making love with me?"

His absolute absence of guile was refreshing. "That, too."

"And what else, *mi amor*? What else is on your mind tonight?"

He waited while she formed her thoughts. "I guess I've finally realized some things about myself."

"Such as?"

She played with the silver medal he was never without. "Such as it occurs to me that all my life I've—I've never felt I measured up. To expectations. To my potential."

"You are an amazing woman. How could you think such things?"

Because she was a constant disappointment to the family she'd wanted to please most. She didn't tell him that. She didn't want to dwell on it. "No matter, the end result was that I settled, you know? Settled for what I thought I deserved."

"You speak of your fool of an ex-husband?" he asked after a moment.

"Yeah. Him, too, I guess. But in general, I've settled for what I needed, but just barely."

He lifted a lock of her hair, wound it around his finger. "How so, Lily?"

She met his eyes in the dark bedroom and finally came up with a comparison. "Okay. Let's try this. If my life were a metaphor, it would be . . . water. Water is good. It's necessary. It's everything I need, but . . . it's not wine."

She kissed the medal, then touched it to his lips. He caught her fingertip with his teeth and she felt that special thrill he generated when his mouth opened and drew it inside. "Until you, Manolo, I never really tasted wine."

She searched his eyes in the dark, kissed him. Soft. Slow. Lingering. "You are wine to me, Manny. Delicious, intoxicating, unique. I want to thank you for giving me that."

The hand caressing her thigh traveled the length of her spine, scooped under the hair at her nape. With his thumbs beneath her jaw, he tipped her face up to his. "I love being your wine, *querida*." He touched his mouth to hers, whispered against her parted lips, "I love that you think of me that way."

A sudden sadness washed over her. They were running out of time. "I have to go back to the States soon."

He bussed his lips across hers. Cradled her face in his hands, then kissed her fiercely. "That does not have to be. Stay with me. Ti amo. Ti amo, Lily. You know that I love you."

It would be so easy to believe him. And so easy to return those words. *Ti amo.* I love you. But a summer fling—and she kept telling herself that's all this was—in an exotic country with an even more exotic young man did not a relationship make. Beautiful as he was, attentive as he was, they had no future. He couldn't leave his country and she couldn't stay.

And then there was the age issue.

"How old are you?" she'd asked before. He'd always danced around answering her. "Tell me this time. No dodging."

When he told her, she groaned.

Eighteen. *Eighteen, for God's sake.*

On some level, she'd suspected. But she'd hoped . . . God, she'd hoped she'd been wrong.

She couldn't stop a laugh. Dropped her forehead to his chest and shook her head. "I could get arrested back in the States for what we've done together."

"Then you have stupid laws in your country—just like in your country, that may be young. Not in mine."

On that he may be right. A boy grew to a man quickly in this part of the world, where life to those in power was not sacred and circumstances sent boys to war. But *eighteen.*

"I know my heart, Liliana," he said defensively, and she realized then that she'd hurt him.

"You have your whole life ahead of you." She pressed her fingertips to his lips, silencing him when he would argue. "I know you think you love me. And I know you care for me deeply, just as I care for you. But love—you have many years to figure out what love is."

She was making it worse. That she would doubt his conviction, that she would not tell him she loved him, too, made it worse. His eyes were dull with hurt.

"You cannot know what I am capable of feeling. You cannot know the things I have done, the things I have lived through. You cannot presume to know."

He was right. But so was she. She lowered her head. Kissed him. "Let's not talk of this anymore. We're here now. We're together now. Make love to me."

She felt him go hard between her legs, knew then that they were well on their way to a pleasurable distraction. When he gave up the fight and smiled for her, she slid down his body and sipped at his skin. Slid lower and took him into her mouth.

His hands knotted in her hair and soon they were lost. *Lost*, Lily thought breathlessly as her love play turned to serious business and they found release in each other.

———

Manny was in love. Deep in his soul, in love. More in love than he'd thought possible. Perhaps foolishly so.

He had always adored women. And women, he'd learned early in life, adored him. Had been adoring him since he'd been born the only boy to a house full of soft hands, warm smiles, and unqualified love from his mother and his sister, who had fussed over his onyx black eyes, played with his dark curly hair, sighed over his handsome features and caramel gold skin.

Whether it was the women in his family cuddling him

close and singing in his ear, his nanny slipping him special treats, or his mother's model friend seducing him, at sixteen, with that first electric taste of physical love, Manny had been surrounded by, loved by, and idolized by the fairer sex.

In turn, he welcomed every opportunity to give back all the adoration that had been lavished on him. Sometimes, to his regret. But with Lily . . . he regretted nothing.

Unless . . . sometimes, he talked too much. He'd confided in her that he was a clandestine operator, often worked with the U.S. government as well as his Contra brethren intent on overthrowing the Sandinista regime. He told her all of this. He put his life in her hands. A dangerous and risky thing to do, as he'd just found out.

Waiting for her back at the apartment, he leaned against the kitchen counter, his arms crossed over his chest, his mind reeling with fear of her, of betrayal.

His chest tightened when the kitchen door finally opened and she walked inside, her arms full of flowers and a bottle of wine.

"Hey, you," she said brightly as she unloaded her things on the counter, pecked him on the cheek, then opened a cupboard door. "I thought you were picking me up today."

"What was Poveda doing at the clinic?"

"Hm?" She glanced at Manny over her shoulder, then resumed her hunt for a vase for the flowers.

He caught her by the arm, spun her around. "Poveda. He was at the clinic when I came for you. I saw you talking with him."

She looked shocked, then confused. "Oh. Oh, right. He was there. But what you saw was him attempting to talk to me, not me talking to him. Manny? You're hurting me."

Only then did he realize there was pain mixed with her confusion. He let her go, felt a sick knot in his gut when he saw the imprint of his fingers on her arm.

"Manny? What's going on?"

"You cannot speak to Poveda of me."

She blinked. Shook her head. "You think I would talk to Poveda about you?"

She looked so hurt, so perplexed, that a fist of self-loathing punched him in the chest.

"I did, yes," he confessed, and knew by the look on her face how wrong he'd been to doubt her. Relief was almost as potent as regret.

"I was wrong to do so. I'm sorry, Lily." Folding her into his arms, he held her tight against him. "It is just that he is already upset with me—because I took you home from his party. I cannot afford to become someone he concerns himself about."

She stiffened in his arms. "What you mean is, you're not certain you can trust me with your secrets."

He expelled a breath heavy with regret. Yes. That is what he'd meant. He wasn't proud of it, but it was true. As his father so often pointed out, for all Manny had experienced, he was not yet fully a man. He had a man's body, a man's appetites, and a man's appreciation for a beautiful, heartbroken woman, but sometimes he led with a boy's heart instead of a man's head.

Lily was the proof of that.

He'd placed himself in jeopardy.

Because he was in love.

"I am so sorry, Liliana. I should not have doubted you. It is just . . . Poveda. He wants you. I saw it in his eyes that night at his house. Not only that. In my coun-

try, one never knows who is friend. Who is foe. It is hard
to trust. Old habits—they are hard to break."

The tension in her body softened as he held her. "I
would never betray you, Manny," she whispered against
his chest.

"I know, *mi amor.* I know. Forgive me?"

She pulled away far enough so he could see her smile.
"Of course."

"Bueno. Está bien." *Good. It's all right.* He breathed
his first full breath of relief since he'd seen her at the
clinic with Poveda hovering near. She understood. All
was forgiven. Now Manny would make certain that all
was forgotten. "We will not speak of this again, okay?"

She nodded. "Okay."

"So . . ." He lifted a brow and the bottle of wine.
"Should we make use of this beautiful wine you brought?"

She grinned. "Make use of? I thought we'd just
drink it."

"Sí. We will drink it. I'll get you a glass."

"What about you?"

"My wine," he said, methodically opening the buttons
on her blouse, "I will drink from you."

He would drink from her forever, if she would just
let him.

———

They were sound asleep when Lily received a page from
the clinic. It was the middle of the night when she
slipped quietly out of Manny's bed so as not to wake
him. After scribbling a note of explanation and propping
it against a vase of flowers on the kitchen table, she went
to help with the emergency.

The sky was breaking to a pearly lavender dawn when she finally returned to the apartment. Puzzled but too exhausted to give it much thought when she found Manny gone, she fell into bed and dropped instantly to sleep. It wasn't until she woke late in the morning and Manny hadn't returned that she began to worry.

"The young Lieutenant Ortega?" A sour-faced representative of General Poveda looked up from his desk at the general's office compound three days later. "Please be seated. I will see what I can find out for you."

Three days. Lily had searched for Manny for three days and hadn't found out one thing. Desperate, she finally had gone to Poveda.

A door opened to her right. She glanced over and saw Poveda himself walk into the reception area.

"Senorita Campora."

Lily stood as he drew her to her feet and kissed the back of her hand. She endured the attention with stoic silence.

"You are asking about Manolo Ortega?"

She nodded, unwilling to elaborate and give the general a reason to question her further.

"You and the young lieutenant are friends?"

Again she nodded, second-guessing the wisdom of coming here.

"Then I am sorry to tell you—Lieutenant Ortega has died in action, I'm afraid. A terrible tragedy, to be sure. He was a fine young officer."

Lily didn't remember much of anything else Poveda said. She barely remembered walking out of the general's office. Wasn't even certain how she made her way back to the apartment.

She sank down on the bed where she and Manny had

made love and had laughed and she'd had her heart stolen by the boy who was so much a man.

And now he was dead.

Terrible tragedy.

Snippets of Poveda's words rang through her mind as she lay back on the sheets that smelled of Manny. She hugged a pillow to her breast and rocked back and forth, tears spilling down her cheeks.

Terrible tragedy.

Manny was dead.

And something inside of her died, too.

CHAPTER 5

When Manny came to, he was lying on his back on the riverbank, covered in dried mud and blood and bugs. He'd been steeped so deeply in dreams of Lily, it took a moment to realize where he was, what had happened.

It came back to him slowly, painfully, like a dull, rusty knife slicing straight through his heart.

Lily had betrayed him.

And now he had to figure out how to stay alive long enough not only to deal with the pain of it but also to deal with her.

The first thing he became physically aware of was the diamond-bright glare of sunlight stabbing him in the eyes. The second was an odor more vile than vomit.

He rolled to his side. Groaned when his body reminded him of what it had been through—then stiffened when he realized his nose was level with a pair of scarred, worn boots not six inches from his face.

"So, look at the ugly fish the river puked out, eh?"

Manny squinted through raw, gritty eyes, twisted painfully to his back again, and followed the length of the legs disappearing into the boots. For the second time in twelve hours, he found a Soviet-made rifle pointed dead center at his chest.

"What's your name, fish?"

Manny's head felt as thick as the mud he'd crawled out of and he drifted toward unconsciousness again— then jerked awake with a groan when a boot connected sharply with his ribs.

"Your name, or I will gut you like the bottom-feeder you are."

He fought to focus as the scream of a howler monkey grated through his brain and a slow-moving cloud covered the blinding sun. Finally, he pulled his swimming vision together and stared at his new tormentor.

Bandoleers filled with ammunition crisscrossed a scrawny, bare chest. A Makarov pistol hung from a canvas belt, the holster tied to a bowed right leg. A steel-handled knife hung from a scarred leather scabbard strapped to his left calf.

Manny's new captor wore the dirt-stained camouflage pants of a jungle fighter. Beneath the brim of a battered bush hat was a face that would break a cupboard full of plates. The man's right eye bugged out like a frosted-glass marble. His left was open only a slit. A thick, jagged scar cut a half-moon from the outside of that eye down to the corner of his mouth and hooked it up into a perpetual sneer. What teeth he had were the color of hemp and as jagged as a rusted saw blade.

Diablo. The devil has found me.

Manny heard a raspy laugh. Only realized it was coming from himself when pain sliced through his ribs.

"For a man about to die, you are very happy, no? Maybe I should just shoot you now. That way I won't have to clean my knife."

"I'm not going to die. Not . . . today. And when have you . . . ever cleaned anything, Enrique?"

Those monster eyes pinned him to the ground. "You call me by name. How do you know this?"

"Only one man I know . . . reeks of rancid pig piss," Manny managed through a throat as dry as dust. "Cristo, Enrique. It's me. Manny. For God's sake, untie me. And then, amigo, you will pay for that boot you planted in my ribs."

But not right now. Right now it was all Manny could do to stay conscious and silently thank God for sending this unlikely angel of mercy.

Enrique Diaz dropped to his knees with a cry of "Dios!" when he finally recognized Manny.

Enrique whipped his knife out of the scabbard and sliced the rope tying Manny's wrists.

Icy hot needles of fire exploded through Manny's hands. He roared out his pain when his shoulders, frozen for hours, fell forward. Then he puked river water until there was nothing left but bile.

And then, mercifully, he passed out again.

———

"So. Do you know who betrayed you, amigo?"

Enrique and his brothers, longtime Contra fighters Manny had trained with, sat around a small campfire deep in the jungle, sharing a sparse meal of black beans and rice. Manny had told them about Poveda's men coming for him.

He stared at the fire as a green iguana skittered across a rust-colored rock and disappeared into the jungle scrub. It was dusk now. Thanks to Enrique, Manny was clean and clothed. His arm and his thighs were bandaged and soothed with salve. His belly was no longer empty.

It was only by good fortune that Enrique and his small band of guerrillas had been in this part of the jungle today. They'd been hunting. Manny was the only game they'd found. No one else would find him here. The camp would not be visible to anyone—including the Sandinistas. The jungle folded around them like a tent of green.

Manny was rehydrated. Enrique's salve had begun to work on the gunshot wound that had started to fester. Manny's headache had dulled to a minor annoyance. In a day or two, his body would be strong again.

His heart, however, would never heal. This he knew with everything in him.

"Manolo?"

He jerked his head toward Enrique, realized he hadn't addressed his friend's question. Manny set his jaw. Stared at the fire. "Yes. I know who betrayed me."

He didn't offer any more explanation. Enrique exchanged a look with the others, gave a slight shake of his head. They knew better than to ask more. Knew that Manny would deal with the betrayal in his own way. In his own time.

"I need to get to Cougar," Manny said. "Can you take me to his camp?"

Cougar was their CIA contact in this war that the United States quietly sanctioned and covertly assisted. Last Manny knew, Cougar was headquartered just the other side of the northern border in Honduras. But that was months ago. And Cougar never stayed in any one place for long.

"Sí." Enrique nodded. "I can get you to him. When you are stronger. First you must rest. Unless we find transportation, it's a five-day march."

Wishing for transportation was the equivalent of wishing for peace. It wasn't going to happen. "We leave in the morning," Manny said, and while he could see Enrique wanted to argue, he only nodded.

It was time to call in favors from the CIA. Manny had been Cougar's informant for over a year, feeding him information so the United States could best support the movement against the communist Sandinistas. Now Cougar would repay Manny for his service.

His cover was blown. He could no longer show his face in the city. No longer see his family for fear they would become caught in the crossfire.

So he would do his fighting from the jungle from now on. And for that he would need weapons, explosives, and men.

———

The CIA agent stood when Manny and Enrique entered the tactical camp just the other side of the border in Honduras five days later. Tall, lean, and as mean as a bull shark, Cougar squinted at Manny through blue eyes as hard as chipped ice, while around them men in U.S. Army camouflage carrying submachine guns and armed to the teeth stood at the ready.

At a nod from Cougar, they relaxed their guard, but only marginally. No man on assignment in this part of the world ever fully relaxed.

Manny estimated Cougar to be in his late thirties. Beneath a camo boonie hat his head was shaved, his eyes hardened, his expression blank.

"Thought you were dead," Cougar finally said, moving a toothpick from one corner of his mouth to the other.

Word traveled fast in the jungle. Manny wasn't the only plant among Poveda's ranks. "There are those who would wish it so."

Cougar grunted. "So it seems. Let's get out of the sun. Tell me what happened."

Manny followed Cougar to a tent stained mud gray and jungle green. Inside, it smelled of must and cigar smoke. Manny sat and told Cougar about his capture, leaving out the part about Lily.

That was for Manny to deal with. For him to know.

For him to regret.

"I need guns. I need men," Manny said point-blank.

The CIA agent reached into a box, withdrew two cigars, offered one to Manny.

Manny shook his head. Waited.

Cougar sliced off the end of a cigar with his bush knife. "No guns. No men."

Manny felt his anger rise but kept it in check. "I risk my life to give you information. This is how you repay me?"

The older man lit the cigar, savored the first puff, then leaned forward, elbows on his knees. "Look, Ortega, you know how the game is played. You're a dead man if you stay in Nicaragua. Any man found *with* you is as good as dead. Poveda's pissed. You duped him. He won't call off his dogs until he finds you. And that makes you a liability to the cause."

It was a truth Manny had been avoiding because he needed to fight, but Manny knew the agent was right. Still, there had to be a way.

"He won't find me. As you said, the word is out that I'm dead."

Cougar shook his head. "Only speculation on their part. Either way, it doesn't matter. The damage is done.

You're useless to me now—and no good to your people with a price on your head. Poveda won't kill the hunt until he finds a body."

Unfortunately, Manny realized, Cougar again was right. Poveda would not stop looking. Would not rest until he was certain that Manny was dead.

"Let me send you to the States," Cougar said, rousing Manny from his brooding thoughts. "Let things cool off down here for a while."

"Go to the States?" Manny glared at the CIA operative. They'd had this conversation before—or one similar to it. "And do what? Hide like a dog while others fight what is my fight?"

"Learn. You'll join the Army. Get more training. And you have my word, we'll bring you back here in a year with an arsenal of knowledge and skill that will do you much more good than any weapons cache I could give you now.

"Think about it, Manolo," Cougar said when Manny remained thoughtful and silent. "You're a smart man. Just think about it," he repeated. "You'll see the wisdom."

What Manny saw, after giving the CIA agent's suggestion some thought, was that he had no choice. Cougar was right. Manny was now a liability.

Which meant he was a failure.

He'd failed his country.

He'd failed himself.

All because he'd been a fool over a woman.

He rose to his feet, gave Cougar a nod, and walked out of the tent. Only then did Manny allow himself to think about her. About Lily. Whom he'd first met in Poveda's excessively opulent house that had been paid for and furnished on the backs of Manny's countrymen.

If he had been thinking with his head instead of his cock, he'd have listened to her words, not her dulcet voice, at the dinner table when she'd agreed with Poveda about the lost cause of the Contras.

If he had been thinking, he wouldn't have told her secrets that could bring him down. Wouldn't have believed her when . . . well. He just wouldn't have believed her.

His father was right. He wasn't a man. He was a foolish boy.

And the next day, when Manny boarded a transport plane that would take him to the United States of America, he felt every bit the boy.

Lily had reduced him to that. She had taken everything that was important away from him. He was leaving his family. Leaving his home and everything he knew. The only thing that kept him from crying like a boy was the promise that he would return.

That and a growing hatred for the woman who had changed his life forever.

PART II

United States, present day

CHAPTER 6

"I guess that does it for the fifty-cent tour, Lily." Howard Rutledge, the balding forty-something Emergency Medicine administrator, extended his hand. "Welcome aboard. I hope the facility measures up to your expectations."

The scream of an ambulance siren bled in from outside. All around them, the emergency center staff attended to the demands of a bustling and well-run ER. Well run, yes, but Lily already had some ideas that would streamline operations even more and improve patient care.

She didn't mention that to Howard, however, who had just taken her on a guided walking tour of the center where, as of today, Lily was officially the new head of nursing. She also didn't mention that she'd stopped having expectations years ago. At least about some things.

And those kinds of thoughts are unnecessary, jaded, and just plain pissy, she chastised herself as one of three ambulance bay doors flew open and a trauma team greeted a blood-drenched gurney surrounded by EMTs.

Chalk up her attitude to buyer's remorse. Wrong sign of the moon. Or most likely, Lily could blame it on worry.

Adam had flown out two days ago. Her baby was halfway around the world in Sri Lanka by now. *Sri Lanka, for God's sake.* She still couldn't believe he was gone and that he'd be spending the summer assisting in the ongoing tsunami relief efforts.

God, when had her little boy grown into a young man? And of all the things he'd inherited from her, why had it had to come in the form of her "save the world" gene?

She snapped herself back to the moment and smiled at her new boss. "It's a great facility, Howard. State-of-the-art. I'm thrilled to be part of the team."

"No more thrilled than we are to have you. I know I've said it before, but your credentials are outstanding."

Lily allowed herself a moment to see her résumé from Howard's perspective as the gurney rolled past them and into a trauma room.

Yes, Lily had earned her way to this position starting with her DWB field experience years ago and her subsequent return to school, where she'd earned her master's, and ending with her previous position in Portland, where she'd set up and staffed a cutting-edge trauma unit—the first of its kind in the city.

Howard checked his watch. "Sorry to tour and run, but I've got a meeting. You need anything, you know where to find me."

Lily folded her clipboard against her breast and laughed. "Well, I'm a little uncertain of that at this point, but I'll figure out the topography soon enough."

Rutledge laughed, too. "It is a bit like a rabbit warren, isn't it? Just follow the yellow brick road and you'll be fine. I'll let you get settled in then."

Lily thanked him and, sidestepping another rolling gurney, picked her way back to her office.

Once behind her desk, she let out a deep breath.

"So," she said, looking around the nicely appointed

and roomy office that now had her name on the door, "this is home."

At least for a while.

It had taken her several tries to screw up the courage to move to Boston. And finding that courage had nothing to do with her new position. It had to do with the surprise of her life and the eight-month investigation that had led her here.

She'd assured herself it was for Adam's sake that she'd stayed in Portland as long as she had. It was tough enough being a teenager without being uprooted every few years.

It was tough being a mom, too. Tough being a single mom with a secret that could change both hers and Adam's lives forever.

On a deep sigh, she told herself not to think about that now. Not yet.

Instead, she indulged in an uncharacteristic surge of self-pity. Her only child was now at the mercy of strangers halfway around the world. And while her parents had never recovered from the shame of their only daughter having a child without the benefit of a father or a husband and had never been loving, involved grandparents to Adam, they'd had plenty to say about her decision to let him go to Sri Lanka. None of it good.

"He'll be fine," she'd assured them, wishing she could be immune to their lifelong disapproval of her career and life choices.

"He'll be fine," she muttered now, telling herself she needed to get to work familiarizing herself with the filing system.

A dozen other students had accompanied Adam, along with qualified student sponsors. She'd personally researched the summer youth exchange program and knew it was credible and safe. Just like she'd thoroughly researched Sri Lanka.

Her globe now wore the imprint of her thumb over the island country that lay just off the southeast tip of India. She'd also checked world weather forecasts. It was *not* storm season in Sri Lanka. And although earthquake activity could not be accurately predicted, there were no indications that another tsunami was anticipated. As for the political climate, while it could be dicey, Colombo, where Adam's host family lived, was far away from any hostile activity that might break out between the Sinhalese government and the Tamil rebels, who liked to stir up trouble. She'd made sure of that, too. He would be staying with a wonderful host family—she'd spoken with the Muhandiramalas twice on the phone—and Lord knew, Adam's experience on this humanitarian mission would be life altering.

Then there was Adam's take on the situation. As he so enjoyed telling her, he *was* sixteen. Not a baby.

Well, he was *her* baby, damn it, and that was never going to change. Opening up a lower desk drawer, she pulled out his photograph and set it on the credenza where she could see it.

Such a beautiful boy. Who would soon be a man. A man who looked exactly like his father.

When she felt a tear threaten, she growled, angry with herself, "Okay. Pity party's officially over."

She settled in to get some work done. In the back of her mind, however, a niggling question—one that had nothing to do with Sri Lanka—played over and over again: How long was it going to take her to work up the courage to follow through with the *real* reason she'd moved to Boston?

As soon as she got her legs under her and her back-bone shored up, she'd face the music . . . and possibly the most difficult confrontation of her life.

———

Two weeks later

"Ms. Campora?"

Lily looked up from her desk to see the charge nurse poke her head in Lily's open office door.

"Hey, Gracie. And it's 'Lily,' okay?"

Lily's first two weeks on the job had passed in a blur of activity. Which was good. When she dragged herself home each night, she was too exhausted to worry about Adam. But she still missed him. That wasn't going to change even though he'd called twice, he was fine, and he was having the time of his life.

"You got a minute?"

"Sure. What's up?"

"We're having a little trouble deciphering your new trauma board procedures. Can you come down and de-code for us?"

"Absolutely." Lily checked her watch—couldn't be-lieve it was almost noon. She reached for her coffee mug, telling herself that since it was still officially morning, she was entitled to another jolt of caffeine to get her through it. "Give me fifteen and I'll be there."

One of the hallmarks of her administrative practices was the open-door policy. That and striking a balance be-tween management priorities and staff needs. First and foremost, she was a nurse. She didn't want to ever forget that. And she wanted her staff to know she never forgot it.

She finished up what she was doing, then hit the floor and headed for Trauma. She'd just rounded the corner into the unit and had the main desk in her sights when she looked up—and felt her heart stop.

A man stood in profile at the far end of the hall; he was speaking with the EMTs who were debriefing an attending on what appeared to be a recent admit. The man was well built, dark, and Latino. And the way he stood . . . the breadth of his shoulders . . . the blue-black of his hair. He looked so much like Manny.

Manny.

Her heart still hurt when she thought of him. Of returning to his sister's Managua apartment all those years ago and finding him gone. Of the days she'd spent searching for him, agonizing over his fate.

Of the moment Poveda had told her that Manny had died in a firefight in some Nicaragua hellhole.

For seventeen years, she'd still seen him in every handsome Latino man she ever encountered. She would spot a man across a room, across a street, on a bus, or even on a plane and her heart would stutter exactly the way it was stuttering now.

God. She'd lost track of the number of heart-stopping times she'd studied a dark male profile with her breath caught in her chest . . . and then he'd turn and she'd be looking at a stranger.

Because Manny Ortega was dead.

For seventeen years.

Only now she knew otherwise.

It still came as a shock—but Manny was alive.

The thrill and amazement and confusion that knowledge always brought coursed through her now, adding to the irregular beat of her heart.

Manny was alive.

He was also the real reason she'd moved to Boston.

He was here. A detective on the Boston PD. He'd *been* here for almost five years now. And Lily had been determined to find him. To find out what had happened. How he'd survived. Why he hadn't contacted her.

A guarded hurt always accompanied that knowledge. Hurt and, if she let it, anger. In all these years, he hadn't contacted her. She didn't know what that meant. And she needed to find out.

It wasn't going to be today, though, she told herself, no matter that this man had given her heart a scare.

He moved on and Lily regrouped. She headed toward the nurses' station. *Soon,* she promised herself. She would go to see him soon. It was still a question of courage. Of confronting a ghost.

She'd taken a huge chance coming to Manny after all these years. True, it wasn't as if she could have contacted him sooner. It was only eight months ago when she was watching an old news documentary on the elite Special Forces that she'd seen him.

Talk about heart-stopping moments. She'd recognized him on the tape immediately even though she'd been stunned to see him alive and had no inkling how he'd ended up in the U.S. Army.

It had taken her months of Internet searches and dead ends to finally locate him, another month to come to terms with the reality of confronting him. And then, when the job opening here at the BMC had come up—well, it seemed like an omen. Karma. Kismet. Whatever.

The offshoot was, she'd moved to Boston. And some stranger who reminded her of Manny had just shocked her into remembering that her search was almost over.

Switching gears, Lily spotted Gracie filing charts. "Hey, Gracie. I'm yours for the next ten minutes. What can I do for you?"

Exactly ten minutes later, the confusion cleared up, Lily headed back down the hall toward her office. A heated debate in rapid-fire Spanish blasted from behind a curtained treatment area and stopped her.

When the "debate" rapidly accelerated to an argument, she headed toward the curtain, whipped it open, and stepped inside.

Her heart bumped up again when she encountered the tall Latino she'd seen earlier. Then as now, he stood with his broad back to her, faced off with a resident and a uniformed officer over a patient lying prone on a stretcher. Both the officer and the resident were agitated and scowling.

"This is a hospital, gentlemen," Lily advised them in a stern but hushed voice. "I'd suggest you work your problems out elsewhere."

They immediately quieted at the authority in her tone; the two men facing her looked sheepish. The Latino's shoulders stiffened. Slowly, he turned around.

And for the second time today, Lily's heart stalled, kick-started, and fired.

Manny.

It really *was* Manny.

Her knees buckled.

He reached out and grabbed her elbow, steadying her. Just as swiftly, he pulled away. Eyes as black as onyx and every bit as hard searched her face, clearly as stunned at seeing her as she was at seeing him.

Time stopped. Shifted to another dimension, even another reality, as she stared, unable to absorb anything but the pure uncensored rancor emanating from him like ice from a glacier. If possible, his eyes grew even harder, knifelike, as his gaze cut into hers.

Finally, she found her voice. "Manny? . . . My God . . . It *is* you."

Just as quickly, she lost the power of speech. When he ripped his gaze away from her, it felt like he'd ripped a piece of her soul along with it.

Reeling again at the force of it, she grabbed a gurney for support and hung on.

"We'll settle this down at the precinct," Manny told the uniformed officer. Then he shouldered around her and, without another word, left—but not before shooting her a look that horrified her.

Rage.

Hatred.

Unqualified bitterness.

They all hit her with the impact of a head-on collision with a train.

Lily couldn't make herself move. Could only stare at the space where Manny Ortega had stood, her thoughts jumbled and stalled, her hands shaking.

Emotions bombarded her—joy . . . disbelief . . . shock. Along with confusion and pain. They circled like a funnel cloud, immobilizing her where she shivered in the wake of his departure that left a chill as icy as an arctic front. The scent of musk and male that even the antiseptic hospital smell couldn't dilute lingered.

"Ms. Campora?"

Startled, she snapped her gaze to the resident and realized he must have addressed her once before.

"You okay? You look like you've seen a ghost."

Oh God. If he only knew.

"Fine . . . I'm fine," she managed, wishing her lie at least sounded credible.

"You and Ortega," the uniform put in, unable to contain his curiosity, "you know each other?"

"Um. Yeah." She nodded, still mired somewhere between a long-ago Central American summer and the improbable reality that was today.

"Long . . . long time ago," she said when she realized both the officer and the resident were waiting for more. "What . . . um, what exactly was the problem here?" she asked, attempting to regain some semblance of professionalism when all she really wanted to do was chase after Manny.

And do what? Let him slice you to ribbons with his glare?

A thousand questions about what had prompted his hatred wove together in her mind, voiding one another out.

"Detective Ortega wanted to question the patient," the resident said.

"Crazy cop wanted to beat the hell outta me!"

For the first time, Lily became aware of the teenage gangbanger lying on the gurney. The bandage wrapped around his forehead seeped blood. She'd been in Boston long enough now that she recognized the scarf tied around his bicep as the colors of a Hispanic gang whose members frequented the ER.

And she'd known that Manny was on the police force. Had actually anticipated a similar scenario . . . running into him in the ER. Having chance take away the necessity of going to him.

Well, chance had done just that.

Nowhere in her imagination, however, had she anticipated his reaction. Shock, yes. Surprise, absolutely.

But hatred?

"Hey—I'm bleeding here!"

The patient's aggravated demand snapped her back to the moment.

"Stow the theatrics, Diego," the officer said. "Ortega saved your sorry ass and you know it.

"I'm sorry, ma'am. I'm Officer Mullnix." He extended a hand.

Lily shook it. "Lily Campora."

"You sure you're okay?" Mullnix asked. "You're shaking."

"Fine. I'm fine," she insisted.

She tucked her hands in the pockets of her white jacket and balled her fingers into fists to steady them. "Detective Ortega—do you work with him?"

"No, ma'am, but we do work out of the same precinct."

"Hey! What about me? I'm still bleedin'."

Lily glanced at the patient, then at the resident. "Are we all squared away here?"

"We are."

"Then treat your patient, Doctor."

She slipped out of the cubicle, then walked straight to her office on rubber legs. She sank down behind her desk, clasped her shaking hands together on top of it, and stared into space.

Manny.

Memories she'd schooled herself not to relive resurrected themselves in vivid, living color and scent and sensation. A hot thrill of awareness arrowed through her. The reality of Manny's reaction doused it like a bucket of cold water.

She ran a still-trembling hand through her hair. *So much for sweet reunions.*

Not that sweet was what she'd wanted. Not after all these years. She'd hoped for cordial. Maybe even affectionate. And yet . . .

She heaved a ragged breath. And yet she'd gotten so much more. He still tripped all those triggers. The damp palms, the weak knees, an almost Pavlovian ache low in her belly. Woman low. An ache she hadn't tended to in more years than she cared to remember.

An ache he'd always known how to satisfy.

At least that beautiful boy she'd known a lifetime ago in Nicaragua had known.

And there was the difference.

Manolo Ortega was no longer a boy. He was, very clearly, a man.

Old. Harder. More gorgeous than ever.

Angry. With her. Guess she had her answer as to why he hadn't contacted her.

She leaned back, breathed deep in an effort to stop the trembling, then dragged her hands through her hair again.

He hated her. God. Violently hated her.

She wasn't mistaken about that. His fast exit added an exclamation point to a very definite statement. And she had no idea why.

She swallowed back a rolling nausea, vaguely aware that her cell phone was ringing. With impatience she unclipped it from her belt and, with clumsy fingers, flipped it open. "Lily Campora."

And just when she'd thought she'd experienced the biggest shock of her life, she received news that gripped her heart with terror.

CHAPTER 7

Manny unlocked the door to his townhouse, walked inside, and shut it carefully behind him—just to prove to himself that he could do something with care. That he had control of his actions when inside, it felt like a bomb was ticking to its final countdown.

That he had control over his life when in reality, life had control over him. Total and complete control.

Lily Campora.

He tipped his head back, breathed deep, and closed his eyes. His heart rate ratcheted up just thinking about her.

"Cristo." Of all the demons from his past that haunted him, she still topped the list.

And she was here. In Boston.

How perfect was that?

He walked into the uncluttered townhouse done in dark woods and blacks and tossed the keys to his SUV on the counter that separated the kitchen from the living area. Then he shrugged out of his shoulder holster and tucked it up into a cabinet.

Several moments later, he found himself standing, hands on hips, staring into space. Wanting to break something.

Wanting, *very badly,* to break something.

Wanting it so badly that he walked purposefully to the fridge and dug around for a Corona.

"Hell, it's five o'clock somewhere," he muttered, and twisted the cap off the bottle.

Lily.

In Boston.

For how long? he wondered, and tossed the cap toward the sink.

He'd lived here almost five years now, and ironically, he was two weeks' notice away from leaving the department and heading south to Florida. Two weeks and a shit-load of restlessness that had prompted him to quit the force and join Ethan Garrett and the crew at E.D.E.N., Inc., as a security specialist.

Two weeks away from being gone.

And he runs into Lily.

What the fuck did that mean?

He leaned back against the kitchen counter, tipped up the beer bottle, and swallowed a long, deep pull.

He believed in fate. Kismet. Whatever you wanted to call it. But by the same token, he didn't want to believe there was a grand plan that involved running into Lily Campora again.

Not after all these years. Not after all this hate.

The clock on the kitchen wall ticked loudly into the utter silence of his thoughts. Because of Lily, the last time he'd seen his family intact was seventeen years ago. He flashed on a memory of watching through the porthole of a U.S. Army transport plane as his homeland was obscured behind a layer of clouds.

He'd left everything because of her betrayal. Left his family. Left a fight he believed in with the promise that he could return and make a difference. Only he never had.

He'd left to become a soldier as Cougar had suggested, had advanced quickly to the Rangers and then on to Special Forces, where he'd worn the Green Beret.

A year came and went. It was finally time for him to return home. And then the unthinkable happened. Congress pulled the funds on Reagan's Contra effort. And just like that, the war was over. The Sandinistas ruled.

Manny's fight was lost. So was his country.

It was ten years before he'd dare sneak back again. To a father who was broken financially and emotionally. A mother who struggled to hold things together. A sister who had been raped by Poveda's men in retaliation for Manny's allegiance to the freedom fighters. She, too, was broken. No longer knew how to trust or smile.

Just as he no longer trusted. Not in women. Not in an emotion he'd fallen prey to because of one woman.

He tipped up the Corona again just as someone knocked on his door and shattered the silence that roared with memories and truths that haunted him every day of his life.

Mrs. Feinstein, he thought with a weary sigh. The old woman had a sixth sense when it came to knowing when he was home. *Or high-powered binoculars,* he thought grimly.

He put up with her daily neighborhood reports because he understood that she was lonely. And because she was a crazy, sweet old bird who sometimes brought him rock-hard cookies that he thanked her for graciously, then promptly tossed in the trash. The woman could not cook.

He wasn't in a mood, however, to deal with her today. Didn't think he could take a twenty-minute dissertation on every squealing tire, every suspicious-looking "thug," and the ever popular state of her bursitis.

He took another pull. Ignored the knock. And felt his heart rate rev and his blood run hot as his thoughts strayed back to Lily.

Not a day went by—*not one day in seventeen years*—that he hadn't thought of her.

And he didn't know who he hated more for that weakness. Himself for giving in to it or her for what she'd done to him and ultimately to his family.

When the pounding finally stopped, he heaved a breath of relief.

Then his cell phone rang.

Annoyed, he slipped it off his belt and checked the incoming number. He'd been prepared to ignore it, too, until he recognized his precinct prefix.

Frowning, he flipped open the phone. "Ortega."

"It's Mullnix. Answer your damn door; I know you're in there."

The line went dead. Manny flipped his phone closed and set it on the counter. Then he stared at the door. Next to Mrs. Feinstein, Mullnix was about the last person he wanted to deal with right now.

He couldn't hit Mrs. Feinstein. He couldn't hit Mullnix, either, but thinking about it gave him a helluva lot of pleasure. The rookie had pissed him off at the hospital with Juan Diego today.

On a resigned breath, Manny walked to the door, wishing he could shake the image of Lily and how she'd looked. As beautiful as he remembered. More so. The years had been good to her. She'd matured with elegance. With incredible beauty.

And she betrayed you, he reminded himself as he felt a slow slide toward sentiment.

He checked the peephole, saw Mullnix's ugly mug on the other side, and swung open the door. "Can't this wait until tomorrow?"

He'd barely gotten the words out when he realized the young officer wasn't alone.

Lily Campora stood beside him. Her eyes were swollen and red, as if she'd been crying; her expression was grief stricken and shocky.

Like the very first time Manny had seen her.

He'd been a fool then. He was no man's or woman's fool now.

Manny shifted his gaze to Mullnix. Glared. "Why the fuck did you bring her here?" Manny snapped, telling himself he wasn't moved by Lily's tears. He'd fallen into that trap once before.

"Don't be angry with him. I made him bring me." Lily shouldered past Mullnix and into Manny's townhouse.

Manny watched her walk inside, then directed a glare at Mullnix. "What? Her gun was bigger than yours?"

The rookie held up his hands. "Always was a sucker for a woman's tears." He gave Manny a mock salute and walked away.

Manny stood at the open door for a long moment. Considered walking the same way Mullnix had and leaving her there. Not coming back until he was certain she was gone.

But she'd just come back. And he would have solved exactly nothing.

He shut the door, drew a bracing breath, and turned to her.

"I . . . I'm sorry to . . . intrude. But I don't . . . I don't have a choice. And I don't have time to do anything but just spit it out. Manny . . . I need your help."

Of all the things he'd expected her to say, that wasn't one of them.

I'm sorry, Manny. Forgive me, Manny. Why are you alive, Manny?

Instead, it's *I need your help*?

But then, she'd used him before. Why not expect that she'd want to use him again?

"And you used to be so subtle," he said, refusing to be swayed by the misery on her face. "If I recall, it's more your style to play things out until I ask if *I* can help you."

Confusion played across her beautiful face. "What are you talk—"

He held up a hand, cutting her off, wise enough now not to let her emotional plea get to him. "Save it. I'm not the baby-faced boy you used in Managua. And I'm not as easily fooled. Whatever it is you think you want from me, I don't have it to give."

"My son is missing." Tears spilled down her cheeks as she blurted out the words. Agony wrestled with the desperation in her eyes. "Please. Manny. Please. I don't know who else to turn to. I don't know what to do."

Lily had a son. Why that cut, why that surprised, he didn't know. Just like he didn't know why he had to brace himself against a renegade urge to wrap her in his arms when a sob wrenched her slight body.

Hate her or not, a child was in trouble. The cop in him took over. Stone cold. Concerned with just the facts. Sworn to do his duty.

"Where and when was he last seen? I'll notify the precinct."

She shook her head, pulled herself together. "No. No, he's not in the States. Three weeks ago he . . . he left with a student exchange program to go to Sri Lanka. But today . . . I got a call today . . . right after . . . well, right after I saw you. He and his host family . . . Oh God, Manny . . . it looks like they might have been abducted."

Because it looked like she might collapse right there, he took her arm, steered her toward a chair. "Sit."

She wrenched her arm away. "I can't sit. I have to do something!" Fire as bright as her tears spilled from those amazing eyes. "I have to find him . . . but I don't know how."

"Have you called the State Department?"

"And the Sri Lanka prime minister's office. Their local police. Everyone I could think of. For all the good any of it did. They'll look into it." She lifted a hand in frustration. "You know as well as I do what that means. Days . . . weeks . . . maybe months of diplomatic red tape and tap dancing. He doesn't have months. He . . . he may not even have days."

Okay, Manny thought. So he wasn't completely immune. He wasn't as dead inside as he wanted to be, because her misery was getting to him. And the fact that he let it pissed him off.

"Look. I'm sorry about this. But why me? Why the *hell* did you come to me? For Christ's sake, why isn't his father looking for him?"

She closed her eyes. Swallowed. When she met his gaze again, it was with a tortured, searching look. "I'm hoping that his father will."

Silence rolled into the room like a live grenade, hushed and deadly, before the meaning of her words detonated with the force of a bomb.

Manny stared at her tearstained face, refusing to believe what he thought she had just told him.

I'm hoping that his father will.

Jesus. Sweet Jesus Christ.

———

Lily watched a range of emotions play across Manny's face. He didn't want to believe her. And yet she could see the struggle in his eyes.

"Are you telling me the child that's missing is mine?"

Tears stung again. "He's amazing, Manny," she said, then gasped when he gripped her upper arms and jerked her up against him.

"Why are you doing this? Why do you lie?"

Seventeen years of feelings and fears and regret spilled out like floodwater. "I'm not lying! We have a son! A beautiful, intelligent, caring young man who doesn't have time for me to convince you that I'm telling the truth."

"The truth? Why should I believe you know the truth? Everything you ever told me was a lie." The conviction in his tone was bitter and unyielding.

"What . . . what are you talking about? I never lied to you."

He made a sound of disgust, then, as if just now realizing he was touching her and finding it repugnant, pushed her away. She staggered, then righted herself as he sank down on the arm of an overstuffed sofa, glaring at her as if she'd just told him the sky was falling.

"Manny . . . whatever happened . . . whatever you think I've done . . ."

She stopped when he jerked his gaze away from hers,

but she wasn't about to give up. Not now. Not after she'd spent the last two hours since she'd received the call from Adam's sponsor finding Mullnix and convincing him to bring her here.

"Manny . . ." Desperate now, she groped for anything that made sense. "You disappeared. I . . . couldn't find you."

His gaze cut into her like a machete. "*I* disappeared? I woke up alone that night. It was you who were conveniently absent when they came for me, *querida.*" He hurled the endearment like a stone.

That night. That horrible night when she'd returned from the clinic and found him gone. "I . . . I got a beep," she explained. "From the clinic. There was an emergency. I didn't want to wake you. I left a note. Jesus, Manny. When I came back in the morning, you were gone."

"And I am to believe that this surprised you?" Sarcasm dripped from each word.

"Surprised? Of course I was surprised. I didn't know where you were. When a day went by, then two, and you didn't show up, I was out of my mind with worry. I looked everywhere. I asked everywhere. They said . . . they told me that you were dead."

Even seeing the hatred in his eyes didn't diminish the pain that always accompanied the memory of that horrible day. "They told me you'd been killed in a firefight."

Another harsh sound of disgust. "It's a good story, when in fact I woke up that night with Poveda's men pointing their guns at my belly and cold sheets beside me on the bed. But you already know that, don't you?"

"Know? Know what? What are you talking about?" She couldn't think past her fear for Adam.

When Manny only glared she sifted through his words.

When they came for me. Poveda's men. Guns. "Poveda? Are you saying that he came after you?"

"Jesus, Lily. Cut the crap. You know exactly what happened."

Finally, it registered—and the realization stunned her. "You think I turned you in? That's what this is about? You think I told Poveda about you?"

His gaze bored into hers, accusing, unyielding, and filled with loathing.

She shook her head, realizing then that there was no defense against the absolute certainty on his face.

"And now you say I have a son." He said it so quietly she barely heard him. "And I am to believe you."

The depth of his hatred became clear to her then. It wasn't based only on anger. It was based on disillusion. On despair. On disappointment. Because of that, she could see that there weren't enough words in the English language to convince him she hadn't betrayed him. And there wasn't enough time in the world to make him see the truth.

Adam didn't have the time. He needed her. He needed Manny, and so did she if she was going to get her son back.

In the process of searching for Manny, Lily had learned what a warrior he'd become. As a Special Forces soldier he'd served in South America, Afghanistan, and God only knew how many other places. Now he served the Boston police force and had built on his reputation as a man to be counted on, a man of integrity.

He was also the only man who could do what she'd asked him to do. Something she could never ask of any other man.

Just like she knew of only one sure way to convince him. She fumbled inside her purse for her wallet. Dug around and pulled out a photograph of Adam. She held it out to Manny with a shaking hand.

"You don't have to believe me. Believe this."

He stared from her to the photograph, then finally took it. For long moments his expression remained blank, his gaze riveted on the picture of a boy who could have been Manny at sixteen.

She watched as his face drained to pale. Finally, he swallowed, closed his eyes. The waiting was interminable, yet even before he finally asked, she knew the photograph had made him a believer.

"What is his name?"

Tears of relief welled up, spilled over. "Adam. His name is Adam."

Again, Manny stared at the photo before slowly holding it out to her.

She shook her head. "You keep it."

He said nothing, yet she could see the emotion he fought to keep in check.

She made one final, desperate attempt to explain why sixteen years had passed and this was the first time he'd seen the face of his son. "I thought you were dead."

"I was," he said with an emptiness that made her heart ache.

Then he rose. "I need to make some calls."

For the first time since she'd received that horrible news three hours ago, Lily felt a tentative sense of relief. Relief was tinged with regret, however. For all the years wasted, for all the pain, all the misunderstandings. Manny Ortega hated her, was convinced that she had betrayed him. Probably wished to God he'd never seen her face again.

None of that was important now. What was important was that he would help her.

He would help her because a father would move heaven and earth to save his son.

CHAPTER 8

Heat radiated in shimmering waves through the tropical island summer, warping the silhouettes of the passengers disembarking from the Sri Lankan Airlines jet. A glut of indistinguishable shapes descended the jet steps and inched like a snake weaving across the tarmac. It was like a picture of Lily's life ever since she'd heard that Adam had disappeared: distorted, terrifying, out of focus.

She couldn't shake the cloying sensation of living a nightmare, knew she had to get her wits about her if she was going to be any good to her son. But she was too wired and too frightened for him to pull it all together.

"There they are."

Lily followed Manny's gaze to see three figures break away from a group of passengers and make their way toward the gate. Like Lily and Manny, they were dressed in white camp shirts and long tan pants with zippered compartments running down the legs.

Two of them appeared to be carrying large camouflage packs on their backs. They were similar to the one Manny wore and referred to as ALICE packs. The third person wore a smaller version of the backpack that resembled Lily's. It wasn't until the three of them reached the gate and she could see them clearly that Lily realized the third person was a woman.

Lily hadn't expected that. Wasn't exactly certain what it meant that a woman had come along.

She was about five-five, five-six. A redhead. Pretty. The men were tall, hard-edged, and handsome. Dark hair, intense eyes, Caucasian. Brothers, Manny had said, although getting information out of him was like pulling teeth.

As close as she could figure, Ethan Garrett and Manny had served in the Special Forces together several years ago. Lily still wasn't clear on how Manny had ended up in the elite U.S. Army's special ops unit, but from the bits and pieces she'd gathered, he'd come directly to the United States after escaping from Poveda's men.

What she knew about Ethan Garrett was that he and his brothers, Nolan and Dallas, and their sister ran a se-curities agency in Florida with the assistance of another ex–Special Forces buddy, Jason Wilson. Because Ethan and Dallas had dropped everything to come to Sri Lanka to help when Manny had called, Lily knew something else. Their bond was blood strong.

Lily studied the redhead. Wondered if she was the Garretts' sister, Eve. Right now Lily felt too jet-lagged and edgy to even attempt to pry information out of Manny. She'd find out soon enough anyway—although "soon" had become a relative term.

The twenty-four-hour flight to Colombo had been in-terminable. It seemed like days instead of hours since she'd slept. She wanted to get to Adam. She wanted to find him yesterday, but they'd had to be content with booking a 4:00 P.M. flight out of Boston with connec-tions in London and Mumbai before reaching Colombo.

She'd stopped at a bookstore on the way to Logan International to meet up with Manny. There she'd hastily bought every Sinhala and Tamil language tape and Sri Lanka guidebook she could lay her hands on. Between short, fitful naps, both she and Manny had alternately listened to the tapes and pored over the books much of the flight, trying to get the lay of the land and a handle on some basic phrases and customs.

She also suspected that Manny was grasping at any opportunity to not talk to her. His hatred for her was like a third entity between them, huge, hulking, ever present. They'd finally touched down an hour ago. Had been waiting in stormy silence for the Garretts to arrive ever since.

Lily had wanted to move on without them. Manny had been insistent that they wait. But then he'd been insistent about other things, too. Like that she stay behind in Boston while he and his former special ops buddies flew to Sri Lanka and searched for Adam.

"You asked me to help. I'm helping," Manny had said, his jaw as pliable as stone when she argued with him. "By advising you to stay here. You're not equipped or trained to handle this kind of op."

This kind meaning "dangerous." On that one thing they agreed. Lily had made numerous phone calls to the Sri Lankan capital of Colombo—all with the same frustrating response: They were looking into it.

She couldn't wait on time-sucking bureaucratic red tape on either the U.S. or the Sri Lankan end; if she did, a search might never get underway. That left only one option: They would launch their own unsanctioned rescue mission.

Dangerous.

Lily knew the risks. She'd willingly take them to find

her son—just like she'd willingly put up with Manny's wrath.

"I'm going," she'd told Manny. "It's not open for discussion. If Adam is hurt, or sick," she'd said, not wanting to think it but determined to be pragmatic, "my medical training could make the difference."

Along with her backpack, she'd packed a duffel full of medical supplies—antibiotics, dressings, suture kits, antimalaria pills, anything she could think of—praying all the while that she wouldn't have to use them. On Adam or Manny or his friends.

She hung on to that duffel like a lifeline and, as was the norm since this all began, watched with an exhausting combination of appreciation, apprehension, and impatience as three new arrivals made their way slowly through the gates.

When the redhead spotted Manny, she rushed forward, shrugged off the shoulder straps of her pack, and threw herself into his arms. He hugged her hard, lowering his face into the hollow of her neck before she leaned back, framed his face in her palms, and kissed him. The kiss was brief, filled with concern and affection. Like a sister would give a brother, and yet Lily felt an unsettling kick of jealousy—as unexpected as it was out of place.

It was the familiarity between them, she supposed. The honest show of love and the obvious connection. And the woman's welcome as well as the men's clearly excluded Lily and established the four of them as a unit.

Nothing new there. Lily lifted her chin, squared her shoulders. She'd been on her own for a long time. She was used to being odd man out. She couldn't imagine what Manny had told them about her. Or maybe she could. It would explain the men's total avoidance of eye contact.

"Lily." Manny turned to her, his arm still around the redhead, and made brief introductions.

The woman, it turned out, was not a sister but Darcy Prescott, fiancée of the tallest Garrett brother, Ethan, who glanced at Lily, nodded a cool hello, then clasped Manny's shoulder.

Dallas managed a curt hello, then turned back to Manny. "Where can I get our currency exchanged?"

"Bank of Ceylon runs a Bureau de Change—just around the corner." Manny nodded in the direction of the bank.

Without another word Dallas headed out. Lily felt her back stiffen even more. It was very clear that they were here for Manny. That was fine. She didn't care what they thought of her as long as they helped find Adam.

And then Darcy Prescott blew through the protective wall Lily had quickly erected by unwinding herself from Manny's side and pulling Lily into her arms.

"I'm so sorry about your son." Darcy hugged Lily tight, her emotions honest and true. "But we'll find him. Trust me. These three will move heaven and earth and they'll make it happen."

Darcy's unexpected overture of friendship caught Lily off guard. Gratitude, fatigue, and jet lag had tears threatening again. She blinked them back. Knew she must look shell-shocked and pulled it together.

"Thank you," she said, pulling away from Darcy Prescott's unexpected embrace. "Thank you for coming. All of you."

"What say we chitchat on the fly?" Ethan shouldered Darcy's pack, slung an arm over her shoulders, and followed Dallas.

Which left Lily to walk beside Manny, a stranger in a foreign land, alone, again, among these four people who, for all of their sacrifice in coming here, regarded her as an outsider.

———

"So, what do you think?" Darcy and Ethan stood by the rental-car desk while Manny, with Lily and Dallas, gathered their gear.

"About what?" Ethan stuffed his wallet back into his hip pocket.

Despite the gravity of the circumstances, Darcy had to grin at this amazing and beautiful man. His dark hair and eyes matched his sober expression. The way he carried himself—tall, composed, proud—reflected his special ops background. But it was his integrity and honor that drew her to him the most. She'd lost him once, but now she was lucky enough to have him back in her life. Lucky enough to have her own life back—in no small part thanks to Manny. And now she was hoping that her background with the State Department might open some doors and help Manny get his son back. A son he'd never even met.

"You're not that good at playing coy, tough guy," she teased, so very, very grateful that Ethan was hers to tease again. "You know *about what*. What do you think about Lily?"

Ethan lifted a shoulder, stoic as ever. "Not here to pass judgment but to find the boy."

"Judgment wasn't what I had in mind, Lieutenant,"

she said, addressing him by the rank he'd worn in the Special Forces when she'd met both him and Manny years ago in Peru. "The fact that you chose that particular word, though, tells me you've put Lily Campora on trial."

Ethan leaned an elbow on the counter, impatiently waiting for the paperwork. "Don't know the woman, but Manny's my friend. And from my perspective, sixteen years is more than enough time to tell a man he's got a child."

"Agreed, but from what you've told me, which is damn little," she pointed out with a leading smile, "I figure there's got to be more to the story."

Ethan grunted. "Honey, we're talking about an outline here, not a story. Until he called, I'd never heard Manny mention Lily Campora's name. Now all I know is that they met seventeen years ago in Managua, had an affair, and Manny hadn't seen her since—until yesterday."

"Like I said," Darcy replied, linking her arm with Ethan's as he accepted the keys to a Suburban and they headed for the rest of the group, "got to be a lot more. Did you notice the way he looks at her?"

Ethan reached into his shirt pocket and pulled out a roll of cherry Life Savers. "Like she's a two-headed, fire-breathing dragon?" He offered Darcy the roll of candy that he was never without before taking a piece for himself.

Darcy popped the Life Saver into her mouth. "Yeah. Like that. A lot of emotion invested in those looks."

Another grunt. "All of it anger."

"Which makes me think there must be a lot of other feelings bubbling below the surface."

Ethan stopped abruptly. He frowned down at her. "This is not a matchmaking mission, love."

She nodded solemnly. "I know. It's deadly serious business. I'm just saying—"

He touched a hand to her cheek, cutting her off. "I know what you're saying. And I agree. There's a lot more going on between those two than meets the eye. But that's for them to work out, not you."

He kissed her forehead, pressed her with a look. "Agreed?"

Okay. So he was right. "Agreed, my pragmatic romantic."

He wrapped an arm over her shoulders as they stepped out into the blinding sunshine and suffocating tropical heat. "When we get back to the States, we're setting a date. I want you to be my wife again. How's that for romantic?"

"A girl couldn't ask for more." She wound her arm around his waist, remembering a time, not so long ago, when Ethan and his brothers and Manny had rescued her from a band of terrorists in the jungles of the Philippines.

Remembering most of all that both she and Ethan had almost died in the process and that she'd been certain they'd never see their families again.

"Let's go find that boy," she said, and together she and Ethan walked across the parking lot toward the rented Suburban.

CHAPTER 9

"Okay, this is what we've got." Manny sped down the left side of the road toward the heart of the city of Colombo. He spared a brief glance at Lily. "Correct me if I'm wrong or to fill in the blanks."

Manny was behind the wheel, Lily riding shotgun, although she was certain he'd rather have her lashed to the top of the vehicle where he wouldn't have to see her. Ethan and Darcy sat in the second seat, with Dallas in the rear of the Suburban with their gear, consulting a map and listening. They understood the urgency and the necessity of finding Adam as soon as possible.

"As I told you on the phone, Adam and the dozen other students are all staying with separate families for the summer through a youth student exchange program.

"Adam's host family." Manny paused and deferred to Lily for help with pronunciation as she handed out copies of Adam's photo.

"The Muhandiramalas," she enunciated for everyone's benefit.

"The Muhandiramalas," Manny repeated, "live in Colombo. Mr. Muhandiramala." Again he paused and deferred to Lily.

"Amithnal," she supplied a first name.

"Amithnal," Manny continued, "is a highly influential member of the governing Sinhalese parliament."

"Which could make him a prime target of the LTTE," Ethan surmised.

Lily glanced at Ethan, as impressed by his knowledge of the political climate as she was sobered by his assumption. She'd thought that the prestige of Amithnal Muhandiramala's position and the fact that the Muhandiramalas lived in Colombo, well away from the troubled Northern Province, would ensure Adam's safety. It appeared that she'd been wrong on both counts.

"LTTE." Dallas frowned from the backseat. "The Liberation Tigers of the Tamil Eelam, right?"

Again, Lily was impressed. Even more so when Manny added, "More commonly known as Tigers. They're big into terrorism. Threat of a renewed brutal and bloody civil war with the Sinhalese governing body here in Sri Lanka is always on the table."

"The Tamils want their own independent state," Lily explained. "Differences based in religion. Sinhalese Buddhists versus Tamil Hindus."

"Although some maintain it's simply about equality," Darcy mused aloud, giving Lily another surprise with her knowledge of the volatile situation in Sri Lanka. "The Tamils are the minority ethnic group. They want to be heard. Still, no matter how you slice it, it's the same ole same ole, though, isn't it? Two inherently peace-loving religions at war. Why does this always happen?"

"One of the most asked questions of our time," Dallas put in cynically from the backseat as they sped toward the market district. "Take a right at the next intersection."

"In any event." Manny flipped his turn signal and darted into the right lane before continuing. "Since none of the other students have been abducted or gone missing, we've got to figure that Amithnal was the target and Adam was just in the wrong place at the wrong time."

"And that the Tigers are most likely the major players here, figuring they can use Amithnal for political leverage," Ethan surmised.

"Ransom demands?" Darcy asked.

Manny shook his head. "None yet."

"I've spoken with Adam's student adviser three times since this all happened." Lily turned in the seat so she could see Darcy. "According to him, Adam and the Muhandiramalas' daughter, Minrada, have been helping to repair the primary school in Matara and make it operational again."

"Matara . . . Matara . . . Wait." Paper rattled in the backseat while Dallas searched for Matara on the map. "Okay. Found it. Southern tip of the island. Looks like it's about two hundred and fifty kilometers from here."

"Amithnal and Sathi, that's Mrs. Muhandiramala," Lily continued, "made plans to meet Adam and Minrada last Friday in Ratnapura. South and east," she added for Dallas's benefit when she heard the map crackle again. "It's about a halfway point between Matara and Colombo."

"Okay, there it is," Dallas said.

"The plan was for the four of them to meet up, then drive on up to the mountains and eventually to Kandy for some sightseeing and to spend a long weekend together." She glanced over her shoulder toward Dallas. "If you're looking, Kandy's due east of Colombo."

Lily had not only studied the globe when Adam had

started planning this trip, she'd also ordered a Sri Lanka map and pored over it, familiarizing herself with the island. She'd wanted to know everything she could about the place her son would be spending the summer.

"Do we know if they met up in Ratnapura?"

Lily couldn't make herself respond to Darcy's question. To her surprise, Manny came to her rescue.

"No. We don't know. No one has seen any of them since they left on Friday."

With his arm propped on the door over the open window, Ethan drummed his fingers on the Suburban's roof. "When were they due back?"

"Amithnal and Sathi were expected back in Colombo on Tuesday afternoon," Lily said. "The kids were scheduled for another workday in Matara on Wednesday, so we're assuming their plan was to head back sometime on Tuesday."

"That's two days ago."

Lily didn't need Ethan's calculations. She knew exactly how many days it was. The knowledge made her heart race with worry and fear for her son.

"Were they camping or hoteling?"

"Hotel." Lily rolled down her window to catch a breeze in the stifling heat. "According to Emory—Adam's sponsor—Sathi likes her creature comforts. But we don't have the name of any specific place. Emory's made several calls but so far hasn't hit the right inn. According to the guidebook there are any number of guesthouses where they could have stayed in an area that covers several hundred square miles."

"Okay, we're talking central highlands here. Not known Tamil strongholds," Ethan reminded everyone pragmatically. "The Tiger operational bases are all supposed to be to the north and along the east coast. So maybe we're leaping to conclusions on an abduction. Maybe they had an accident or just got lost."

Manny had purchased an English version of a Colombo newspaper while they waited in the airport. He picked it up from the seat between them. A St. Christopher medal swung out of the open collar of his shirt when he twisted around to hand the paper over the front seat to Ethan.

Was it the same one, Lily wondered, that he'd worn all those years ago? She flashed on a memory of Manny levered on his elbows above her, his eyes closed, his face taut with desire as he pumped into her, the round silver medallion gently tap, tap, tapping against her breast.

"Check it out," Manny said, the gruffness of his tone snapping her back to the grim reality of the present.

"Well, hell," Ethan muttered after reading the front-page article chronicling a foiled bomb plot in Kandy. It had "Tiger" written all over it. In addition, there had been uncharacteristic sightings of Tiger rebel squads in the Nuwara Eliya district in the mountains south of Kandy in the past few weeks.

"It wasn't known Tamil territory," Manny restated Ethan's point with a glance in the rearview mirror, "until three days ago. About the same time Adam and the Muhandiramalas disappeared."

Which pretty much cemented their original assumption. Tamil rebels, ruthless, unscrupulous, notoriously brutal, were most likely at play here. And most likely, the Muhandiramalas *had* been abducted. Possibly killed, Adam included.

Suddenly it all caught up with Lily. The worry. The fear. The helplessness of first being so far away and now being so near and unable to see or touch her son.

"Adam's not dead. He can't be dead."

She hadn't realized she'd said it out loud until she felt Darcy's hand squeeze her shoulder.

"We'll find him," Darcy assured her.

Lily closed her eyes. Nodded. More thankful than she could have imagined for the presence of this woman she'd just met. With nothing but cold indifference coming from Dallas and Ethan, and waves of brittle hostility emanating from Manny, Darcy's warmth helped shore Lily up.

Dallas glanced up from the map again. "And what's the reason the Sinhalese government isn't on top of this?"

"Let me tackle that one," Darcy said, then surprised Lily again with her on-point accurate assessment. "Because of the civil unrest between the Tigers and the Sinhalese, and because there is constant infighting between the Sri Lankan president and the prime minister, I'm thinking the government is bottlenecked over getting involved. They're probably dragging their feet on organizing a rescue mission because they're afraid intervention could result in all-out civil war and topple the precariously built cease-fire they've been coddling for the past three years."

Lily blinked at Darcy and hung on to the door handle when Manny made another sharp turn.

"In a not so distant former life," Darcy explained with a smile, "I worked as vice-consul for the U.S. Embassy— most recently in Manila."

Darcy exchanged a meaningful glance with Ethan before going on. "Old habit. I still keep abreast of political issues in this part of the world. And I know all too well how these struggling democracies work—or don't work, as the case may be. Plus we pulled everything we could find on Sri Lanka off the Net before leaving West Palm and we all read the material at least twice on the flight."

"Slow down." Dallas glanced around the bustling Colombo street. "We should be getting close."

Some of the vendors were preparing to close up shop for the day, but many still hawked products ranging from fruits, to vegetables, to fish, to sarongs—anything imaginable—from open-fronted stands lining the streets. Some sold out of two-wheel carts running single file down the middle of the stationary stalls.

The locals wore everything from the traditional saris and sarongs in blazing white, to rich, jewel-toned colors, to Western dress or a combination of both. Ox- and donkey-drawn carts competed for parking with hundreds of vehicles. Jeeps, Cadillacs, VWs, and even one old pickup that might have rolled off an assembly line in the early sixties lined the curbs.

Lily understood why Sri Lanka was a tourist's dream and an increasingly popular vacation spot for both Europeans and Americans. Colombo was exotic, vital, and a charming mix of old world and new. The scent of fruits and fish and suntan lotion and bug spray bled in through the Suburban's open window as they made their way slowly through the glut of color and culture.

Another time, another life, she might have enjoyed, even relished, exploring the markets and bazaars. The richness of it. The romance. The thrill of discovery.

But there was no romance in abduction. No richness

in fear. And there was no thrill in knowing that the man with whom she'd once shared lazy nights of love and laughter now regarded her with a wariness and trust reserved for pit vipers.

"There—that's it." Dallas's voice broke into her thoughts. "Pull over in front of that print shop. We'll see if my sources came through."

Manny double-parked and Dallas rolled out of the backseat. "Sit tight." He slapped a hand on the roof of the vehicle, then, dodging traffic, jogged across the street.

Lily watched as Dallas ducked inside a small shop. Inside the Suburban all was quiet. No one said a word—yet Lily got the feeling that to a person they all knew what Dallas was after, all but her.

The tension heightened to bowstring tautness. Perspiration trickled down her back as they waited, all of them sticky hot, all of them tense.

"What's he doing?" she asked when she couldn't stand it any longer.

Manny glanced over his shoulder at Ethan, who gave him a go-ahead nod.

"Making a deal." Manny propped his elbow on the open window frame, flexed his fingers on the steering wheel, and stared straight ahead. "If we're lucky."

A deal. There was only one commodity Lily could think of that required sources and deals. Weapons.

Both relief and panic hit her full bore. Relief that they weren't going after her baby without an arsenal. Panic that the illusion she'd secretly harbored of finding Adam and bringing him home without a deadly confrontation had just been shattered.

These men—these warriors who had fought for freedom, fought for peace—harbored no such delusions.

Her child was in grave danger. And everyone who went after him was in danger, too.

———

Same time, somewhere in the mountainous Badulla district, UVA Province, Sri Lanka

"Do you have any idea where we are?" Adam whispered. He didn't want to attract the attention of the armed guard who watched over them at the entrance of the cave.

Minrada lowered her head to her knees, where her bound wrists rested. She turned her head, blinked at Adam through the long curtain of thick black hair that fell over her eyes. "Still in the mountains. But south maybe. UVA Province? I'm not sure. It is cool. It is dry." Looking weary to the bone, she gave her head a slight shake. "Other than that, I do not know. There are caves all over in this area."

Adam could barely make out Minrada's features in the darkness. The cave was bone cold and midnight black. They'd been moved here from someplace outside of Kandy during the night. Bound and gagged, they'd been thrown into a rusty pickup, ordered to lie down, and covered with a filthy tarp. He didn't know how many kilometers they'd bounced along, their faces grinding into the rusted metal of the truck bed. The air had been thick with dust and sweat and the shift and grind of gears.

Beside them in the cave, Minrada's parents slept. Both were exhausted. Sathi was frightened and Amithnal held her, comforting her. Shit, they were *all* scared. Although, to look at her, you'd never know Minrada was a captive of this group of twenty men who were as short on explanations as they were on food and water.

She was cool, composed, and utterly calm. Adam had never known anyone so brave.

And he'd never felt so useless. The assholes who attacked them had come out of nowhere. They wore Tamil Tiger uniforms, Minrada had whispered when she and Adam were hauled into the truck. One minute the four of them—Adam, Minrada, Sathi, and Amithnal—were listening to the constant chatter of birds and admiring a temple ruin; the next, a dozen men with semiautomatic weapons, their faces covered with black scarves, surrounded them.

He should have fought them. No matter how many times Minrada had assured him no good would have come from it, Adam knew he should have fought.

And he *would* fight them. When the time was right. But now, he had to wait. His ass was asleep. The rock was cold and hard as steel beneath him. He had to bite his tongue to keep from bitching and moaning like a baby—probably would have done plenty of both if it hadn't been for Minrada. He'd thought he was tough. She'd taught him a thing or two about the word.

He'd never met anyone like her. She was twenty. Soft and curvy and only four years older than he was—and yet she had what his mom would refer to as an old soul. Old and strong and beautiful. Nothing like the girls he knew back home who were all about makeup and hair and stupid things. Baby things.

Minrada was . . . amazing.

"It's a pretty name," he'd told her one day when they'd been working side by side painting a classroom in a newly reclaimed grade school in Matara. "What does it mean?"

"My mother says it means 'she who gives wisdom and love.' "

"It fits you." It had taken Adam a long time to screw up the courage to say so.

When she'd smiled for him, he'd gone weak in the knees. No shit. He'd felt all rubbery and faint—*him*—and his face had burned hot. Probably turned as red as a ripe melon, too. He hadn't been able to speak to her again for a full day. What a dweeb.

He glanced toward the mouth of the cave. Studied the black silhouette of the soldier guarding the door. Kidnapped. Shit. He'd come to Sri Lanka for the adventure. For the experience. Because it was a cool thing to do. And yeah, because after reading about the tsunami victims, he'd wanted to help. But then he'd met Minrada. And in addition to the adventure, he'd fallen in love. With her soft black eyes. With the dark, inky silk of her hair. The warmth of her smile and the amazing generosity of her heart.

She was a woman. Until her, all he'd known was girls.

He let his head drop back against the cave's wall, let his eyes drift shut. When they got out of this—*if* they got out of this—he was going to tell her.

He was going to look into eyes as soft as a summer night, as dark as a deep mountain spring, and he was going to tell her he loved her.

Damn. And how was it that the thought of confessing his feelings to this woman scared him more than facing another night in the hands of hard men with big guns who were just looking for a reason to blow him to pieces?

"I pray that your saint is protecting us," Minrada whispered.

Adam let out a long breath, thought of the silver medal his mother had placed over his head before he'd boarded his flight.

"What's this?" He studied the medallion, then searched her face, trying not to be embarrassed that his mom was about to cry in the middle of a crowded airport terminal.

"St. Christopher. Patron saint of travelers."

He had to grin. "Mom . . . we're not Catholic," he pointed out gently.

And that made her grin, too, thank God, because things were getting real close to watery.

"Humor me. Wear it anyway. It's like the one your father wore. It's important to me that you have it. Especially now."

"Fine. Don't get all blubbery about it," he said, refusing to admit, even to himself, that he felt a little burn behind his eyelids, too.

"Adam?"

Minrada's soft voice filtered out of the darkness and brought him back to the bleak, hard darkness of the cave.

"Yeah," he said, just as softly so as not to rouse the guard's attention. "I hope the medal works, too."

He lifted his bound hands, touched the medal. Thought of his mom. Thought of his father. Wished he'd known him. Wished he knew more about him.

"I spy something . . . black," Minrada's voice whispered across the cold stone walls.

Despite the trouble they were in, he smiled. They played the old standard children's game often while they worked side by side at the school in the sweltering heat in Matara. It passed time while they painted or repaired plaster or cleaned. It was silly. It made them laugh.

She spied something black, all right.

"Everything," he whispered back, and hoped she heard the smile in his voice.

"Excellent. You win an all-expense-paid trip to anywhere but here."

Again he grinned, then sobered abruptly when the guard stood at attention and two additional silhouettes filled the opening of the cave.

What now? Adam wondered as his heart stumbled. Someone struck a match, and a flare of a torch lit the dank cavern and temporarily blinded him.

"You, come," one of their captors said in Tamil.

Shit, Adam thought, and dutifully started to rise. A boot in his chest knocked him back to the floor. He cracked his elbow hard on the cave floor and bit back a cry as pain exploded and nausea rolled through his belly. When the guard reached for Minrada and dragged her to her feet, Adam forgot all about the pain.

"Leave her alone!" He struggled to his feet again. "Take me."

The butt end of a rifle slammed into his midsection. It doubled him over, sent him tumbling to the ground. A bell rang in his head when he hit the cave floor. Stars floated like trailing rockets through his vision. And then nothing.

Nothing but black and more nothing and pain.

CHAPTER 10

Colombo

"Well, you tried. It was worth a shot," Manny said an hour later.

Dallas had made his connection at the print shop and scheduled a time and place for an exchange of cash for guns. Since then they'd met with Emory, Adam's student adviser—who was as panicked as Lily and had nothing new to report. They exchanged phone numbers with promises to update each other with any news, then moved on to the U.S. Embassy, where they were now.

"I expected more," Darcy grumbled as she climbed into the Suburban and Ethan shut the door behind her. Because of her embassy connections, Darcy had been granted an after-hours consultation. That's as far as the favor had been extended.

Manny tried not to focus on or be moved by the disappointment and anxiety tightening Lily's face as he checked for oncoming traffic, then pulled out onto the street. A plea to the embassy for help had been a long shot; the thumbs-down had been all but a foregone conclusion. But they'd had to try.

"Their resources—human and otherwise—have been stretched thin since the tsunami," Darcy said in defense of the embassy staff as they rolled along the rutted streets back toward the market district. "They're doing what they can."

"Which basically means we're on our own," Ethan said.

"It's just as well."

Manny glanced in the rearview mirror when Dallas grumbled from the backseat.

"Not that I don't appreciate your attempt at diplomacy, Darcy, but—"

"Yes, Dallas, I know, *but* what?" Darcy said.

So did everyone else. Neither the U.S. Embassy officials nor the Sinhalese government could sanction a rescue mission by Americans that would most likely involve a show of force. The *but* was that it didn't matter to any of the individuals in this vehicle. They would proceed with or without a blessing.

"We need to get out of Colombo." Lily's voice was on the shrill side. "We need to be looking for Adam."

Manny glanced sharply at her. She looked like she was nearing the end of her rope. He understood. They'd been on the ground for almost two and a half hours and they still weren't looking for her son.

For *his* son.

God. Manny was still wrestling with, adjusting to, *reeling* over, the fact that he had a child. A child he might never get to meet if they didn't get some leads, and fast.

His fingers tightened on the steering wheel while his stomach knotted in both anger and loss.

"Take it easy, Lily," he said, taking his frustration out on her. "We can't go off half-cocked and unprepared. We need to lay in supplies. In the meantime, we can't connect with Dallas's contact for another two hours and we can't head into this unarmed."

Her dark eyes met his and he steeled himself against

the raw pain he saw. Finally, she nodded, drew in a settling breath. "I know. I know. It's just . . ."

"It's okay, Lily." Darcy cast Manny a quick glance, a
silent plea to ease up a little. "We're all on edge. We
know what's at stake here."

At stake was a boy's life. A family's life.

His son's life.

*Damn Lily. Damn her for . . . for what, Ortega? For
not telling you about Adam? The woman thought you
were dead.*

Yeah. She'd thought he was dead, he reminded himself before he cut her some slack, because she'd turned
him in to Poveda.

"Take a left up there," Dallas said from the backseat.
"I saw an army surplus store. We should be able to get
the rest of what we need in the form of gear there."

"And once we do, let's work on losing the tail before
we make our next connection."

Four pairs of surprised eyes turned to Ethan.

"That's right, children. We've got company. White
VW. Picked him up when we left the embassy."

"Who? Why?"

"Good questions." Ethan flashed Darcy a tight smile
before checking the rearview mirror. "Someone was with
the Suburban at all times, right?"

"While you and Darcy were in the embassy? Yeah."
Manny knew what Ethan was asking. Had anyone had
an opportunity to plant a tracking device on the vehicle?
"No one came within ten meters of us."

"Well, someone wants to get up close and personal
now," Ethan pointed out unnecessarily. "The question is
do we want to find out who it is or fly blind?"

Manny glanced at Lily wondering about the calls

she'd made. "How bad of a time did you give the Sin-halese officials?"

"My son is missing in their country. How bad of a time do you think I gave them? I begged. I threatened. I screamed at them."

"So they probably had you on a watch list before you even set foot in the airport."

"Why would they care that I'm here?" Frustration colored her voice. "We're doing their damn job, for God's sake. We're searching for their people and my son."

"They would care for the same reason they won't act to find Adam and the Muhandiramalas," Darcy said with a sympathetic look at Lily. "Any action on their part could risk the peace with the Tigers—that's how volatile the cease-fire is. People are tired of the fighting. The prime minister is worried about public opinion. She doesn't want to take unnecessary risks that might reignite the blaze. Plus, it's an election year."

"Well . . . God forbid we screw up an election," Lily sputtered, angry and frustrated.

She fidgeted absently with the seat-belt buckle and Manny worried again that she might be nearing a breaking point.

Not that he cared about her, he reminded himself, but they couldn't afford to have her flip out and jeopardize their operation.

"Okay, here's the way I see it," Dallas said after a moment. "If it is a local government enclave checking up on us and we confront them, they'll know we're on to them, right? So we'd be forcing their hand. I'm not sure we want to do that. They might decide that to save face they'd need to give us a short, sweet bon voyage party and ship us home, FedEx.

"On the other hand," he continued as everyone mulled that over, "if we don't let on that we know they're watching us, maybe they'll be content to just play spy."

"And by the time they figure out we've got their number, we'll have lost them," Manny concluded.

Dallas's grin held little humor. "You always were a quick study, Ortega."

"Yeah. That's why they pay me the big bucks." Manny managed a tight smile.

From the corner of his eye he caught Lily's reaction. She smiled, too—a nervous "yeah, okay, we need to lighten up" smile. It was the first smile he'd seen her give up since this whole thing started. And despite the gravity of the situation, it made him think of a faraway Nicaragua summer. The smiles they'd shared. The love they'd made.

For an instant, his heart ached as much for that loss as for the loss of the son he didn't know.

He turned his head. Met her eyes, wondered if she was thinking the same thing, and abruptly looked away.

"And what if they aren't government people?"

Ethan glanced at Manny, shook his head. "Then that means someone else cares that we're here. Another player—one we hadn't figured on. And what *that* means is that we've got bigger problems than the threat of civil war."

Manny pulled into a parking spot across from the surplus store. *A problem bigger than war.*

There was a time in his life when he couldn't have imagined a bigger problem than war.

But now Lily was back in his life. Now he had a son. And the idea that his own flesh, his own blood, could be forever lost was as unimaginable as the idea of the woman he had loved betraying him.

———

Making certain he wasn't followed, Dallas rounded the corner and headed for the prearranged meeting spot. The contrast between the bland back alley and the multi-colored brilliance of the street vendors at the open-market bazaar two miles away was absolute. They'd gone from a vibrant, lively cacophony of sound and scent and tactile sensations to a seedy unseemliness that made up too much of life in too many parts of the world.

The transformation of tone and intent was sobering.

As was this leg of their journey. If something went wrong here, they were royally fucked.

Manny had skillfully lost their tail a little over an hour ago. And now, as directed by his contact, Dallas approached the back door of a decrepit building in the Slave Island section of the city while Ethan and Manny and the women waited around the corner in the Suburban. Dallas knocked twice, then four times in rapid succession. And then he waited.

Dallas didn't know the boy. Didn't know Lily Campora—hadn't yet decided what he felt toward her other than resentment. Manny was his friend. And it was to Manny that Dallas attached his loyalties. Most recently, they'd been through a minor war together helping Ethan rescue Darcy from an Abu Sayyaf terrorist cell on a southern Philippine island. Darcy and Amy Walker.

As it always did, the memory of Amy—broken and scarred both physically and emotionally—caught Dallas off guard. It had been almost three months since Amy had appeared, then disappeared from his life.

And he hadn't been able to let go. He should have.

But he couldn't.

She'd suffered. Suffered bad. Both Amy and Darcy had been held hostage. Both had been changed because of what they'd gone through.

In the dark of night, in places like this that reeked of the worst life had to offer, Dallas could still see Amy's delicate blue eyes—empty of anything but fear and pain. He could still see her face, bruised and bleeding, framed by snarled and matted blond hair that he'd mistaken for brown until the first time he'd seen it clean.

Yet he could still feel her spirit—shaken but valiant as she'd grappled with trust. In him. In herself. In a world that had turned her over to the animals who had raped and abused her.

She hadn't deserved what had happened to her. Just as Adam Campora didn't deserve what had happened to him. And it was Adam who needed Dallas's help now. Wherever Amy Walker was, he couldn't help her. But he could help Adam. He wanted to get to that boy. Get him out of whatever hell he was going through—because Dallas knew a thing or two about hell himself.

He was getting damn sick of the flashbacks. And they were coming on him more frequently now, blasting him out of sleep some nights with the concussion of a live grenade. Flying rock. Splattered blood. The screams of men.

And he felt himself sucked into the nightmare again.

He shook his head.

Don't go there. Not now.

Christ, he couldn't deal with that now.

He slapped his face. Hard. Then again to snap himself back to the present when he heard footsteps behind the locked door. The door creaked open. Dark eyes set in a brown leathery face glared out at him.

This snake of a man didn't give two shits about saving Adam Campora's life. This man, like so many others in the warmonger business, cared only about cash. In the Sri Lankan underground, rupees were the universal language of "how to make things happen."

Dallas suspected that in this particular back alley, money had made a lot of things happen. His background in Force Recon could make things happen, too. And his quick study of languages would assist in the process. Provided he could keep his shit together.

Dallas pointed to himself. "Dallas Garrett. Jahan mah-mah, e-vah-nah-vaah." *Dallas Garrett. Jahan sent me.*

The man peered outside and glanced around. Apparently satisfied that Dallas was alone, he nodded. "Sahl-li?" *Money?*

Dallas patted his breast pocket.

The man held out his hand.

Dallas could play this game. He shook his head. "Na-ha. Pah-lah-mu-wah-nah pan-sah-lah." *No. First see pencils.*

He'd been cautioned not to refer to the commodity they were bargaining for as guns. In keeping with the print shop front, he was here to purchase pencils. It would have been laughable if lives weren't hanging in the balance.

After a brief hesitation, the man gave a slight bow and stepped aside. "A-thul ve-nah-vaah." *Enter.*

Dallas bowed as well, then followed him into the dank-smelling building. More important, Dallas entered into critical negotiations for the means to save a boy's life.

———

Badulla district, UVA Province

Sathi had stopped crying. Amithnal held her close and shushed her, soothed her, whispering that everything was going to be okay.

Adam hoped to hell Amithnal was right. It felt like hours since their captors had taken Minrada—in reality, probably no more than an hour had passed. In the dark of the cave, time crawled like ants. Adam didn't know if it was day or night.

But he did know one thing. He'd kill the bastards if they hurt Minrada. Kill them with his bare hands if he had to. She was everything good and fine and special. And they were animals.

He lifted his bound wrists to his face and rubbed at his swollen eye with the heels of his hands. Blood from the hit he'd taken to his temple had caked and clotted and clouded his vision. His head throbbed. His gut and ribs ached where they'd clubbed him. It hurt like hell to bend his elbow.

He supposed he should be good and scared now, but what he was, was pissed. If they hurt her. If they—

The sound of approaching voices brought his head up. His heart started pounding. A small ray of light gradually grew to the yellow-rose glow of a torch beam and filled the cave. Shadowy silhouettes, distorted and wavy, formed on the striated rock walls before two guards came into view.

Minrada wasn't with them.

Adam planted his shoulder blades against the cave wall and levered himself to a standing position. "Where is she? Where's Minrada?"

The guards said something to each other in Tamil, then laughed. On the floor of the cave, Sathi cried out, a grieving sound of a mother for her child.

Adam's adrenaline kicked him full in the gut. "If you bastards touched her I'll kill you!"

The guards grabbed him by the arms and dragged him toward the mouth of the cave. Behind him, he could hear Amithnal calling out to them. Adam didn't understand his words but knew without a doubt what he was saying.

He was pleading. Pleading for his daughter's life. Pleading for Adam's life. Offering to give them anything they wanted if they would spare the children. Sathi's sobs, muffled against her husband's chest, followed Adam out of the cave and into the sun's blinding glare.

He bit back bile as the pain lancing through his head made him nauseous. And then instinct and adrenaline kicked in. He started fighting. With everything in him, he fought. He dragged his feet, swung his bound wrists. Used his head to butt, his shoulders to dislodge. His knee to gouge.

But he was one. Against two. Then two more who came running out of their tent, laughing, like it was sport, as they wrestled him to the ground. Spent, he went lax when they lifted him, then carried him by his feet and his hands and tossed him into the depths of yet another cave.

Sprawled facedown on damp rock, he groaned at the

pain. Panted. Cursed. Blood ran into his eyes again. His ears rang.

"Adam?"

Minrada.

He stilled when the sound of her voice whispered out of the darkness. And felt his first pulse beat of hope since they'd taken her away, when the touch of her fingers grazed the back of his hand.

————

Outskirts of Ratnapura

Green, green, and more green. Verdant. Fertile. Lush. Another time, Lily would have appreciated the beauty. The birdsong. The wild, tropical uniqueness of the countryside. Now she just wanted to get somewhere, anywhere, she had a chance of finding her son.

The sun was gone now. The heat remained, forceful, unrelenting, saturated with the promise of a heavy night dew. With Manny still behind the wheel, silent and stoic, they'd covered the one hundred kilometers from the coastal region of Colombo to Ratnapura in what Lily suspected was record time.

As soon as Dallas had concluded his gun deal and they'd been certain no one was following them, they'd lit out of town like bandits. It still hadn't been fast enough for her even as the Suburban ate up the coastal highway, then veered east to the winding road that passed by the paddy fields cloaking the valley floor. As they climbed steadily higher in altitude, rubber tree forests interspersed with acres of tea bushes flourished on the hillsides and scented the air.

Life—rich and vibrant—surrounded them. Yet all she felt was anxiety and frustration.

She heard movement in the second seat, where Darcy and Ethan had been sleeping for the last hour or so. Dallas was sacked out farther back. Provisions and Dallas's contraband weapons and ammunition were stowed in every available space inside the Suburban. More supplies were lashed to a carrier on the roof.

There had been no sign of a white VW in the Suburban's rearview mirror.

"What are the candles about, do you suppose?" Darcy asked around a yawn as they passed several older houses in the small village of Kahangama.

Lily glanced back to see Darcy stretching as she sat up. "Traditionalists light candles at dusk and leave them on the doorstep. They believe the candles keep evil spirits from entering their homes."

Lily turned back to the side window, searching the dark, always looking for a sign to lead her to her son. She wished that all it took was a lit candle to protect Adam. He could use some help warding off evil. And she could use some protein, Lily realized—something to counteract the fatigue leaning on her like a hundred pounds of lead. But she couldn't make herself eat. Just the thought of food made her nauseous.

She was exhausted, but anxiety over Adam kept the adrenaline at spike level and prevented sleep. From a physiological standpoint, she understood that adrenaline was pretty much all that kept her going. She wasn't sure what gave Manny his stamina.

Wearily she offered to drive.

"I'm fine," he said without so much as a glance her way.

"Always were a stubborn SOB." This from Ethan,

who had also roused himself. "Pull over, Rambo. Catch a power nap. I'll take a turn behind the wheel."

To her amazement, Manny pulled over. They all took the opportunity to get out of the Suburban and stretch—all but Dallas, who lifted his head, then laid it back down when Ethan uttered a quiet, "Chill, bro."

It was Ethan who caught Lily's arm when she wobbled and almost went down. But it was Manny who stepped to her side and steered her toward the backseat.

"Climb in the back with Darcy." The gentleness in his tone surprised her and undercut the stern set of his mouth. "You need to sleep."

She would have argued, but Darcy was suddenly beside her, guiding her into the vehicle. "Adam's going to need you rested. You won't be any good to him if you drop over from exhaustion."

Lily actually managed a smile. "Okay, now I understand why you had a career in the diplomatic corps."

"Don't even think about arguing with her." Ethan settled in behind the wheel while Manny climbed into the passenger seat, slumped down low, and closed his eyes. "It's a no-win situation."

"Why, thank you, Lieutenant." Darcy smiled and made room for Lily to lie down on the seat beside her. "Next time we square off, I'll remind you of that little concession. Save us both a lot of time and trouble."

Ethan grunted and shifted the Suburban into gear. "Fixed my own wagon with that one."

Easy. They were so easy with each other, Lily thought as she folded her hands beneath her cheek and closed her eyes. That was the way with love. She'd longed for that once. Longed for that gentle, flirty teasing. Those knowing looks. The ones that said there were no secrets—at least not from each other. The ones that said there were no lies.

The closest she'd ever come to what Darcy and Ethan had was a summer a lifetime ago. With a man who now considered her a traitor.

Manny had been a loving, playful young man when she'd known him then. He'd worn his heart on his sleeve, his emotions in his eyes. He'd been a warrior then, too—but his heart had been gentle.

There was nothing gentle about him now.

Not even his speech. She used to love his lushly romantic Spanish accent. Now even most of that was gone. Seventeen years in the United States had added a crispness to his enunciation and speech patterns. Seventeen years had added a deepness to his voice.

Seventeen years. Lost.

Like her son was lost. Like more hours were lost in her search to find him.

Like she felt lost . . . until she felt the warm comfort of Darcy's hand on her shoulder.

It was a small gesture. A huge expression of understanding. One she'd craved in this hostile country amid all these quietly hostile men. One she welcomed.

Against all odds she drifted off to sleep as a warm, wet tear trickled from the corner of her eye.

CHAPTER 11

On the road to Kandy

"Be lucky if the sonofabitch doesn't jam on the first round," Ethan sputtered. Well-hidden in a copse of trees, he lifted the seen-better-days AK-47 to his shoulder and sighted down the barrel.

It had been a bitch of a day. And this was the first chance they'd had to inspect the weapons and ammunition up close and personal.

"Yeah, well, you can pick your friends, but you can't pick your friendly neighborhood black-market weapons suppliers," Manny heard Dallas say with a grunt. "Or the weapons he supplies. At least not all of them. Trust me these are better than the ancient AK-74s the bastard wanted to pass off as 'superior quality.'"

They were "pseudo" camping in a public campground, well back from the main contingent of campers, acting like tourists, playing down their presence, drawing as little attention as possible. And taking a little time to regroup and figure out where to go from here after a full day in Ratnapura.

Arms crossed, knees locked, feet set wide, Manny stood back in the shadows as his friends examined the weapons Dallas had bargained for in Colombo. Manny had just come from the communal shower in the center of the campground. His hair was still wet. His shirt hung open and free of his cargo pants.

The late-afternoon breeze felt fine against his exposed skin where it funneled in through the open placket of his shirt. It was the only thing that felt fine.

He agreed with Ethan's and Dallas's assessment of the weapons. The rifles—funny how Soviet-made weaponry turned up in every war-torn country he'd ever been in—were functional at best. The handguns were a step up but still a far cry from the state-of-the-art firepower they'd had available when they'd staged Darcy's rescue mission on Jolo three months ago. There they'd had contacts with the U.S. spec ops boys stationed in Manila, who'd gladly let them "borrow" an arsenal that would make a five-star general drop to his knees and weep with fucking joy. Here they had a back-alley deal—with back-alley quality—at Wall Street prices.

Manny glanced toward the darkening sky. The morning had started off cool; it had been a brief respite for what had morphed into a scorcher of a day. They were at a higher altitude now. The night would cool down to tolerable.

Right now, they were all whipped. What sleep they'd gotten last night had been in the Suburban—if power naps could be called sleeping. The guys were okay. Manny was concerned about Darcy and Lily, though. Today in Ratnapura had been long and grueling, but they hadn't wanted to attract any more attention than necessary by checking into a hotel tonight.

The plan was to rest a few hours here tonight, then hit the road before first light. There'd be time for sleeping once they found Adam. In the meantime, each hour was a loss on so many counts. Not that they'd wasted any time. Today they'd spread out and split up into three groups: Ethan with Darcy; Dallas on his own, which he preferred; and Manny had taken Lily by default.

It wasn't that Manny wanted to be with her. Hell no. What choice had he had? She might not be safe on her own, and Dallas and Ethan clearly didn't want to be saddled with her. Manny's friends' reaction to Lily was barely veiled disdain.

He watched a painted stork swoop lazily across the sky, told himself he didn't need to feel any guilt over the way they treated her. That both Ethan and Dallas were solid in the character judgment department and were forming their own conclusions.

He lied.

The guys were his friends. His brothers. They'd disliked Lily on general principle from the moment he'd told them about Adam. And they were taking their cues from Manny. At first he'd felt justified in their response. Lily deserved to be treated like a pariah. He was entitled to their anger on his behalf.

But he could see how their cold shoulder affected her. It wounded. Yet she took it on the chin. The look in her eyes said, *The hell with you.*

It was hard not to admire her for that, he admitted grudgingly. Or for her single-minded determination to find her son. She loved that boy. Would move mountains, rivers . . . hard-faced men to find him. And she was running on empty. But she didn't complain. She had to be out of her mind with worry—but she didn't boo-hoo and wail.

Instead, she looked stoic and determined and so goddamn beautiful it made him ache.

Bad.

So, yeah. It was hard not to admire her—even though he didn't want to. He wanted to keep feeding his anger—yet the sharp edge had dulled and doubt had set in. Maybe he'd been wrong. Maybe . . .

Hell. He tipped his head back. Glared at the canopy of leaves shielding the setting sun, breathed deep of the forest loam and the distinct scent of tea leaves that filled the humid air. It royally pissed him off that the resentment wasn't nearly as potent as it had been before she'd shown up after nearly two decades.

And it ticked him off that they hadn't made any major strides in finding Adam. They'd canvassed the city of some forty thousand all day. No clues. No leads. No ideas of where to go next.

It wasn't until a little over an hour ago, when they'd about decided the day would come up empty, that they'd finally gotten their first break.

The Rest House was a colonial-style inn that sat on the top of the hill that dominated Ratnapura. The manager of the inn, the son of a gem dealer who owned the property, had seen Adam.

"Yes, yes, American boy," he said, pleased to help when Manny showed him Adam's photo. "Tall. Like this?" He'd held his hand above his head—which wasn't all that far, considering he barely reached five feet.

When Lily had nodded, the innkeeper had hurried on, eager to assist. "He and a young lady, they come on the bus. A man and woman—the lady's mother and father, from Colombo, I think—met the children here for dinner. They laughed much. I heard them mention Kirindi Ella Falls and the game preserve on the way to Kandy."

It wasn't much more than they'd already known, but at least someone had seen Adam and his host family. Whether they made it to Kandy was still up for grabs, but it was a place to start tomorrow.

Manny hadn't wanted to be, but he'd been moved by the mixture of relief and renewed worry that crossed Lily's face when she heard the news. Just like he didn't want to be impressed now, as she marched past him and joined Ethan and Dallas by the cache of weapons.

Manny stood at attention when she picked up a Browning Hi-Power P35, then proceeded to handle it like she toted the damn thing every day of her life.

Jesus Christ, look at her.

Life threw him few surprises these days, but, as she had since she'd reentered his life a few short days ago, Lily knocked the ground out from under him again when she grasped the semiautomatic handgun. She tested its weight with the familiarity of a seasoned shooter, then sighted down the barrel using a two-handed grip.

The weapon looked big in her small hands, but not clumsy. She racked the side like a pro, said something to Ethan that Manny couldn't hear, then with a nod pocketed a box of ammo and shoved the gun into the waistband of her khaki pants. And he felt an ache tighten and twist low in his groin.

Dallas and Ethan exchanged a look that encompassed surprise and awe—as well as an unspoken, *Make a note not to piss* her *off.*

No shit.

Manny had many memories of Lily Campora. Most of them involved her naked in his bed. None of them were of a pistol-packing Amazon with a grim-reaper look on her face. A look that spoke volumes of both the strain and the unwavering resolve of a woman focused on one and only one thing: finding her son.

Despite the way she'd expertly handled the gun, Manny had to ask. When she would have walked past him back to the Suburban, he stepped in front of her.

"That's a lot of firepower. You sure you're up to handling it?"

She looked dead ahead, avoiding his eyes. "I'd prefer a .45, but the 9mm will do. The action's pretty much the same as my Springfield."

Manny blinked. "Your Springfield?"

"Springfield Armory 1911. It's a copy of the Colt semi-automatic that used to be the military's service pistol—"

"Whoa, whoa. I know what it is," he said, cutting her off. "What I don't know is what the hell are you doing with a Springfield?"

Still avoiding eye contact, she rolled a shoulder. Dismissive, impatient. "There's a lot you don't know about me."

She was right about that. He didn't want to know, either, he told himself. He knew everything about her that he needed to know. Nothing good would come of asking more.

And yet, damn if he didn't. "Like what?"

She glanced at him then, like she questioned his motives for asking. Hell, so did he.

In the end, she shrugged again. "I've been alone a long time."

The weariness in her tone suggested that "alone" hadn't necessarily been part of her plan. He decided not to think about that.

"I sometimes feel the need for protection. The Springfield provides it."

Her eyes held a hint of defiance. A full measure of resolve. And, though she would never admit it, a boatload
of fatigue.

She was a woman on the brink of collapse.

"When was the last time you ate?" he growled, more
upset with himself for caring than with her for not taking care of herself.

"Not your concern." She moved to walk past him.

He wrapped his fingers around her upper arm. And
realized his mistake too late.

He hadn't intended to touch her. Had never intended
to touch her again. He hadn't wanted to resurrect, recon-
struct, or in any way renew memories of what her warm
flesh felt like beneath his hand. To be amazed by the
satin softness of her skin. To imagine what it would feel
like to sink into the giving, gloving warmth of her lush
body again after all these years.

He closed his eyes. Insane. He was in-fucking-sane.

"Eat something," he ordered, and let her go, his body
practically humming from the electric rush. "Then get
some rest. You aren't going to be any good to yourself or
your son if you don't keep up your strength."

She turned with a sharp look, seemed about to say
something, but abruptly walked away instead.

The fact was, she hadn't had to verbalize what was on
her mind. She'd transmitted her message loud and clear
with one look from those incredible eyes: It wasn't just
her son's life on the line here. It was *his* son's life, as well.

His son.

Manny thought of the photograph Lily had given him.
The one he now carried like a talisman. He'd memorized
the boy's face. Saw himself in it so clearly it made his

throat ache. And he wondered, *Does Adam even know my name?*

Manny hadn't realized he'd clenched his jaw until it started to cramp. Slowly, he let off on the pressure while residual tension built and bred in his gut, coiling in on itself like a spring.

He'd hated Lily Campora for half of his life. Had never wanted to see her again. And now her life was embroiled so intricately with his, it was as if those years had never existed.

Except they had.

He had a sixteen-year-old son whose existence said they had.

And here he stood. His hand still tingling from touching her. Wanting to go after her. Wanting to ask . . . hell, a million questions. Why was she alone? Why wasn't there a man in her life now? Manny was half-crazy wondering how many men there had been after that Nicaragua summer when she had been his.

When she had been his.

Manny looked south toward the distant peak of Mount Pidurutalagala, unaware that he'd clenched his jaw again until he felt it pop. She swore she hadn't betrayed him. That she'd searched for him. That she'd been told he'd died in battle.

He had no reason to believe her. And now, just because she insisted he was wrong, just because every time he looked at her his gut twisted and he wanted to bury himself deep inside of her, he questioned everything he thought he'd known about her. Questioned every motivation he'd ever owned that had been fueled by his hatred.

"Dios," he swore under his breath, and walked toward

Dallas and Ethan to stake a claim on an AK-47 and the
Czech CZ-52 he'd spotted in the mix.

He was no better than that boy who had been seduced
by an older woman with eyes that cried and a body that
had made him weep. Even now, his cock reacted to the
sight of her. To the memory of her. To the reality that
Lily was no longer a raw, gut-wrenching part of his past.

She was part of his present.

And he was certifiably insane, because more than he
wanted to hate her, more than he wanted to justify that
hate, he wanted something else.

He wanted her.

And if that didn't make him out of his fucking mind,
he didn't know what did.

————

Lily stowed the Browning and ammunition in the bottom
of her medical bag, steeling herself at the thought of using it. Then she ate—not because she'd been ordered to,
but because she'd be damned if she'd give Manny or the
Garretts a reason to blame her for slowing them down.
And then she slept for an hour—for the same reason.

She even bit her tongue to keep from railing at them to
move out and resume their search in Kandy. But common
sense told her they all needed some rest. She was restless
now, though, so she walked through the thickening dusk.

All day long, she'd gotten the feeling that Manny had
bitten the proverbial bullet and taken responsibility for
her. Like she was a liability. Or an encumbrance.

Their little exchange a while ago cemented that notion.
She'd missed an opportunity then to set him straight on

that point. To make certain he knew she could hold her own and didn't need him running interference for her.

But she'd gotten sidetracked. And she wasn't proud of herself over the reason why. There he'd stood. Wet from a shower, his shirt open, his skin glistening. The cool silver of his St. Christopher medal lay in stark contrast against the warm butter bronze of his skin.

He'd been a handsome boy. He was a stunning man. Shockingly so.

So shockingly it had momentarily insulated her from the real world. And in that moment, all she could think, all she could feel, was the knot of desire twisting low in her belly, the tingling in her fingers with the need to touch him. Just . . . touch. Just reclaim what once had been hers for the price of a smile.

There were no smiles from Manny Ortega now. And she was . . . what? Baffled? Ashamed? Annoyed with herself?

All of the above, she settled on finally. She shook herself out of her little side trip to lust and cut herself a little slack. She was desperate to find Adam. Desperate, also, for some relief from the constant and grisly thoughts that plagued her. Manny, regardless of his feelings for her, offered diversion.

Well, she didn't want diversion from him right now. She decided on the spot that she wanted to clear the air—something she should have done earlier. She'd missed an opportunity then to tell him she was up to here with his tight-lipped, stiff-backed, regard-her-like-she-was-a-leper attitude and to get over it.

So she went looking for him. To confront him. To set him straight or give up trying.

Instead of just Manny, however, she found all three men together. It was hard not to be moved by the picture they made. Their dark good looks contrasted with the white shirts they all wore; their expressions were intense, their eyes hard, as they huddled over a small fortune in cash like thieves over stolen loot.

Jesus.

It was a huge sum of money—money that Lily suspected she wasn't supposed to have seen. But there it was. Three big piles on the ground between Ethan, Dallas, and Manny that they appeared to be divvying up.

Finances hadn't been at the top of her concerns when she'd asked Manny for his help. Yeah, she'd known she'd owe someone money when this was over. She just hadn't realized how much.

"I . . . I'll repay you. I . . . I don't know when," she stammered, still stunned by the amount of cash that lay on the ground at their feet. "But I'll pay you back."

Three pairs of eyes snapped her way. Even in the fading light, she could see their surprise transition to resolve.

Ethan and Dallas glanced at Manny. "You explain it," Ethan said, and he and Dallas picked up their share of the bills and walked away.

Which left Lily with Manny—only suddenly it didn't seem like such a good idea to be alone with him.

Not because he frightened her. Not even because he hated her.

It was a bad idea for an entirely different reason. One that shouldn't have come as a surprise but blindsided her just the same—just as it had earlier.

It wasn't just the visual of all that cash that had her heart rate soaring off the charts. It wasn't even the visual he made—all Rambo commando male perfection.

No matter how she tried to tell herself it was all about the physical pull, it came to her now that there was so much more.

It was him. The whole man. It had *been* him since she'd seen him in the ER what now seemed like years ago.

He'd become a craving to her—body and mind. Satisfying it had been amazing. No one—before or since, although there'd been damn few of either—had touched her, pleased her, moved her, like Manolo Ortega.

Perfect. Just . . . perfect.

She didn't get it. She wasn't a masochist. And she didn't make a habit of clinging to something that wasn't hers. Maybe it was because she was so worried. So mired in concern over Adam. It made her vulnerable.

Well, hell. She'd rather choke than apply that word to herself, but if she was being honest, it was true. She *was* vulnerable right now. And raw. With emotions and fear and a growing regret for all the lost years, all the misunderstandings and unfulfilled dreams.

"The money," Manny said, snapping Lily out of her funk as he folded the huge wad of cash into his wallet, "is not an issue for you to worry about."

"Excuse me?" Why she laughed, she didn't know. Nothing about this was funny. "Not an issue? There had to have been a hundred thousand or more on the ground a minute ago."

"Closer to two hundred K," Manny admitted, "but as I said, it's not an issue."

"Why? Because if you tell me where it came from you'll have to kill me?" Now that *really* wasn't funny. But she so didn't care.

She was frustrated and confused over the way she reacted to Manny—which was the way she had *always* reacted to Manny. She couldn't look at his mouth without wanting to own it. Couldn't see the pulse beat at his throat without wanting to heighten it. Couldn't look into those black Latin eyes and not wonder if he still wanted her, too.

And it was all pointless, Lily realized, beyond frustration and exhaustion and worry.

It was the wrong place.

Wrong time.

Wrong . . .

Just wrong.

CHAPTER 12

"We have a benefactor, okay?" Manny said. "It's that simple."

Lily shot him an incredulous look, worry for Adam rolling over the guilt she felt for her knee-jerk physical reaction to this man. "A benefactor?"

He shoved his wallet into his hip pocket. "One who can afford to bankroll us."

"Because he thinks you're . . . special?"

On any other man, in any other light, the slight tightening of his lips could have been mistaken for a smile. But Lily had seen Manny Ortega's smiles. This wasn't even close.

It was a grimace. Of impatience, she suspected. A save-me-from-this-insufferable-female smirk.

"Nolan—Ethan and Dallas's brother—once saved the life of a very rich man's daughter."

"A rich man's daughter? Does the daughter have a name?"

He hesitated, then told her. "Jillian Kincaid. Jillian Garrett now."

"Kincaid? As in Kincaid Publishing?" There were perhaps seven or eight major players in the publishing industry. Kincaid was at the top of the list.

"The same."

Lily might be a little sleep deprived—a condition she'd like to blame for this glut of physical reaction to Manny—but she managed to put it together. "So Nolan now has a rich father-in-law."

"Who is eager and willing to back certain . . . operations."

"Operations." She repeated the word as if mulling it over when in fact her temper flared like a flash fire. She was closer to the edge than she'd thought, because the distant, cold mechanics of the word had her seeing red. "My son is *not* an operation."

"Yes," Manny said after a long moment in which he seemed to be taking her measure. "He is. That's how we get him out of this. By keeping it impersonal. By keeping it real."

"Real? *Jesus.* You want real?" It was too much suddenly. Emotions that had been balancing on a thin, frayed line teetered, toppled, and plunged. "This is what's real. My son—*your* son—is in danger. We don't know where he is. We don't know who took him. What they're . . . what they're doing to him."

She stopped, tried to collect herself, and fell short. She covered her face with her hands, then on a deep breath raked the hair back from her forehead. "We don't know if he—if he's hurt. Or sick. Or, God, if he's even—"

"Lily." Manny's voice was hard, cautionary, as she spun around, paced away, paced back again.

He wanted her to settle down. She wasn't in a settling mood. "He's a boy! He . . . he is not an *operation,* got it? He's *my* child—"

Strong arms banded around her, dragged her flush against a chest as unyielding as her anger.

The sound that came out of her mouth was primal, raw, unrecognizable as her own, as she keened out her heartache and frustration.

"God. Oh God, Manny. He can't be dead. He can't be d—"

He cupped her head in his big hand and pressed her face against his shoulder. Holding her steady. Holding her still.

Holding her together with his arms and his body and his heartbeat that pulsed against her cheek.

She'd lost it. God, she knew she'd lost it. Just like she knew he was holding her to quiet her, not to comfort her.

That should have angered her, too. Should have shamed her. Should have had her pushing out of his arms and dealing with her outburst on her own.

But she was weaker than she'd thought. And that was as demoralizing as it was defeating. Defeating to know that she needed this from him—no matter what the reason. Needed his arms around her. Needed the reminder that once there'd been something magical and good between them, when now everything was horrible and scary and she felt so damn helpless.

But for the strong, rough cadence of his heart beating beneath her ear and the sound of her own ragged breaths, all was suddenly silent around them. Even the unceasing song of the birds quieted.

For too long she let him hold her. For too long she leaned on him. Counted on him. On this man who knew her more intimately than any other.

On this man who hated her.

And suddenly that hurt cut her like the slice of a knife. She'd been dealing with it, trying to tell herself it didn't matter. But it did.

It hurt. Too much.

She tipped her face up to his, hadn't even been aware that she'd gripped his St. Christopher medal in her fingers and was hanging on tight. He searched her face and her heartbeat quickened. With wonder and surprise— even with hope—when, in the fading light, she saw much more in his dark eyes than she'd expected. The anger was gone. There was compassion there now. But most shocking of all, there was need. Riveting. Intense. Real.

So real she moved closer, sensed, with a razor-sharp awareness that only lovers feel, that he wanted to lower his mouth to hers. Taste. Rediscover. Reclaim.

And he was about to. With everything in her she knew he was about to . . . but then his body stiffened. He closed his eyes, tightened his jaw, and swore under his breath. When he met her eyes again, a dark cloud of restraint had dropped like a curtain.

And she was persona non grata once again.

She'd never felt so raw. So exposed.

Pride, however, was an amazing thing. It swept over her like a trauma team, swift and efficient, finding each insult to her psyche and applying salve on the wounds he'd just opened.

"I'm . . . I'm sorry," she said, pretending she'd never seen his desire, never felt her own, as the medal fell from her suddenly lax fingers. "That was . . . well. That was pretty pathetic is what it was."

She made to push away, but his arms tightened, then loosened abruptly. It happened so fast, she wondered if she'd just imagined that swift, protective pull before he let her go.

Wishful thinking? Desperate thinking?

God. She *was* pathetic.

"You're entitled to a meltdown," he said, his face as hard as the arms that had held her.

Entitled?

Well, damn.

Just when she'd felt a small concession on his part, he hit her with another reminder of what he thought of her.

With mercurial speed, her ragged emotions shifted again. Her hackles rose . . . like those of a dog whose chain had been yanked too many times.

"I can't tell you what it means to me to receive your blessings." Sarcasm dripped like acid from each word. "But next time save your absolution for someone who might actually appreciate it, okay? I don't need it. Not from you."

His brows knit together. "That's not—"

She cut him off. "You're not my judge, Ortega. You're not my conscience. And you sure as hell aren't someone whose approval or permission I need."

Sick to death of him and of her pointless feelings for him, she spun around to leave.

A firm grip on her arm stopped her. "I just meant—"

"I know exactly what you *just* meant." She glared at him over her shoulder. "You meant that even a bitch like me deserves to be cut a little slack. Well, I'm up to here with your judgmental bullshit, all right? You think I turned you in? Fine. Think what you want. But think about this, too. What reason would I possibly have had to turn you over to Poveda? What *possible* reason?

"God, Manny." Frustration buzzed through her like a saw blade. "Think about it. I abhorred the man. Abhorred all he stood for. When did I *ever* give you any indication that I hated *you*? When did I ever do anything but *give* to you? When was I ever anything but *there* for you?"

For long moments she stared into his eyes, searching for some indication that he was folding on that point. Nothing. He gave her nothing. Because, she finally realized, he had nothing to give.

"Let go of my arm." She had to get away from him before she did something really stupid—like beg him to forgive her for a sin she hadn't even committed.

Silence sang between them like a bowstring, taut, quivering, suspended until he finally let her go. He gave no indication that he'd understood or even considered the sense in her words.

"We'll rest here for another hour. Then we're heading for Kandy."

She blinked. Blinked again. "That's it? That's all you have to say?"

A muscle in his jaw tightened.

She shook her head, almost feeling sorry for him. "You are so wrong about me." She no longer cared that he had the ability to hurt her. "And so help me, if Adam spends even one more second in harm's way than is necessary because of *your* problems with *me,* I'll never forgive you. And when you finally figure out the truth, you'll never forgive yourself."

———

"Hey, you okay?"

Lily hadn't seen Darcy approach her. She was pretty much lost in an anger that blocked everything around her.

She'd stomped away from Manny—yes, stomped, although she wasn't exactly proud of it—to the Suburban, where she'd sat down on the grass, cross-legged, and leaned against the front bumper. Fuming. She'd figured no one would notice her there.

"I'm fine," she said without glancing up.

A moment of uncertain silence passed. "Want some company?"

It was on the tip of her tongue to say "Thanks but no thanks" when Lily realized she would actually welcome the opportunity to vent with someone who had something other than testosterone running through her system. And Darcy had been kind. More than kind. She'd been the only one in the lot who hadn't judged Lily.

She motioned to the ground beside her. "Enter at your own risk."

"He's having trouble coming to terms with things," Darcy said as she eased to the ground beside Lily.

Lily didn't pretend to misunderstand. They were five people in close confines. The others had to have heard, if not actually witnessed, her little—in Manny's words—"meltdown."

"He's pious and judgmental." She let her head fall back against the bumper, made a sound of frustration.

"And maybe hurting?" Darcy suggested carefully.

Lily shook her head but finally conceded, "Okay. Yeah. Maybe."

They sat in companionable silence for a while before Darcy turned to her. "Tell me to bugger off if you want to, but I've got to ask. What's the story with you and Manny?"

Lily glanced over at Darcy, saw sincere interest and concern on her face, and decided what the hell. At least she wanted to know. That was more than anyone else in camp.

"I was working with a Doctors Without Borders team

in Managua," Lily began at the beginning. "We met at a state dinner—a media event orchestrated by the Sandinistas. A command appearance—we saw it as insurance that they wouldn't pull our visas before the team's work was done."

She breathed deep of the cooling mountain air, smelled campfires and pine and the earthy loam of the forest floor. "I'd lost a friend that day. A nurse who went down on an evac chopper that I was supposed to have been on."

"That's a tough one." Darcy's pretty green eyes were filled with understanding.

"Yeah. No matter how often I replay it, it always comes down to I should have been the one who died."

Even though the gradual coolness of the night was refreshing, Lily shivered. Swatted a mosquito off her neck. "That night . . . well, I was hurting pretty badly . . . pretty messed up, you know? And then, out of the blue there was this amazing young soldier who wanted to make me forget. Who promised to do things to me to make sure I forgot. And because I needed some promises that night . . . I stepped out of the box. Big-time. And I let him."

"A man like Manolo Ortega could make a woman forget a lot of things," Darcy said with a soft, knowing smile.

Lily actually laughed, though there was nothing remotely funny. She stared into space, remembering how he'd taken her breath away.

He still took her breath away.

"Yeah," she said with a slow nod. "He could. He did. We were together a week. It was pretty intense. And then he just disappeared. I looked for him. Was finally told by the Sandinista general in charge that he'd died in a firefight."

She shook her head. "From what I've pieced together

since, the Sandinistas figured out he was a spy for the Contras and arrested him. Manny's convinced I'm the one who turned him in."

"But you didn't."

Lily glanced at Darcy again, not surprised exactly but certainly pleased that Darcy had made a statement, not asked a question.

"No. I didn't. I searched for him, but, like I said, they told me he was dead." Even now, even after she'd found him, seen him, knew he was alive, that memory had the power to shake her.

"I was already back in the States when I realized I was pregnant. And I didn't know until a few months ago that he was alive." She expelled a deep breath. "He'd actually arrived back in the U.S. before I left Nicaragua. And he'd never contacted me."

She drew her hair over her left shoulder and absently brushed at the snarls with her fingers. It still hurt to know that. Ached deep inside . . . an ache that had intensified since he'd accused her of betrayal.

She glanced at Darcy. "All those years. He was alive. Hating me."

"I think maybe he's rethinking things, Lily." Darcy's voice was thoughtful in the darkening night. "He hasn't said anything. He wouldn't, but . . . sometimes I'll catch him watching you. It's not with the eyes of a man filled with hate. Anyway, I think maybe he's figuring out that he was wrong about you."

Lily tugged at a blade of grass. "Yeah, well, if he's figured it out, he's sure not giving me any signs."

"No. I don't suppose he is. I don't expect he can. Not yet, anyway. It's not going to be easy for him to let go of those feelings. Add to the mix that he hasn't yet had time to adjust to the idea that he has a son . . . well. It's a lot. Even for a man like Manny."

Yeah, Lily thought. It was a lot. It had been a lot for her to absorb. "I was scared to death to come looking for him," she confessed. "When I realized Manny was alive, I was . . . hell, I don't know what I was. Shocked. Elated. Hurt. Scared."

"I imagine it takes a lot to scare you."

Lily pushed out a grunt. "I'm not so sure about that anymore. I used to think so."

"And I imagine it took you some time to come to terms with all of those feelings about Manny."

Lily closed her eyes. "Yeah. It took some time."

Darcy touched a hand to Lily's shoulder. "Give him some time, too, okay? I know it hurts. But give him some time."

Darcy was right. Manny did need time. But time to what? To decide if he wanted Adam to be a part of his life? To decide if he wanted to pick up where the two of them had left off?

She didn't think so. She didn't even know if she wanted that to happen. Couldn't see the sense or the wisdom in it. She suspected that he couldn't, either. Chemistry—even chemistry as explosive as theirs—did not a relationship make, regardless of their emotional connection. She was ten years older than him, for God's sake. Ten years and a vast chasm of cultural and lifestyle differences between them.

Besides, there was the survival factor. She'd lost Manny once. She hadn't even loved him and the pain had been crippling.

She hadn't even loved him.

Okay. So she'd been *pretending* she hadn't loved him.

Working her damnedest to convince herself she didn't love him when, in fact, she was over the moon for the beautiful boy who was so much a man.

What about now? Was she pretending again? Was that what this was all about? Was she still in love with Manny Ortega and half scared to death with it?

And if she was, could she bear to admit it? To herself? To him, when she was fairly certain there could be no happily ever after in a story that involved the two of them?

"So . . . what's the story with Ethan and Manny?" she asked, because she didn't want to think or talk or consider her history—or her present—with Manny anymore. And because she needed something to take her mind off the ever present fear for her son.

For the next half hour, Lily did manage to forget about Manny's hostility. She even stopped thinking about Adam for a moment or two as she listened in fascination while Darcy told her about Ethan and Manny's history in the Special Forces. How Darcy had met both Manny and Ethan in Peru, where she and Ethan had gotten married, how their marriage had crumbled several years ago, and how, as fate would have it, the Garrett men and Manny had recently rescued her from a terrorist cell in the Philippines.

"That's why I know they'll find Adam," Darcy assured her again. "They found me. Against impossible odds. These guys don't know defeat, Lily. They never will."

"I pray to God that you're right."

The night had settled in like a tepid, damp blanket. The muffled, undistinguishable conversations of distant campers, the rustle of the wind through the trees, the residual weight of the day, encompassed them.

Somewhere out there was her son. It would soon be over seventy-two hours since it was discovered he'd gone missing. Each additional hour, she knew, diminished the chances of finding him alive.

A sick longing filled her chest as she looked toward the sky. Was he looking to the sky for answers, too? Was he alone? Was he afraid? Was he sick or hurt or . . . She couldn't think that way. She had to think positive.

More than anything in the world, more than she needed to sort things out with Manny, she needed Adam back. And she needed to believe he was alive.

CHAPTER 13

Outskirts of Kandy

"Okay, here's the plan." Manny pulled up to the gates of a small airport just outside of Kandy at 4:00 A.M. He cut lights and the motor. "We split up here."

Lily couldn't hide her surprise. "Split up?"

"So we can cover more ground." The overhead light came on as Ethan opened the door and got out. Dallas did the same, followed by Manny.

So that's why they'd been divvying up the money, Lily thought as she joined the men and Darcy at the rear of the Suburban. They'd hatched this plan back at the campground last night.

The situation had always been urgent. This shift of tactics, however, spelled out exactly how urgent. These men knew things about terrorists and hostage situations that most people would never have to know. They knew they were racing a clock here. Trying to get in under the wire to save lives. To save her son's life.

With Ethan holding a flashlight, Dallas dug into his ALICE pack and pulled out three phones that looked like forerunners to the modern cell phone. "Satellite phones," he explained when Lily frowned. "Not the newest models, but we should be able to stay in touch with these."

The men did a quick check to make certain the SAT

phones were working. Then the others helped Dallas stow a disassembled rifle into his pack along with a handgun and various provisions.

"Wait," Lily stopped him, and raced around the vehicle for her medical bag. She quickly pulled some of everything from her stash of supplies. "Take these. Just in case."

With a nod of appreciation, Dallas tucked the supplies into the pack.

"Later," he said, shrugged into the backpack, and headed into the slowly lightening horizon toward a hangar just the other side of the fenced-in airfield. Spotlights shined on three small, ancient aircraft and one lone helicopter that sat on the tarmac. A huge For Hire sign shined under a light on the side of the corrugated-tin building. Inside the hangar, a light flickered on.

"Where's he going?" Lily asked.

"North. Jaffna Peninsula." Ethan's face was grim in the shadows as he watched his brother walk away.

"Jaffna?" Darcy's concern was evident in her voice. Lily understood why. Jaffna was the hub and stronghold of the Tamil movement.

"He'll be fine," Ethan assured them. "And if he's lucky, he might even find a connection or two among the ranks."

"Our boy gets around," Manny said in an attempt to ease everyone's minds.

"He knows some of the Tamil fighters?" Darcy looked skeptical.

Ethan grunted as he packed a duffel similar to Dallas's and nodded toward Darcy to throw some of her things into it as well. "More like he knows someone who knows someone whose name might open a door or two. At the very least see if he can shake any monkeys out of the trees."

"In other words, it's a long shot that he'll find any-thing out to help," Lily surmised as she made another trip to her medical bag and assembled a medical kit for Darcy and Ethan.

Manny looked grim. "Long shots are about all we've got at the moment."

"At daybreak Darcy and I will hit all the touristy places in and around Kandy." Ethan broke into the silence Manny's stark declaration had bred. "If there's anything to shake loose, if anyone's seen them, we'll find out. And I think it might be time to find out who our new friends are."

"Fuck," Manny swore under his breath. "We've got another tail?"

"Since we left the campground," Ethan confirmed. "Which is another good reason to split up. One vehicle can't tail us all."

"Be on the lookout for an all-night car dealer," Manny said as they piled back in the Suburban and took off down the road again. "We'll need a jeep. Odds are they'll follow you in the Suburban and leave us alone," he added with a glance in the rearview mirror at Ethan.

Before Lily could ask, Manny supplied the answer to her next question. "You and I will head for the hill country."

The hill country. The hill country had caves. Temple ruins and sacred cities. Jungle groves and wildlife sanc-tuaries. Miles and miles, acres and acres, of mountains and wilderness and tropical forest where it would be easy to get lost—or easy to hide hostages where no one would think to find them.

Her son was a hostage. It was still hard to think about. Was he hidden away in a small, dark cave? In a filthy mud hut? In an insect-infested jungle where snakes and night creatures and God only knew what kind of predator might attack him?

It had been a long time since she'd put much faith in God. She wasn't sure who had caused that break. Her or Him. But for the first time in a very long time, she felt a need to breach it.

Please, God. Please let him be okay. Please, please, let us find him before whoever took him hurts him. Before whoever is following us tries to stop us from finding Adam.

———

Victoria Reservoir road south of Kandy on the way to Nuwara Eliya

Shielding her eyes against the blinding morning sun's glare, Lily stood and peered over the windshield from the passenger side of the topless and, at the moment, disabled jeep—circa older than dirt.

They'd bought the jeep for a song in Kandy. Apparently, a song had been too much, but the pickings had been slim.

Currently they were three hours south and west of Kandy. Instead of taking the main road to Nuwara Eliya, they'd been following the Victoria Reservoir road on a sketchy lead Ethan and Darcy had picked up in the city.

Unfortunately, the jeep had just sputtered, lurched, then belched up a burst of steam that now spewed out of the motor like fog.

Darcy swatted at a fly that buzzed her. This was so not what they needed. Not now. Not when they may have gotten a break.

A mile or so back they'd met an old man and a little

boy lugging sacks of potatoes and carrots. As Lily and Manny always did when they encountered locals, they'd stopped. Manny had shown them Adam's photograph. They hadn't seen him. But they had seen a group of soldiers yesterday, some driving a pickup truck, some in a beat-up van, traveling together, heading south.

"Tamil?" Manny asked.

The old man had shushed the boy with a look. Lily understood. The locals were friendly to tourists. Ask them about a temple ruin or a holy shrine and they talked like magpies. Ask them about the Tigers and they closed up like clams.

Sri Lanka was a country of many cultures. Besides the majority Sinhalese and the lesser contingent of Tamil, the island was populated with Moors, Malays, burghers, and even some Christians, none of whom wanted to get caught in the crossfire between the two warring factions. The best way to do that was to simply keep a low profile.

Lily, however, hadn't given up.

"What was in the truck?" she had asked.

"Blan-kaht-tu-vah," the boy answered before his father could stop him.

"Blan-kaht-tu-vah?" Lily repeated, then took a stab at translating. "Blankets?"

The boy nodded.

"Blankets?" she wondered out loud. "Or tarps? Tarps covering a pickup bed?"

"Which could hide anything from supplies, to ammunition, to hostages," Manny speculated, following her line of thought.

It wasn't much, but it was in keeping with a lead Ethan and Darcy had called them about, so they had pressed on.

Until the jeep had given up the ghost.

"What's wrong with it?" she asked, wiping the dust from her forehead with the back of her hand, then crossing her arms over the top of the windshield.

"It's not working," came Manny's mumbled response from underneath the open hood.

Well, yeah. That much she'd figured out. Just like she'd figured something else out. Ever since Manny had let his guard down at the camp last night and held her, he'd gone to extremes to keep his distance—both physically and emotionally.

Okay. She got it already. He wasn't pleased that he'd been nice to her. Was ticked that he'd actually felt some empathy for her—maybe even more than empathy—when his big bad self was determined to play the hate and loathing card every chance he got.

Give him some time, Darcy had said.

Lily was trying. Just like she was trying to keep calm in the face of what could be a major disaster. It was their third day in Sri Lanka. They weren't any closer to finding Adam. Her nerves were splintered. Her temper on a very tight leash.

And now this.

"I know it's not working." She dug deep for patience when his long fingers clamped around the edge of the hood. "What, specifically, is the problem?"

His face was hard as he rounded the jeep and reached into the backseat. Sweat trickled down his jawline, disappeared in the open collar of his white shirt as he dug into his ALICE pack that held their share of food, supplies, and weaponry. "Busted radiator hose."

She wasn't heavy into car mechanics, but from the grim set of his mouth as he rifled through the contents of the pack, she could tell that wasn't good.

"Can you fix it?"

Coming up empty, he swore, then zipped up the pack with a disgusted scowl. "Not without a new hose or a damn good sealant, neither of which we seem to have."

"Sealant? As in tape?"

"If I had some, yeah. That'd do it." He planted his hands on his hips, looking all male and macho and mad—which triggered a response she couldn't have stopped if her life depended on it.

"I thought you special ops types never went anywhere without your duct tape."

The driver's side door opened; his weight bounced the jeep as he wedged his big body behind the wheel and cut her a sharp look. "Clearly, you've been watching the wrong movies. Unless there's a service station over that hill, and I wouldn't make book on it," he said with a hitch of his strong chin down the curving road, "we're walking from here."

Despite the seriousness of the broken hose, after being made to feel like a liability for days, Lily was actually going to enjoy what happened next. She turned around, stood on her knees on the front seat, and reached for the medical bag she'd stowed on the floor behind her. When she surfaced it was with a roll of wide white adhesive tape. "Will this work?"

Manny jerked his gaze her way. He spotted the tape. His eyes didn't exactly brighten. He didn't exactly smile. But he came close. *Damn close.*

"You're making me look bad here."

Miracle of miracles, he did smile then. Slow. Reluctant. Dazzling.

Something inside Lily's chest gave like a sigh. Something that had been coiling and knotting since she'd seen

him in the ER back in Boston. Something that gripped
like a fist clenched so tight it had become painful.

One smile and the fingers of that fist slowly uncurled.

That's all it took to ease the hurt. Ease the stress. Ease
it just a little. Just a very critical little.

So little, she almost didn't smile back. Didn't quite
trust herself to believe the monumental significance of
that smile. But it *was* significant.

He'd just extended an olive branch. A small, fragile
peace offering. An end to the hostilities.

Give him some time, Darcy had said.

It seemed too much to hope for, but maybe that time
had come.

Almost light-headed with the prospect of relief from
his unrelenting anger, Lily dipped another toe in untested
waters. "Yeah, well, 'Be prepared.' That's my motto.
Mine and the Boy Scouts'. But then you know that. Being
an old Boy Scout and all, right?"

He snagged the roll of tape that she dangled toward
him on her index finger and gave up another quick grin
that sent her heart racing and launched a series of little
electric pulses humming through her system.

"It's not nice to rub salt in a wound, Liliana."

Liliana.

He'd called her Liliana. She doubted he even realized
it. It had just come out. Spontaneous. Unguarded.

Liliana.

It took her back. Took her away from the urgency of
their search. God, how she used to come unglued when
he said her name in Spanish. Of course, she was usually
naked and he was usually inside her, or under her, or
kissing her with a carnal dedication that made her weep.

She almost wept now. Almost cried with joy over his

ever so unexpected transition from hostility to good humor. But she kept it together. Replayed the brief exchange again and again until she was convinced it had actually happened.

And as he went back to work under the hood, Lily clung to the promise of a minor but meaningful shift in the wind between them.

———

Manny steered the jeep around a rut as they bounced down the winding reservoir road. So far, the tape was holding on the radiator hose. So far. According to the map, the next town was just a mile or two over the next ridge.

Town. Hell. More likely a village—one of a few remote little settlements dotting the mountain road. He didn't hold out a lot of hope that they'd find a replacement hose there—or a fuel pump, as theirs, he suspected, was in the throes of a long, gasping death.

The jeep was a piece of shit. He'd known it when he'd bought it, but since it was the only piece of shit on the lot and there'd been no time to look for another, he'd had to take a chance.

Time was king now if they were going to find Adam alive.

Manny gave Lily credit for keeping it together in the face of that very obvious fact. She was smart. She knew the score. And yet she kept her head.

While he was losing his.

Over her.

Christ.

He drummed his thumbs on the steering wheel, resisting the urge to glance over at her. Lost the battle.

Even in the mountains and this close to the reservoir, the temperature must be pushing one hundred degrees Fahrenheit, the humidity closing in on 90 percent. The wind whipping over the windshield and funneling around the open jeep was hot, wet, and scented of the rain that would most likely arrive midmorning out of the blue and then dissipate as quickly as it came before retooling for an afternoon shower.

This part of Sri Lanka was much like Nicaragua that way. It made him think of home. Of family. Of loss.

As the jeep rumbled down the road, the wind licked his hair wildly, played rough with Lily's, tugging stray wisps and slapping them across her face even though she'd twisted the mass of it into a thick, lush knot and tucked it up under a ball cap.

Despite the protection of the cap's brim, the sun had painted her cheeks and nose pink. She was hot and tired and her white camp shirt was wilted. Yet even with the weight of the world on her shoulders and the sweat of the day beating her down, she was beautiful.

She should look fragile. But she was solid and steady and . . .

Jesus Christ, he wanted to hate her.

Needed to hate her.

Had hated her for so long now.

But he was damn weary of the battle.

Was he falling under her spell again? Was that why he wanted to smile for her instead of snarl? Walk toward her instead of away?

Cristo.

He didn't know what was happening. He just knew that one way or another, he needed to clear the air. He couldn't breathe anymore with the way things were between them.

Swearing under his breath, he jerked the wheel hard left and pulled over to the side of the road. Gravel peppered the underbelly of the vehicle when he slammed the brake into the floorboard; dust plumed around them.

Beside him, Lily braced one hand on the roll bar, the other on the dash. Her eyes were wide, her mouth poised on the brink of screaming.

But she didn't. Because she was Lily. Strong. Brave. True.

How he wanted to believe that she had been true.

The jeep rocked to a stop and she turned her dark eyes on him. She must have read something in his face, because she didn't rail at him. Didn't demand to know what the hell he was doing. She simply sat and waited.

"I have something to say," he said at long last— because, Jesus, he'd turned into a cur dog of a coward all of a sudden.

Her wary looks shot an RPG of guilt dead center through his heart.

"I've been an ass," he said, staring at the dusty, bug-streaked windshield because he couldn't look her in the eye.

He'd been a boy when he'd faced off against the Sandinistas. A Special Forces soldier when he'd battled the ruthless drug cartel in Ecuador, the Taliban in Afghanistan. Boston had been rife with its own brand of terrorists. And yet he didn't have it in him to face this one small woman.

Beside him, she was very quiet. He was sure she wanted to put a punctuation mark on the "ass" part of his admission, but to her credit, she didn't.

She quietly said, "Tell me why. Tell me all of it."

He dragged a hand over his lower face, realized he was squirming, and sucked it up.

"When they came for me that night," he began, needing to work this through as much for his benefit as for hers, "they said it was you. They told me that it was you who told Poveda."

"They lied," she said with a quiet conviction that made him want to believe.

He gripped the steering wheel tightly with both hands. Only realized he was pushing it toward the dash when his biceps started to burn.

He loosened his hold. Finally worked up the courage to look at her. She stared straight ahead, her hands clutched together in her lap; a single, silent tear trickled slowly down her cheek. She quickly wiped it away with the back of her hand, as if making it disappear would erase what she probably considered a show of weakness.

"It no longer matters," he said, realizing it was true.

Her head whipped to the side to meet his gaze, her dark eyes puzzled and a little wary. "No longer matters? How can it no longer matter? What changed, Manny? What changed after all these years that it no longer matters?"

What had changed was that after seventeen years of hate and belief in Lily Campora's betrayal, he was ready to let it go. Needed to let it go.

On a hot, dusty road thousands of miles from home, in a broken-down jeep, on a life-and-death search for a boy who didn't have time for a "man" to come to terms with his new reality, Manny was suddenly ready to forgive her.

Maybe he was just tired of hating her. Maybe, like the boy he'd been then, he was so dazzled by her now, it was simply easier to forgive her.

"You came back into my life again. That's what's changed." He wasn't sure of much else, but that, at least, was the God's honest truth.

Silence, as weighty as the worry over their son, crowded into the open jeep with them.

"So . . . this isn't about believing me? It's about accepting? Forgiving?"

His silence was her answer.

She shook her head and he could see the frustration in her eyes along with the heat of anger. Anger that transitioned to sorrow. "Well, I'm sorry. That's not good enough," she said after a long moment. Her eyes looked as sad as she sounded. "Not nearly good enough."

He worked his jaw, as angry, suddenly, as she was miserable. "What else do you want from me?"

She pinned him with a look of tempered steel. "I want you to believe me. Why is that such a hard thing for you to do?"

"And why is it so hard for you to just admit it?" he shot back. "Christ, Lily. I told you things I'd never told another living soul. Not even my family knew for certain that I fought for the Contras. No one but you had access to Poveda. No one but you could have turned me in."

"And what was my reason for doing this?" she demanded, her anger matching his. "What was my reason?"

He jerked his gaze away from her burning black eyes; he didn't want to see her reaction when he threw the truth in her face. "You don't have to pretend anymore. I know what was going on. I know that Poveda was your lover."

CHAPTER 14

If Manny had said, "I know you are an alien," Lily couldn't have been more stunned. It took her a moment to find her voice.

"My lover? You think Poveda was my *lover*? For God's sake, Manny, *why* would you think that? After all we'd done together? All we'd been to each other? Granted, we were only together for a week, but we shared everything. Did you *really* not know me? Did you not have even a clue who I was?"

"I didn't then," he said quietly, and a muscle in his jaw worked. "I only figured it out later."

She actually laughed. "Well then, by all means, enlighten me. Who was I?"

He had the balls to actually try to be patient. "You were a woman with a hatred for men," he said with a grim conclusiveness that stunned her.

"Hatred? What are you talking about?"

"Your ex-husband. Men before him." He lifted a hand. "You told me. They all let you down."

"God, Manny." *Unbelievable.* "That made me disappointed, not deceitful."

"And distrustful. You did not trust my love for you. You never trusted it."

Now, as it had then, she could see that it hurt him.

"Because you were a boy," she pointed out, still reeling over his conclusions. "You couldn't have known your heart."

"Yes. I was a boy. Who was easily fooled."

She didn't even know what to say anymore. It was all so preposterous. But somehow she needed to make him see that.

"So let me see if I'm following this. Because I hated men, I fooled you into loving me? And the reason I did this was because in my deep hatred for men, I wanted to—what? Make you pay for being one of them?"

His jaw tightened. A building breeze sent dust skittering down the side of the road.

"And in my quest to wreak havoc on *man*kind," she continued, unable to stem the sarcasm, "I pried secrets out of you, then told them to my 'lover,' General Poveda, who I hated, *but,* vindictive bitch that I was, used those secrets to bring you down. Does that about sum it up?"

But for the wind rattling through the trees she was met with more silence.

"Manny. Do you realize how ridiculous that sounds?" She lifted a hand, let it drop in frustration. "I could *maybe* understand a boy rationalizing such a load of crap. But you're a man now. An intelligent man. With a man's experience. A man's head, for God's sake. A man's heart. Can you look at me and honestly think I could have done such a heinous, horrible thing?"

She watched his sullen profile. Watched the muscles in his neck work when he swallowed. Watched, heart in her throat, when he finally turned to her. His dark eyes were bleak, penetrating, and bored straight into her soul.

"When I look at you, Liliana . . . I can only think of having you."

Silence rang in the wake of his hushed confession. A small dust devil skittered around the open jeep, spinning pine needles and leaves with the fine soil at the side of the road before it rose and twirled away.

"And if I can have you," he continued as if the admission sliced scars in his soul, "then nothing else matters."

She was still reeling over the stunning shock of his statement when he turned the key, shifted into gear, and, spraying gravel like a wake from an outboard motor, tore out onto the highway.

――――

Jaffna Peninsula

Dallas knew he had company even before he heard the single warning shot from the Kalashnikov.

"What took you so long, boys?" he muttered under his breath, and, stopping in the middle of the road, raised his hands to either side of his head.

He was hot, he was dry, and he'd been walking this parched, dusty road since the pilot had reluctantly set down on a pocked airstrip a few miles out of Jaffna an hour ago. The terrain was flat and empty but for bomb craters in the fields and burned-out shells of vehicles littering the roadside.

Dallas was in the middle of what looked like a war zone. In truth it *had* been a war zone and in all likelihood would be again. Such was the way of life in Sri Lanka.

He wasn't surprised when two AK-47-wielding Tigers

appeared on the path in front of him. Four others closed in on all sides, rifles locked and loaded.

None of them looked older than sixteen. And he knew of only one thing that would keep their testosterone-charged fingers from squeezing a few rounds into the American trespasser.

Just like he'd known they would come. Had counted on the cadre of rebel forces to be curious about the single-engine airplane that had landed, then taken off, all in a matter of minutes.

"Take me to Ponnambalam Ramanathan," he said in Tamil.

As Dallas had hoped, just the mention of their revered leader's name drew exaggerated looks of curiosity.

"Take me now," he repeated more forcefully, "and may your God have mercy on your souls if you put a bullet in the man Ponnambalam Ramanathan calls brother."

As they motioned for him with their guns to start walking, Dallas prayed that Ramanathan was still alive and, if he was, that he wasn't still pissed about that little matter of a "bungled" arms deal in Afghanistan three years ago.

———

Manny's SAT phone rang just as he pulled up to a gas pump in Marassana. On the map, it wasn't more than a tiny ink dot. In reality, "tiny" was an exaggeration. The main street was narrow. On either side were houses made of brown mud walls topped with thatch roofs. Surrounding and towering over the houses were green gardens and greener trees.

A peddler, the back of his bicycle full of toys, napped in the shade of a banyan tree, its gnarled roots worn bone gray and smooth by centuries of human traffic. A dog sat on its haunches beside the bicycle, vigorously scratching its ribs. Other than that, not much life stirred.

"Ortega," Manny said into the receiver as he surveyed a roadside fruit stand, what appeared to be a tourist information center, and this single petrol pump. Overhead, the sky had turned gunmetal dark.

"We've got a lead on something solid." Ethan was all business on the other end of the line.

"Go." Manny listened without another word, aware of Lily's dark eyes, anxious and intent, as she waited to hear not only if it was Dallas or Ethan, but also what he had to say.

Manny waited until Ethan finished before filling him in on their location.

"Wait a sec." Manny could hear Ethan relaying the information to Darcy. "She says that according to her map, you're half a day from there if you stick to the highways. A couple of hours if you go off road."

Manny motioned for Lily to hand him the map. When she held it out to him, he spread it open over the steering wheel and got a fix on the coordinates Ethan had given him.

"Okay. Got it. I'll be back in touch."

"Watch your six, man. We're heading your way. Can't be more than three hours behind you. Don't do anything until we get there."

"Roger that."

Manny disconnected.

"What?" Lily hitched herself sideways in the passenger seat and searched his eyes.

She hadn't had much to say to him since he'd made his little confession. In fact, they'd ridden in silence until now.

"Darcy and Ethan took a chance on meeting with a local politician in Kandy," he said, understanding Lily's focus was all on Adam now. "She played the diplomacy card, conveniently forgetting to mention that her position in the State Department was inactive and her last post was Manila, not Colombo.

"The offshoot was she got a meeting with a city councilwoman who was sympathetic to your situation and, swearing she'd deny it if asked, slipped Darcy the name and cell number of a covert operative who has extensive, real-time intel on Tiger activity in this area.

"Long story short," he said after handing her the map and pinpointing the location Ethan had given him for her, "they've been in contact with the operative and he gave them a fix on the biggest known Tiger camp in the area."

Lily checked the location on the map, brows furrowed in impatience. "That's hours from here."

"We can take a chance," he said, "and cut across country. If this piece of shit holds up we can cut the time in half."

"Then that's what we do," she said adamantly.

Manny wasn't nearly as certain as she was. He jumped out of the jeep, opened up the hood. The tape was still holding on the hose. He checked the oil—two quarts low—then headed inside the small station hoping there'd be something other than bottled water, rice, and curry for sale.

"Aah-yu-boh-wahn?" *Hello?*

The place smelled of incense and curry and gas and

wasn't much bigger than a phone booth lined with tar-paper, with a very few auto supplies and bottled water. A small, wrinkled man who seemed to perfectly fit the confines of the aged wooden structure popped up from behind a counter where it appeared he'd been taking a morning nap.

"Aah-yu-boh-wahn," he greeted Manny with a sheep-ish grin that revealed widely split front teeth. As was the custom, he gave Manny a courteous bow.

Manny also bowed. "Thel?" *Oil?*

There was much head shaking and several attempts before Manny conveyed that he was looking for motor oil, not cooking or lamp oil.

Finally, with two quarts in hand, he returned to the jeep. "Why don't you buy some of that fruit while we've got the chance at something fresh?" He dug into his hip pocket for his wallet and handed Lily some bills.

While he added the oil and refilled the radiator, she headed for the fruit stand. The wind whipped up; a few splatters of rain hit the dust around her feet as Manny watched her walk away.

He couldn't take his eyes off the no-nonsense jut of her chin. The slight sway of her slim hips that even her baggy shirt and pants couldn't conceal.

When I look at you, Liliana . . . I can only think of having you. And if I can have you, then nothing else matters.

He dusted off his hands, walked inside, and paid for the oil and gas, still burned with himself over what he'd admitted to her. What he'd admitted to himself.

And no matter that he tried to ignore them, *her* words packed even more punch. He heard them over and over in his head.

I could maybe *understand a boy rationalizing such a*

load of crap. But you're a man now. An intelligent man.
With a man's experience. A man's head, for God's sake.
A man's heart. Can you look at me and honestly think I
could have done such a heinous, horrible thing?

Standing in the open doorway of the petrol station, he
tipped back a bottle of water, all the while watching Lily
finish up her purchases beneath a sudden downpour.

She was right about one thing. His life back then had
been filled with trickery and deceit. He'd lived it.
Breathed it. Almost died because of it. And yes, it had
colored his perceptions. Still did. There were few men
he trusted. Fewer women.

He wanted to believe her . . . but what other explanation was there? Who else would have turned him in?
Who else knew? His Contra brothers whom he fought
with against the Sandinistas every day? No. They would
not have turned against him. They would have died for
him—and he for them.

Just as swiftly as it came up, the rain stopped, leaving
behind the damp-dust scent of ozone. He tossed the
empty water bottle in a refuse bin and stepped outside,
still thinking about what Lily had said.

She was so passionate in her denial. So determined to
convince him he was wrong about her.

And if he was wrong, did that also mean she was right
about him? Was it still the boy reacting? The boy who'd
lost his love, lost his home and his family, and needed to
lash out at the one who caused him pain? Was it the boy
who had lived, breathed, and dreamed the nightmare of
her betrayal who demanded that the man not give himself permission to believe her?

Thoughtful, he walked back to the jeep, shut the hood,
and washed the windshield.

Had the Sandinista soldiers lied about Lily? Had Poveda discovered their affair? Manny had seen the way Poveda had watched Lily the night they met. He understood exactly what had been on the general's mind. That's why Manny had been so ready to believe Lily was Poveda's lover. But she insisted they weren't involved. Maybe that was Manny's answer. Poveda had wanted her. Wanted her so much that maybe he'd come for Manny out of jealousy, not even knowing that Manny was working against him.

Or was it someone else? For the first time, Manny allowed himself to seriously consider a possibility that had been swirling like smoke in the back of his mind since Lily had first claimed her innocence.

Cougar. The CIA operative was known for going to extreme lengths to get what he wanted. He'd wanted Manny for some time. Every time they'd met, Cougar had tried to talk Manny into going to the States, to become an elite soldier, then return and fight the fight.

In the end, that's exactly what Cougar had gotten. Could he have orchestrated Manny's arrest, banking on Manny escaping and coming to him for help?

God. He didn't know. And now wasn't the time to sort it all out. Later. There would be time later. After they found his son.

And they would find him, Manny resolved with the single-minded conviction that had kept him alive in Nicaragua and Afghanistan. And on the streets of Boston, another, but just as deadly, type of war zone.

He was ready to go when Lily came back with bananas, cashews, and mangosteens, a sweet, apple-sized reddish-yellow fruit that tasted like a combination of strawberries and grapes. Her white camp shirt was plastered to her lush body; her dark hair, which she'd woven into a single, thick braid somewhere along the way, was damp and glistening from the brief shower.

A single rain droplet rode the ridge of her cheekbone, hovering on porcelain skin the sun had kissed to a rose petal pink.

She was so fucking beautiful.

Men grew distinguished. Women just grew wrinkles.

One of his lovers had once said that. She had been wrong. At least she'd been wrong about a woman like Lily. The seventeen years, yes, they'd changed her, aged her, but there was a soft sensuality to her body now, a body that had always been lush and responsive and honed with the demands of her work. He'd loved her body then. He craved her body now.

The small, fine lines around her eyes should have detracted from her beauty, he supposed. Instead, they added a lived-in grace, a wisdom born of experience. In spite of the stress she was under, regardless that her face was free of makeup that would soften and hide imperfections, she looked more beautiful than he had even remembered.

When I look at you, Liliana . . . I can only think of having you.

He had never spoken a greater truth. And he had to get past it.

"Manny, about what you said earlier—"

"Forget it," he said, cutting her off.

He had to think. He had to focus. And he couldn't do either when she looked at him that way.

"Better put on more sunblock," he said, and stowed some extra containers of bottled water in the backseat.

Avoiding her puzzled eyes, he climbed back behind

the wheel. A bad sunburn might be the least of what happened to her if they encountered the rebel stronghold. He'd already come up with a contingency plan for that.

"Here's the route I think will work best." He spread the map out on the seat between them as the sun broke through the clouds and the early-morning shower rumbled on to the north.

"I'll leave the navigation to you," she said after a moment in which she must have decided to leave well enough alone. "Let's just get going."

"We need to talk about that. Darcy and Ethan shouldn't be more than three hours behind us." He checked his watch. "Maybe four. When they arrive, you need to be here to intercept them—"

"Whoa." She held up a hand. Pinned him with a look. "Don't even think about it. I'm going with you."

"Lily, someone has to—"

"Steer Ethan in the right direction? Get serious. Ethan Garrett doesn't need anyone to get him where he needs to go. So if this is some lame attempt to keep me out of harm's way, it's not going to work.

"This is my son," she stated firmly when Manny opened his mouth to argue. "My. Son."

She pressed a tightly closed fist between her breasts, holding it to her heart. "I don't care if we meet with the devil himself, no one is going to stop me from getting to him."

CHAPTER 15

Jaffna Peninsula, outside of Navatkuli

They untied the blindfold and jerked it away from his eyes. Dallas blinked against the sudden light—although "light," in this case, was a relative term. A single dim bulb hung from a cord dropped from the twenty-foot corrugated ceiling. It was the only illumination in the approximately thirty-by-thirty-foot room.

Even before they'd removed the blindfold, he'd known he was inside a metal building from the hollow ring of doors opening and closing behind him and from the tinny echo of his own footsteps across a concrete floor. And nothing, *nothing,* was as hot under a midday sun as the interior of a building covered by a tin roof.

When his eyes focused, he realized he was standing in an area that, in a stretch, could be called a situation room. Road maps, topography maps, and aerial surveillance maps of every district of Sri Lanka plastered the walls. Tacked-up notes littered a briefing board. Weapon diagrams and instructions for their use papered another wall.

Dallas didn't figure it was a good sign that he'd been brought here. He highly suspected that anyone who had ever seen the inside of this room with all of its tactical information was either a trusted loyalist to the cause or marked as a dead man who would never live to see the light of day again. There was little question into which category he fit.

In the middle of the room was a desk. Behind the desk, with his back to Dallas, sat a man. His dark hair was graying now, his shoulders were rounder than when Dallas had seen him last, but there was no mistaking whose presence Dallas was in.

"Don't suppose you could convince your boys here that they can untie my hands now?" Dallas asked without greeting or preface.

Gen. Ponnambalam Ramanathan, the elusive and reclusive leader of the LTTE, slowly swiveled around in his chair. Other than his trusted inner circle, only a handful of people had seen Ramanathan's face in the past ten years.

"Hello, my friend," Ramanathan said from behind clasped hands as he observed Dallas with a mildly calculating look. "It has been a while."

Dallas nodded, would have been heartened by Ramanathan's use of the word "friend," had his inflection not dripped with cynicism.

"And yet it seems like yesterday," Dallas said with a grim smile. "Why is that, do you suppose?"

Ramanathan lifted a shoulder, lowered his hands. "Perhaps it is because we are meeting under much the same circumstances."

"I don't recall being your prisoner back then."

"Perhaps you should have been." The Tiger leader dropped all pretense of politeness. "You cost me a great deal of money. I have been looking forward to the opportunity to extract some form of restitution."

Dallas smiled. This was the tricky part—if he didn't

consider being held at gunpoint by a squad of soldiers and marched five miles blindfolded with his hands tied behind his back tricky.

"The deal was solid, General," he said, giving the rebel leader the respect his rank deserved. "Might I suggest it could be wise to look among your own ranks for the source of the problem?"

He was bluffing, of course. Dallas had made certain the arms deal—a shipment of twenty SAMs—had gone sour when he'd brokered it three years ago. Posing as a rogue CIA agent when he was stationed in Lebanon with his Force Recon team, he'd infiltrated and happily thrown dozens of wrenches into the works before buyers and sellers alike had gotten wise and he'd had to get the hell out of Dodge—or in that case, Beirut. Same difference. Both were Wild West towns. Both lawless.

"And why would I be *wise* to believe you were innocent and someone else was to blame?" the general asked, casually fishing a knife out of his pocket, then using it to clean his stained fingernails.

As threats went, the knife was none too subtle. Dallas had to appreciate the show, if not the intent.

"How many deals did I successfully broker for you? Ten? Fifteen?" Dallas asked to remind the general that he had come through time and again. Of course, those very calculated shipments of weaponry were of the type the general would have acquired with or without Dallas's help. The SAMs had been another story. Those he'd had to intercept.

"And your point?" Ramanathan asked.

"My point is, someone fucked me over on that deal, too. The SAMs were my bread-and-butter deal. It was going to set me up for a very long time. The screwup cost me everything. I had to relocate. Reinvent. I'm still not up to speed again."

"And I'm to believe that's why you disappeared along with my surface-to-air missiles."

Dallas rolled a shoulder. He was hot. He was dry. The forced march had given him too much time to think. Given his psyche too much time to play and remind him of other ops men who hadn't been alive when the dust had settled.

He had to keep his shit together. He was pinning not only his future but also Adam's on his ability to BS his way out of yet one more dicey situation.

"You're no fool, General. You'll believe what you want. But ask yourself this: Why would I risk coming to you now if I were guilty of cheating you? I'm bold, but I'm not stupid. And make no mistake—it wasn't an accident that I met up with your posse today." He lifted his chin toward the soldiers who continued to hold him at gunpoint. "I came looking for you."

Ramanathan glanced at his lead man. From the corner of his eye, Dallas saw him nod, confirming that Dallas had, in fact, asked to be brought here.

Long moments passed. Perspiration trickled down Dallas's back; the rope binding his wrists swelled with the heaviness of his own sweat.

The general's signal was so subtle that Dallas almost missed it. But when the guard moved, his knife drawn, Dallas understood that something crucial was about to happen.

He braced himself, then breathed his first breath of relief when the knife sliced through the rope and his hands were finally free.

"Talk," Ramanathan said. "Convince me why that blade would not have been better used to pierce your heart. And why it shouldn't yet be used for that purpose."

———

Badulla district, UVA Province

It was midmorning—or so said the angled slant of sunlight burning bright as fire as they were herded toward the cave entrance. Minrada was so quiet. Worried, Adam watched her walk ahead of him. Quiet but not defeated. Her shoulders were squared, her head held high.

Her posture was a message to those bastards. *You cannot break me,* it said. The pride he felt in her swelled in his chest, overrode the pain that pulsed through his body.

His left eye was swollen shut, the cut above his brow caked with dirt and blood. He didn't know what a broken rib felt like, but he suspected the stabbing pain that jabbed like a knife every time he took a breath told the tale. And when they'd jerked him up by his arm to march him out of the cave, it felt like they'd dislocated his swollen elbow.

Physical pain. He'd discovered in the past days that he could handle it. Just like he could handle the hunger. What he couldn't take was the look on Minrada's face when he'd asked her what they'd done to her.

Her beautiful eyes that shined with laughter and light had grown cold. Distant. And she'd looked away.

An oily, sinking sensation rolled in his gut every time he thought about it. He wanted to cry for her. But a man didn't cry. And if he was going to get them out of this, he had to be a man.

He would kill the bastards. He would kill them all for stealing what was hers to give.

He stumbled when they reached the opening of the cave, temporarily blinded before his pupils adjusted to the sunlight. He caught himself, then startled when he heard Minrada's soft cry.

"Ahm-maah." *Mother.* "Thaath-thaah." *Father.*

Amithnal and Sathi were waiting for them at the foot of a cliff face; three armed guards lorded over them with rifles.

Sathi started to cry when she saw Minrada. Minrada rushed to her mother, who looped her bound wrists over Minrada's shoulders and pulled her close. Adam felt a lump lodge in his throat as the women wept.

It was the first time he'd seen Minrada cry. Feeling helpless and for the first time in his life feeling hatred for another human being, he lifted his gaze to Amithnal. The man looked destroyed as he watched his wife and daughter. Moments later, Adam understood the reason why.

A soldier motioned with his rifle for Adam to join the Muhandiramalas, then shoved him hard when he didn't move fast enough.

Lined up like targets on a rifle range, they were all forced to kneel. Adam watched with a rising sense of awareness as the soldiers slipped black masks over their heads, then picked up their weapons.

It was surreal. Like he was watching this happen to someone else. Someone else who was held hostage in a foreign land where terrorists slaughtered at will in the name of their God or their cause.

Six soldiers lined up behind them. Pointed the rifles directly at the heads.

His heart exploded. This was it, he thought. The soldiers were going to kill them.

He looked at Minrada. Silent tears trickled down her cheeks as she met his eyes.

They stayed like that for what seemed like forever. Gazes locked. Hearts pounding so hard it felt like thunder. Dreams, desires, loss, and love flashed through Adam's mind. Anger, guilt. His mother's face. His mother's smile.

"Ki-yah-vah-nah-vaah." *Read.*

The single word shocked Adam into lifting his head . . . and seeing, for the first time, a video camera.

"Ki-yah-vah-nah-vaah!" the rebel repeated, stabbing an index finger at the piece of paper he'd shoved into Amithnal's hands.

Minrada's father was shaking so hard he couldn't hold the paper still.

Cursing under his breath, a soldier snatched it away from Amithnal, faced the small digital camera that Adam now understood was filming, and began to read himself.

Adam didn't understand much of it. Couldn't tell from the reaction on Minrada's face what was being said. Was barely aware that the soldier had finished, that they were being ordered to stand again, and that the camera had been shut off.

Adam's blood pumped like crazy as the four of them were marched back to the cave where he and Minrada had been held. His gut told him to attack. To head butt, kick, and bite any guard he could lay into.

His head told him it wouldn't work. There were twenty of them. Only one of him. And they had guns. All he had was hatred . . . that bred and grew when he was once again shoved into the dark without food or water.

"What did they say?" he whispered for fear of the guards overhearing him.

A long silence passed before Minrada whispered back, "They have given the Sinhalese government until midnight tonight to turn over control of both the UVA and the Central Province to the LTTE."

"And if they don't?"

"Then they will kill us."

Near the Wahala-purha temple ruins

Butterflies and bayonets. Songbirds and soldiers. The contrasts, Lily thought, as she searched the Tiger encampment with Manny's field glasses, were chilling. As starkly frightening as they were frighteningly stark. Mud brown tents, rusted vehicles, tired-looking soldiers—mostly boys. With weapons. All of them with weapons, the gunmetal gray color of death.

At the bottom of the gorge where the camp was set up, smoke from several campfires spiraled into the trees; the pungent scent of burning wood permeated the air. Above the scent of smoke hung the deep floral fragrance and decay of the jungle. The rain forest thickened a hundred yards to the left of where she and Manny lay on their bellies on a black stone outcropping.

Tufts of tall, blade-thin grass shielded the crest of stone. It rustled in the wind like stiff satin and provided cover while they assessed the Tiger camp eighty yards below.

They'd left the jeep a half a mile back, deep in a

ravine and hidden in a copse of Palu trees. Then they'd
hiked to the rise. To Lily's surprise, the jeep had handled
the rough off-road trek that had taken them over rock-
strewn hillsides, through scrub brush and forest, and
across small, meandering creek beds where the tumbling water had licked at the floorboards and sucking
sand had threatened to mire them, wheel-hub deep.

Yeah. The jeep had held up well.

She, however, wasn't doing so hot. She'd counted
thirty—maybe thirty-five—rebel soldiers milling around
the camp. She refocused the glasses and counted again,
her heart pounding as she searched for a sign of Adam.

But all she saw was soldiers and weapons and the
things she'd imagined she'd find in a paramilitary camp.
Transport trucks, jeeps, tents, lines for clothes, fire pits,
and targets at the far end of what appeared to be a
makeshift firing range. Two types of vehicles were no-
ticeably absent. No pickup truck with or without blankets or tarps in the bed was anywhere to be seen. No
beat-up van.

She didn't know what that meant. Had they brought
Adam here, then left? Had they brought him here at all?

"I still count thirty or so," she whispered to Manny,
who had rolled to his back and pulled the SAT phone out
of one of the many compartments on his ALICE pack
and was trying to reach Ethan. Manny's rifle and his
heavy pack lay beside her lighter one in the tall grass.

"Watch the angle of the glass," Manny warned as he
dialed. "If the sun catches it and they spot us, we're up
shit creek without the proverbial paddle."

Lily cupped her palm over the top of the field glasses,
shielding the lenses from the midmorning sun. "What
are they doing?"

"Waiting," he said, giving up on making a connection and rolling to his belly again. His St. Christopher medal clinked softly against the rock when it fell out of his shirt. "The question is, for what?"

Gaze still riveted on the camp, Lily tracked the glasses more slowly over the area. "I don't see anything but soldiers. God. They look so young."

"That's because they are," Manny said with a stoic look, and held out his hand for the glasses. "SOP."

Standard Operating Procedure. Yes. Manny would know about that. He'd been young, too, when he'd joined the Contra movement. Young men boiling with testosterone, bloodlust, and passion made the best recruits. Some things never changed. Adam was sixteen—the same age as Manny when he'd joined the resistance against the Sandinistas. But Adam was her son. He was mentally strong. She counted on that. And he had spirit—like his father. Frankly, she didn't know if that was a good thing in this situation. She didn't want Adam doing anything foolish. Anything heroic.

"Do you see anything significant?" she asked because she had to quit thinking about what might be happening with Adam and concentrate on what she and Manny could do to find him.

Manny continued to scan the area. "I don't know. Something's not ringing true here. They seem kind of ragtag—even for rebels. And it's a big camp for less than a third of a company of soldiers. It's set up for more. Looks like the main purpose of the camp is training, but I don't see much evidence of any going on."

He lowered the glasses, frowned. "Maybe they're just here to do recon. The question is, are there more of them? And if so, where are they?"

"The question is, do they have Adam?"

Anxious and restless, Lily wondered what would happen if she walked down the hill and asked them. She'd never find out. Manny had made it clear; they were here to recon, not act, until Ethan arrived.

"I'm thinking no." Manny lifted the glasses again. "If they had hostages, they'd have a guard posted by one of those tents. Instead, they've got a heavily armed squad stationed by whatever it is that's under that tarp."

She'd wondered about the tarp. It was big enough to cover a large truck.

"Maybe provisions?" she suggested.

"In need of guards? I don't think so," he said calmly. "We'll watch. We'll wait."

"And then what?" She asked the question she hadn't wanted to ask but suddenly needed to know the answer to. "What if Adam is there? What do we do then?"

"Exactly what I said we'd do. We wait for Ethan and Darcy." He lowered the glasses. "Then we go talk to them."

"Talk? You know Tamil?"

He shook his head. "Don't have to. I know a more universal language. Money."

CHAPTER 16

Outskirts of Kandy on the road to Marassana

"What are we going to do?"

Ethan glanced in the rearview mirror, signaled a left turn, and headed back into the city.

"Haven't made up my mind yet, but I'll tell you one thing. These assholes are really starting to piss me off."

Darcy and Ethan had been trying to get out of Kandy and meet up with Manny and Lily for the past hour. It wasn't happening, though, because the white VW was back. The car had been sticking to their tail like the heat that clung to the city and beat relentlessly down on the Suburban.

"Are they getting bolder or are they just stupid?" Darcy asked as Ethan sped down the street searching for the best way to ditch these losers.

"I vote for stupid," Ethan said with disgust. "But we can't risk leading them—whoever they are—to Manny.

"Try to raise him on the SAT phone again, would you? Let him know we've been held up."

"Still no good," Darcy said after several attempts to connect. "Do you suppose they're out of range?"

"Could be. As soon as we deal with our new best friends, I'll check the unit.

"Hang on." He jerked the wheel sharp left.

The Suburban careened around the corner on two tires.

"Still with us," Darcy reported when Ethan cut another corner.

"Good." He pulled into an alley.

As he'd figured it would, the VW sped past the alley, braked with a squeal of tires, and backed up.

"Uh-oh," Darcy said when she saw the VW turn into the alley and creep toward them.

She glanced at Ethan. He was smiling as he pulled a pistol from the glove box and checked the clip. It was not a smile that would warm hearts.

"Oh. You *wanted* them to find us."

"Damn straight." He never took his eyes off the slowly approaching vehicle. "It's time to have a little come-to-Jesus meeting. At which time," he added with a dark look, "I plan to deliver the gospel according to me."

He glanced her way and offered her a Life Saver before popping one into his mouth. "Get down, babe. This might not be pretty."

"Get down? I don't think so, Lieutenant. No way am I leaving in the middle of this movie."

He was gearing up to get all protective and bossy when the car pulled up behind them and cut the motor.

"Showtime," she said, and with her heart beating in her throat, watched as another vehicle pulled into the other end of the alley and slowly rolled to a stop.

They were blocked in.

And they were outnumbered four to two.

"Now what?" Darcy watched as all four men got out of their cars and slowly approached them.

"Now we hope that that official-looking seal in the front corner of each windshield means what I think it means."

"Police," Darcy said, recognizing the symbol on the seal now that the cars were close up. "That's a good thing, right?"

"That's what we're going to find out."

Ethan reached under the seat and withdrew a handgun Darcy had heard him refer to as a Czech CZ-52. He set it on the seat beside him, slipped off the safety, and covered the gun with a map.

"Gentlemen," Ethan said in English when the four men approached them. "Is there a problem?"

Yes, as it turned out. There was. A very big problem.

Four problems to be exact. All of them semiautomatic. All of them drawn. All of them in the hands of some hard-faced men who would not, Darcy was certain, hesitate to put a bullet through the center of each of their foreheads.

"Step out of the vehicle and come with us, please." A short, swarthy Sinhalese with close-set eyes and a pocked complexion flashed a badge. "We wish you no harm. And as long as you keep your hand away from the gun you have hidden beneath the map, no harm will come to you."

"I have friends at the American embassy," Darcy said. "Friends who are aware we are here."

"I assure you, Ms. Prescott, we are well aware of your friends—in fact, they have sent us to escort you to our international crime headquarters."

Darcy cut an uncertain glance at Ethan. He shook his head.

"Then you wouldn't mind giving them a call—letting us talk to them."

To Darcy's surprise, someone produced a cell phone, then punched in a number and handed it to her.

The phone rang several times before a woman picked up. "Vice-Consul Griffin's office."

"This is Darcy Prescott. I—"

"Ms. Prescott," the woman interrupted. "Mr. Griffin's been waiting for word from you. Hold on please; I'll connect you immediately."

Ethan watched her with hooded eyes. She nodded to let him know she'd reached Griffin's office.

"Darcy?"

"What's going on, Griff?"

"Jesus, Darcy. Where are you?"

"At the moment? We're being detained in Kandy by some lovely gentlemen with shiny badges and big guns."

"It's okay. I've had them tailing you to make sure you stayed out of trouble."

"You put the tail on us? They have guns, Griff. Big ones."

"Sorry about that. I just gave the go-ahead for them to move in and detain you—guess they got a little overzealous. Look, Darcy, we've had a development on the Adam Campora situation."

She felt her heart turn over. Reached out and latched on to Ethan's hand. "What's happened?"

"We just received a video via e-mail."

She wasn't aware that she'd dug her nails into Ethan's palm. Was only aware of the difficulty breathing as Griff told her about the content of the tape that had been shot earlier today and e-mailed to the prime minister's office within the past hour.

"Oh God." She disconnected and turned to Ethan. "We've got to get ahold of Manny."

"Nothing," Ethan said after attempting to call. "I'm still getting a no-service message."

"Try Dallas."

"Already on it," he said with an urgency in his tone that matched hers as he dialed Dallas's SAT phone.

Dallas, Darcy thought, and closed her eyes.

Based on the news Griff had just given them, Dallas had walked into the devil's kitchen with little more than a match when what he really needed was a flamethrower.

And Adam and the Muhandiramalas had less than ten hours to live if the Sinhalese government didn't turn over control of the UVA and Central Province to the Tigers by midnight.

The chances of that happening were the same as those of peace breaking out in the Middle East in the same time frame. Which meant that the odds of saving Adam's life had just narrowed to a window roughly the size of the head of a pin.

———

Near the Wahala-purha temple ruins

"How much longer do we wait?"

Lily was impatient. Manny understood that. She was probably also hungry and stiff. They'd been fixed on their bellies on the stone, watching the camp, for the past hour.

"As long as it takes," he said, although he'd pretty much come to the conclusion they were barking up the wrong banana tree.

He'd seen nothing to indicate there were hostages in the camp. No tents were under guard. There were no regularly scheduled spot checks to any particular location in the camp that would indicate concern over a hostage rescue.

The only thing that seemed to be of any consequence in the camp—aside from the fact that it was set up for a lot more personnel than were currently there—was the heavily guarded tarp.

He rubbed his palm over his jaw where a two-day stubble had started to itch. Guns, he was guessing. They probably had a shitload of guns—possibly some RPGs—stowed under the tarp. Which continued to make him nervous as hell. There was room under the canvas for enough weaponry to stage a major coup.

Which led to the logical question: Why would they need that much firepower unless they were preparing to launch an attack? And why would the Tigers risk it in the middle of Sinhalese territory? It wasn't their style—and with good reason. Their military—regardless of this cache of weapons—was outnumbered ten to one.

If they were stupid enough to launch an attack, though, just where did that land Adam and the Muhandi-ramalas? Were they insurance? Or were they a catalyst for some brewing martyrdom plot? And if Manny was right about his suspicions that Adam and the rest were being held at another location, why did it appear that this particular camp may be planning a major battle so far away from the northern territory?

Christ. None of it made sense. Manny thought about Dallas. Wondered if he'd successfully breached the Tiger headquarters in the north and found any information of use. Dallas could handle himself; still, Manny couldn't help but wonder if Dallas was all right. And hope to hell he was able to make some connections that would both clarify and help in Adam's rescue.

Manny couldn't worry about Dallas now. He had enough to deal with right here. He scanned the area again with the field glasses, and, not for the first time, it struck him how much Sri Lanka reminded him of Nicaragua. And not just that the people lived under the constant threat of war. Everything from the lush jungles, to the climate, to the coastal ports made him think of home.

The last time he'd been home as a citizen of Nicaragua, Lily had filled not only his nights and his bed but also his every waking thought. He was a U.S. citizen now. Glad for it. Proud of it.

But other things, he realized with weary acceptance, never changed. Lily still filled his head—though she no longer shared his bed. Right, wrong, somewhere in between, when this mission was behind them, that was going to change.

A lot of things were going to change. He was a father. He would know his son.

And his son's mother—well. Other than fear for her child, frustration with Manny, and the occasional look that made him think she may be as aware of him as he was of her, he didn't know what their future held. And other than having her in his bed, he wasn't certain what he wanted from her.

"Why do you think Ethan hasn't checked in yet?"

Lily's question broke into his thoughts, jarring him back to the ridge.

"Wish I had a good answer for that. The simple one is that something's interfering with our satellite link."

"And a not so simple answer?"

Manny didn't think she'd want to hear the not so simple answer. And he didn't want to think about the possibility that whoever had been tailing them might have made a move and Ethan was not in a position to make contact. Manny didn't want to think about that any more than he wanted to think about what was happening with Dallas.

Manny rolled a shoulder, then his neck, working the burn out of muscles grown stiff from holding the same position for so long.

"Whoa—" He stilled when sudden activity, lots of it, had soldiers scurrying every which way in the camp. "Something's happening."

He adjusted the focus on the field glasses, watched as the camp commander—Manny had spotted the rank of captain on the Tamil officer's uniform—talked into a two-way and barked orders.

"Shit," Manny swore when one of the fighters joined the officer and both of them trained field glasses on the rim where he and Lily were hunkered down. "Looks like we've been made."

"They've spotted us?"

Before he could answer, a dozen rebel fighters ran toward the tarp. They quickly undid the bungee cords that held down the canvas and rolled it back.

"Moth-er-fuck-er," Manny muttered when he got a bead on the piece of artillery perched on the ground like a great beached whale. It was a goddamn cannon! An M-102 howitzer, for chrissake. Talk about overkill. No wonder they had a two-and-a-half-ton truck. They needed something that big to tow it.

What the hell were they doing with that gun? More to the point, where did they get it? The M-102s had seen a lot of action during the Vietnam conflict, but the U.S. Army, for one, had pretty much deep-sixed those bad boys from their arsenal twenty-plus years ago. How one had ended up in the Tigers' hands was anybody's guess.

He refocused the field glasses and damn near swallowed his tongue when they shoved a 105mm round into the breech and prepared to strike the primer. Then they set a trajectory that aimed dead center at the rock where he and Lily were lying.

The bad news: If the sucker was functional, Manny and Lily were charred toast. The good news: The gun was a relic. The chances were good that the rebels could smoke themselves if the weapon misfired.

He wasn't going to wait around to find out who came out ahead in this deadly game.

"Move it," he ordered, scrambling backward. He grabbed both his pack and hers along with his rifle. *She'd make a good soldier,* he thought as they crab-crawled at warp speed down the back of the slope. She didn't question. She just moved—although she was falling behind him.

And then all he could think about was keeping her alive when he heard the unmistakable report of the big gun being fired.

He grabbed her ankle, jerked her down the slope toward him, and lunged on top of her all in one motion. Then he covered her head and prayed there'd be enough left of him to get her out of the line of fire when the smoke cleared.

The mortar round whooshed overhead, then detonated with a ground-shaking concussion that exploded through his eardrums like a pack of cherry bombs in a bucket of water.

He made a cave of his arms and hunkered deeper over Lily's head, waited for the pain, for the rain of rock and dirt and blood that would follow.

Nothing.

The only thing moving in the aftermath of the explosion was the woman beneath him; the only sounds were the ringing in his ears, Lily's muffled, "I can't breathe!" and the unmistakable crackle of a roaring gas fire.

Stunned to be in one piece, he rolled off of her, made a quick recon of the immediate area, and saw not a blade of grass out of place. "What the—" and then he saw it. Smoke. Thick, black, and boiling out of the ravine behind them.

The ravine where they'd left the jeep under the copse of Palu trees.

"What *was* that?" Lily half-whispered, half-croaked, as she struggled to get her breath back.

It registered peripherally that he must have knocked the wind out of her when he'd thrown himself on top of her.

"That," he said, grabbing her hand and dragging her to her feet, "was one big mother of a gun. And that fire you see," he continued as he led her at a run down the hill, away from the burned-out jeep and toward the jungle, "was our ride."

"Oh God," she gasped after a quick glance in the direction of the fire.

"Guess we know where the rest of those soldiers were." He jumped a piece of deadfall, racing for the nearest copse of trees. The additional troops must have been out scouting, running a training exercise—whatever—and had stumbled across the jeep. They'd evidently radioed back coordinates for the mortar round.

Manny hoped to hell he and Lily made it to the cover of the jungle before they became the next target of the big gun.

"Where are we go—"

"Just run!" he barked, eating up ground as fast as he could with his pack and hers and his rifle slung over one shoulder and her hand latched in a death grip in his other. "With a little luck, they won't spot us."

The static, tattoo report of automatic weapon fire broke out not more than a hundred yards behind them. The rounds whistled past his left ear just as he ducked and rolled and dragged Lily with him.

Ho-kay. So luck wasn't on the table.

And Mother Nature picked that exact moment to unload with a late-morning downpour. The clouds that had been milling overhead like swarming bees opened up, burst like popped water balloons, and drenched him and Lily to the skin just as they ducked under the thick, green canopy of the rain forest—a squad of Tiger rebels hot on their trail.

———

Tiger headquarters, Jaffna Peninsula

"You're a popular fellow," Ramanathan said dryly as Dallas's SAT phone rang.

It was the second time in as many minutes. Dallas had no doubt it was Ethan or Manny. He also had no illusions about the wisdom of answering. He had an audience with the head of the LTTE. In Sri Lanka, that was on the scale of an audience with the Pope, only Ramanathan would never be confused as a holy man in a civilized world.

"My brother," Dallas said, referring to his ringing phone. "Most likely he's worried about me."

"As well he should be," Ramanathan said with a sardonic smile. "Now tell me what it is you braved death to ask of me."

"We have lost something. Something precious. The speculation is that you may . . . be in a position to help us locate it."

"Something so precious that you risk your life. Interesting. Tell me more."

Dallas would like nothing better than to lean across the desk and wrap his hands around the slimy little bastard's neck. Instead, Dallas leaned back in the chair that had been provided for him and crossed his ankle over his knee. He flicked at the dust on his pant leg and played the game.

"A boy. An American. Adam Campora. He's in Sri Lanka on a humanitarian mission."

"How noble. And this concerns me how?"

Dallas met Ponnambalam Ramanathan's cold eyes. "He's disappeared. Amithnal Muhandiramala, his wife, Sathi, and their daughter, Minrada, Adam's host family, have also disappeared."

Ramanathan toyed with his knife, turning it over and over in his hand. "And you assume I have something to do with this—"

"Disappearance? No." Dallas shook his head, understanding that an outright accusation of abduction would only meet with more resistance. "I have high hopes, however, that you might have some information that would assist in recovering both the Muhandiramalas and Adam."

"Muhandiramala," Ramanathan mused. "Why is that name familiar? Oh wait. It comes to me. He's a member of the Sinhalese parliament, correct?"

Dallas simply met Ramanathan's hard stare. The general knew exactly who Muhandiramala was and his importance in the Sinhalese government.

"You are a fool on a fool's mission," Ramanathan said at last. "I know nothing of this."

Dallas didn't bat an eye and played his trump card. "Word is that you've suffered some setbacks . . . financially," he said without missing a beat.

Ramanathan's sharp gaze latched on to Dallas like an infrared beam. "And you wish to make a contribution to the cause? How generous."

"I could be generous, yes," Dallas agreed. Unspoken was the *provided you tell me where Adam is*.

A slow grin slid over Ramanathan's face. Then he threw back his head and laughed. "You've got a set of balls on you, Garrett. You come to my house and offer *me* a deal if *I* play nice with *you*?"

He leaned back in his chair, sobered abruptly. "I know nothing of your lost boy. But I will make you a deal. I have lost something, too. Something that is very valuable to me."

"A howitzer?" Dallas repeated after Ramanathan told him what he'd lost. "How in the hell do you lose a cannon?"

"The shipment arrived in Trincomalee," the general explained, referring to a port city on the east coast and north of the Bay of Bengal. "It was intercepted at the docks by men dressed in Tiger uniforms."

"Only it wasn't your men," Dallas surmised. "When did this happen?"

"Three days ago. I want my gun back. And because I like you, Garrett, I'm going to give your brother a chance to find it. If he does, I just might let you live.

"Now answer your phone," he said when the phone rang again. "Your life may depend on it."

"Yo," Dallas answered the phone, never taking his eyes off Ramanathan.

"We've got a ransom tape," Ethan said, wasting no time.

Dallas had figured this was coming. "And they want what?"

Ethan told him.

"Hold on." He tilted the phone away from his mouth and studied Ramanathan. "Interesting," he said, addressing the general, "that you know nothing of Adam Campora and the Muhandiramalas' disappearance, yet the prime minister's office is in possession of a video showing Tiger fighters holding them at gunpoint and promising to execute them if the Tamils' demands aren't met."

Ramanathan frowned. "I know nothing of this tape."

Whether it was the unguarded shock on Ramanathan's face or the stunned tone of his voice, for some reason Dallas believed him. "If your camp didn't make the video, then who?" Dallas pressed.

Ramanathan stroked his chin, thought. "This I do not know, but one wonders . . ." He let the thought trail off.

Dallas completed it. "One wonders whether, if your gun was found, we might also find our lost boy."

"What's going on?" Ethan asked on the other end of the line.

"I'm not sure," Dallas said as, brows lowered in thought, the general reached for the phone on his desk, "but I think we may have just found an unlikely ally. And I may have just gotten my ass out of a sling."

"Explain."

"Seems General Ramanathan's missing something, too." In the background, Ramanathan barked orders.

"Well, fuck," Ethan muttered after Dallas filled him

in on the missing howitzer. "Just what we need. Another complication."

"Yeah," Dallas said. "That's kind of the way I see it, too."

By his calculation, they had a little less than ten hours left before the deadline expired.

Ten hours that could mean the difference between life and death.

CHAPTER 17

Somewhere in the jungle

Rain dripped in Lily's eyes as a steady deluge beat down through massive palms and towering pines, finding its way through the tall canopy trees, then down to the shorter palms, and finally to the ground. Twisted, stunted trees struggled in vain against hardier palms draped in mosses, ferns, and thousands of brilliantly colored orchids. The vibrant fuchsias, pinks and shades of yellow, zipped past her field of vision as she and Manny half-ran, half-hacked their way through foliage that was sometimes so thick, she lost sight of him if he got so much as a yard away from her.

A stiff vine slapped Lily in the face, shooting a fresh wave of pain through her bruised cheek as she trudged behind him. Her skinned knees stung; so did her arms where fern fronds and palm leaves had sliced tiny cuts on their mad dash through the slippery underbrush.

Her hair had long since been pulled, tugged, and torn loose of her braid. It lay heavy on her back; sodden tendrils fell across her face. She was soaked to the skin.

She was hungry, she was tired, and she probably ought to be scared half out of her mind, but all she could think of was keeping up with the man who set a pace that made the Boston Marathon look like a cakewalk.

She wasn't sure how long they'd been running from the rebel forces. Or if they were still being chased. Only one thing was certain. Manny wasn't slowing down— and that told her they were far from out of danger.

Not long ago, he'd pulled a long, lethal-looking knife out of his pack—that was right after they'd heard the roar of what sounded like a very big cat. *Leopard,* Lily suspected, and wished she hadn't read as much about the Sri Lankan jungles as she had.

Leopards, too many varieties of poisonous snakes to count, wild boars, sloth bears, and jackals headed the list of "critters" she wished she didn't know about. Oh, and leeches. God, she didn't even want to think about the leeches.

Above them, noisy troops of toque macaques with their comical thatch of hair parted down the middle of their heads competed with langur and shaggy-hair monkeys on the decibel-level scale. Hundreds of the long-tailed primates swung from treetop to treetop like teams of runners in a relay race. Only the birds—their caws and trills constant—came close to rivaling the monkeys and the rain for noise.

But the sounds that remained etched in Lily's consciousness as Manny hacked a path for them through trailing vines and foot-grabbing roots were the sounds of the explosion that had destroyed their jeep and the too-close-for-comfort whiz of bullets flying past her head.

He stopped so suddenly Lily ran smack into his broad back. She was too winded and weary to do anything but stand there, leaning against him, struggling for breath, while his big, wet body held her upright.

His chest heaved with his deep breaths. He lifted a hand, wiped rain and sweat from his eyes with his forearm.

"Why are we sto—"

His quick "Shush" quieted her.

He was listening, she realized. Attempting to determine if they were still being followed.

She closed her eyes, pressed her forehead against his back, and concentrated on quiet breaths while her heart pumped blood through her veins like a locomotive to feed oxygen to her deprived lungs.

She heard nothing but her own heartbeat.

He, apparently, heard something else.

He tapped her on the shoulder. When she looked up, he held his index finger to his mouth, then tossed their packs under a huge, low-hanging banana palm leaf to the left of the trail. Then he motioned for her to duck in beside the packs.

If possible, her heart beat harder. It was then that she realized what was wrong. It wasn't what Manny had heard—it was something he *hadn't* heard.

The monkeys had stopped their chatter. Even the incessant song of the birds had ended. The silence interspersed with only rain was more unnerving than the noise. And more meaningful.

They had company. Enough to quiet the noisy masses into a silence bred by curiosity. Or by fear. Whichever. Lily understood. Her blood was running with plenty of both.

Manny didn't have to tell her twice to hide. Like a good soldier, she hunkered down beneath palm leaves bowed and heavy with rain—where she waited, water dripping in her face. And she told herself they weren't going to die here. They couldn't die. Adam needed them not to die.

Very carefully, she dug into her pack and withdrew

the Browning. She shoved a full magazine into the grip. Then she slipped off the thumb safety, pulled the hammer back to full cock, and with a cartridge in the chamber, prepared to fire.

Across the trail, looking dark and deadly with his unshaven face and the assault rifle cradled in his arms, Manny gave her an approving nod. Then as quiet and stealthy as the big cat she'd heard growl earlier, Manny ducked behind a moss-covered boulder on the opposite side of the trail that he'd cut. Not more than a yard away from her, he squatted, sank his knife into the forest floor, then dug up mud with his fingers and smeared it over his face, arms, and shirt.

Even with the rain washing down his face and diluting the mud, it was frightening how fast he made himself disappear. Frightening how the warm, dark licorice color of his eyes transitioned to obsidian. Cold, hard, soulless. If she hadn't known he was the same man who had once touched her with a lover's hands, the same man who had just sacrificed his body to protect hers from a mortar round, the deadly look in his eyes would have had her running in the other direction.

A sound—the faint, muffled snap of a breaking twig—registered through the steady drip of water funneling from leaf to leaf like a meticulous series of channels and spouts.

Eyes wild, she sought Manny's. He touched a finger to his lips again, then pointed back in the direction they had come from.

Before she even nodded that she understood, he disappeared. He'd gone back to intercept whoever was following them.

It crossed her mind that it was a good thing she was

sitting on her butt. The impact of discovering Manny had gone after them on his own would have knocked her there. Suddenly it felt like she had an adrenaline drip mainlined into her bloodstream. Her face flushed hot. Her limp-noodle limbs burned with the need to fight. Her finger trembled over the trigger guard of the Browning. She ignored the water running into her eyes, weighing down her clothes and her hair. She focused. She waited.

She'd felt comfortable with her Springfield. Felt confident in her aim. But that had been on a firing range with paper targets. From the moment she'd picked the Browning out of the cache of weapons Dallas had purchased in that back-alley deal, she'd known that if she ever used it, she wouldn't be firing at paper.

She'd been asking herself ever since if she could use it on another human being. She wasn't asking anymore. To protect her son, to protect herself, to protect this man who didn't yet believe in her but who wanted her anyway, she'd do whatever had to be done.

She was stone-cold certain of that fact.

And when a single shot rang out, not twenty paces back along their trail, she knew that the involuntary flinch that jerked her body had nothing to do with fear.

It had to do with necessity.

It had to do with purpose.

It had to do with the certain knowledge that despite the fact that he still didn't believe her, if they put so much as a scratch on Manny Ortega's caramel-mocha skin, if they so much as split a single strand of his beautiful black hair, she was going to blow them to kingdom come.

Gripping the Browning in both hands, she raised the gun, sighted down the barrel, and, steady as a rock, waited.

And waited.

By the time she heard the telltale rustle of leaves behind her, it was too late to even scream. One hand clamped
over her mouth; another wrestled the gun out of her hands,
then pushed her to her back and pinned her there.

———

"Easy. It's me."

Every muscle in Lily's body went as lax as cooked
pasta. She stopped struggling. The air slogged out of her
lungs as Manny leaned over her. Very slowly, he unpeeled
his hand from over her mouth. The scream trapped in her
throat escaped on a low growl as knee-jerk anger nipped
at the heels of relief.

"You scared the hell out of me!" she whispered fiercely
as her body reacted to the fright with a series of tremors.

"Yeah, well, you looked like you wanted to shoot something real bad. Couldn't take a chance that it'd be me."

She let out a shuddering breath.

"Can you stand?"

"Yeah," she said, then made a liar out of herself when
he rose and offered a hand. She stood—and her knees
buckled.

He caught her before she went down, and pulled her
up against his chest.

Through his sodden shirt and pants she felt the hard
breadth of his chest, the lean line of hip and thigh. Felt his
body heat steam through wet clothes and counteract the
rain. His heartbeat, fast but steady, pulsed against her
cheek.

"Steady," he whispered, telling her they were far from
in the clear. "Take a second. Get your feet under you."

"My feet aren't the problem," she muttered, embarrassed by her sudden weakness. "What happened back there?" she asked when she felt herself level out.

He reached around in front of her and retrieved her Browning from the jungle floor. Before handing it to her, he did what he could to wipe it dry.

"What happened is that we need to move out," he said, his face expressionless. "That shot is going to draw the rest of them like flies."

She tucked the gun into her waistband, then met his eyes. Saw in them the answer he had avoided giving her. He'd shot someone. Someone who had been intent on killing him . . . or her . . . or Adam.

Someone who was probably a boy. God. All of this was so senseless.

"We can't . . . can't just leave him."

"Yes," he said, his eyes as vacant and hollow as an empty vault, "we can. You're not here on a mercy mission, Lily. And his friends don't give a rip that you're only here to find your son. Me, they'll just kill if they catch us. You . . . they'll let you live a long time before they're through passing you around. By that time, you'll wish you were dead."

If his intention was to scare her, it worked. When he took off, she reached for her backpack and fell into step behind him. A new level of fear fortified her with a burst of adrenaline.

They slogged on for another hour. The underbrush thinned some, making walking a bit easier. The trade-off was that the terrain had grown steep and the rain no longer had to filter through a canopy of trees. It was like taking a cool, pulsing shower with their clothes on. Not a speck of mud remained on Manny's face or hands. Even his clothes and hers had been washed clean—which made them stark white targets against a dark green terrain.

They were almost to the top of a long, rocky knoll, using tree limbs and thick, woody vines to help pull themselves up the steep, rain-slick grade, when they heard voices behind them.

Lily glanced over her shoulder when Manny swore; not thirty yards behind them at the foot of the hill was a troop of soldiers, all carrying semiautomatic weapons. She could hear their shouted orders and figured they'd be fanning out and combing the area and would not give up until they found her and Manny.

"Go, go, go!" Manny ordered with a quiet urgency that sent her scrambling to keep up with him.

If the rebel troops spotted them, they'd pick her and Manny off like sitting ducks.

When she slipped and slid a few feet backward, Manny reached back and grabbed her hand. He jerked her up beside him and catapulted them over the rise. The momentum sent them flying over the rim of the hill—which dropped off at a drastic angle. She was vaguely aware of Manny wrapping himself around her as they tumbled down the hillside like Jack and Jill on their botched attempt to get water.

Lily didn't have time to think, let alone scream. It was all she could do to keep hold of her pack while they rolled, bounced, skidded, slipped, and careened down the steep embankment like a runaway tire. She felt like she'd been caught up in an amusement park ride—only she had no idea when this one would stop and let her get off.

They bounced hard enough to jar Manny's arms loose and he flew one way, she another. She landed flat on her face at the bottom of a ravine, a bed of ferns and moss cushioning her fall. For several seconds, she just lay there, catching her breath, assessing for damages. When she was relatively certain she was in one piece, she pushed up to her knees—to see Manny spread-eagled on his back five feet away.

His eyes were closed. He wasn't moving. And then she saw the blood. Lots of it, covering his right temple.

Oh God.

She scrambled to his side on all fours, decayed leaves and fern fronds rustling in her wake, the rain, if possible, pouring down even harder.

"Manny," she whispered, and checked for a pulse—*strong, thank God*—then lifted an eyelid. He flinched. Another good sign.

"Manny!" She tapped his cheek with an open palm, trying to rouse him.

He groaned and rolled his head to the side.

Relief that he was coming around zipped through her chest like fresh air.

"Come on," she urged him, kneeling by his head to inspect the cut. It was nasty. He must have hit a rock on the tumble down the hill. A two-inch gash sliced through his scalp, just inside his hairline. That accounted for the blood. Head wounds bled like blazes. The knot roughly the size of a robin's egg beneath it accounted for the unconsciousness.

"Come on," she pleaded this time, trying to rouse him. "We've got to get out of here."

His eyes opened then. He tried to sit up, swore, and went slack again. "Whoa. Spin cycle."

God. He couldn't run in this condition. She had to hide them. Fast. And he wasn't in any shape to help her.

Frantic, she looked around, spotted his rifle and AL-ICE pack through the pouring rain. Crouching low, she slipped and slid her way to retrieve them. Once she'd gathered all their gear, she searched for a place to hide.

Ten feet away, she spotted a thicket of wiry brambles butted up against one of the many man-sized boulders scattered along the jungle floor. Trailing vines, ferns, and thick, lush orchid stems made a curtain around the boulder. At its base a natural hollow, like a bowl, almost like a narrow set of root cellar steps, cut a cove of sorts. A cove big enough to hold a man.

And a woman, she thought, *if they didn't mind getting up close and personal.*

Knowing it was only a matter of minutes before the rebels popped over the ridge, she scrambled back to Manny.

"Help me," she ground out as she worked her hands under his armpits and, employing every ounce of strength left in her, started dragging him toward the boulder.

He weighed a ton, all muscle, solid as stone, and mostly deadweight. He made valiant attempts to dig in his heels and push, but his weight tore at her burning muscles. She thought she heard a shout—and adrenaline kicked in again and helped her drag him the rest of the way.

He was holding his head up and trying to roll to all fours when, panting from the exertion, she left him next to the stone steps and scrabbled back for their packs and his rifle. When she returned, she tossed the packs into the hole for a cushion.

"Survival . . . blanket," he muttered, poised on his hands and knees now, head hanging as blood dripped onto the ground between his flat palms and slowly seeped away in the rain-saturated ground. "Camo. In the pack. Get it."

Her wet fingers flew as she dug inside his pack, found the blanket, and tugged it out.

"Hurry . . . we've got to get down there." When he didn't move fast enough, she gave him a none-too-gentle shove.

He landed on his back on top of the packs with a grunting groan. Wasting no time, Lily piled in on top of him, dragged the rifle down into the hole with them, then covered them with the blanket.

Lying as still as the earth surrounding them, Lily tried to regulate her breathing. Then she held her breath altogether and covered Manny's mouth with her palm when the distinct sound of boots on the ground—lots of them, very, very close now—drowned out the rapid-fire beat of the blood rushing through her ears and the rain pummeling the blanket.

CHAPTER 18

Nothing but the thin camouflage blanket above her protected Lily and the 180 or so pounds of hard, bleeding male beneath her from the rebel forces.

Seconds passed. Minutes. Each one felt like an hour.

She could hear the shouts of the rebel squad scouring the area. Died a hundred deaths when she thought of the marks Manny's body had to have made when she'd dragged him across the jungle floor, which must surely point like an arrow to their hiding place. And then she prayed that the rain washed the signs away—and that this hole didn't fill up and drown them.

Beneath her, Manny groaned and struggled to sit up.

"No . . . no, shush," she whispered, desperate to silence him, recognizing he was most likely disoriented and confused, because he'd been half-conscious when she'd shoved him into the hole.

"Have to stop them—"

She covered his mouth with her hand, pressed her cheek against his. It had been a while since a razor had touched his face. His whiskered stubble felt like sandpaper against her skin. She welcomed the stinging abrasion. Welcomed the reminder that he was strong—would be strong again as soon as he shook off the effect of the blow to his head.

She breathed deep. He smelled like rain and jungle loam and blood. Like sweat and man and things she'd been missing in her life for a very long time.

God. Sex? She was thinking about sex when they could be heartbeats away from death. Okay. She cut herself a little slack on that one. She'd worked enough trauma to know that an adrenaline rush could supercharge all the senses. Libido included. Nothing like a little brush with mortality to trigger a knee-jerk need to experience all the good things soon to be gone. And sex with Manny had always been a very good thing.

He shifted again and she pressed herself deeper into him.

"Manny, be still," she murmured. "Lay still. Please, please. You have to stay quiet."

He stilled abruptly. The tension-wrought confusion in his muscles eased. And then he said her name. "Lily."

His gruff whisper wasn't a question. It was a statement of relief. Of recognition.

He let out a breath, deep and long, said it again. "Li-ly."

Memories . . . of long, loving nights and deep, rich emotions filled her chest with tender longing. So tender, it brought tears—for all that had been. For all that could never be.

She turned her head ever so slightly toward his, their warm breaths meshing, their heartbeats pounding. Against her belly, she could feel the length and strength of an erection that told her his thoughts had gone the same way as hers.

His physical reaction to her had always been instant and intense. Even now, with rebel forces surrounding them, practically walking on top of them, and Manny drifting in and out of consciousness, he recognized her body, wanted to claim it as his.

"Liliana," he whispered, and touched his lips to hers. "I'm with you now."

Then he kissed her with a longing that accelerated the already rapid-fire beat of their hearts. A longing so big, it made her heart hurt, her throat swell.

"I'm with you now," he repeated against her mouth, then touched a hand to her hair. "Tell me what's happening."

It took her a moment. A moment to snap herself out of the unexpected sexual heat he'd ignited with one kiss, one whispered word—*Liliana*—and not a single stirring from his honed, muscular body. A moment to regroup and come back to the reality that death could come quickly and she would never have the chance to tell him she had loved him. Never see the face of their beautiful child again.

"We fell," she whispered shakily, willing herself to pull it together, "into a ravine. You hit your head. Here." Very carefully, she touched her fingertips to the wound and felt the sticky wetness of clotting blood. "You were unconscious for a few minutes. We're in a . . . I don't know . . . it's like a bowl at the base of a boulder, hiding from the rebel soldiers."

"They're gone," he said after a moment.

She cocked her head. Listened. Heard only rain. "You're right. I don't hear them. They've moved on."

"They'll be back," he said with absolute certainty.

"I need to check your head."

His hands on her waist stopped her when she tried to get up.

"Not yet," he said. "There could be trailers."

She didn't argue. With great care, she eased back down onto him. Aware now of every breath, every heartbeat, every pulse point where their bodies brushed and melded. Of the erection that hadn't slackened an inch.

And then she allowed herself to think about the moment when he'd kissed her. Allowed herself to relive it, savor the memory of the supple pressure of his lips. The adrenaline-tinged taste of his mouth. The end to a drought of sensations she'd experienced with only him.

A lifetime ago.

"Are you okay?" He ran his hands up and down the length of her. While it was clear he was assessing for injuries, the feel of those strong hands heated her body in ways the close jungle heat could never do.

"F . . . fine," she finally managed. "A few bruises. That's all."

His hands lingered over her hips, no longer assessing, not quite possessing.

The very air stilled around them. And for the first time, Lily noticed that the rain had started to ease up. Not so the pressure of his pulsing erection against her belly.

She sucked in a fractured breath, realized he'd done the same, and met his eyes in the hooded darkness beneath the blanket.

"I'd better check things out," he said abruptly.

"Um . . . yeah," she whispered, part of her thankful that at least one of them—the one with the head injury, no less—had his wits about him. The other part, however, wanted to shut out the threat of terrorists, of possible capture and death, and just stay wrapped under the blanket and in his arms and pretend everything that led to this point was just a bad nightmare.

He shifted her to the side. Then peeling back a corner of the blanket, he raised his head just enough to see at ground level. "It's clear."

Lily scooted to the side as he braced his hand on the side of the boulder for leverage. She froze the same time he did when the screeching scrape of stone against stone rent the air.

Manny stared from the boulder to her. "What the hell?"

"Did that boulder just move?" Lily couldn't believe what she'd just seen.

He glanced back at the boulder and pushed again. This time it moved a good foot.

Incredulous, Lily tested it herself. It moved again. "How can that be? It has to weigh tons."

He shifted around so he was on his knees in the hollow. As he faced the boulder, his big hands roamed and felt it all over before he reached under the bottom of the huge stone.

"It's hollow," he said, and pushed again.

This time the boulder swung wide.

"It's a door," Manny said, reaching for his ALICE pack.

He rummaged around inside and came up with a palm-sized flashlight. He released a handle on the light, cranked it several times, then turned it on.

A slim beam of light illuminated what appeared to be a series of steps that led to a passageway of sorts.

"Is it a cave?" Lily asked.

He nodded. Pointed the light upward where intricate drawings—frescoes actually—high on the ceiling led down the halls to a room. At the far end of the room sat a statue of a benevolent Buddha.

"A cave that was once used as a *dagoba*," he said.

"A temple." Before Lily could decide if she was

spooked or intrigued by their discovery, they heard voices again.

The rebels had returned.

She didn't understand what they were saying, but there was no mistaking the tone of their voices. They were pissed. And they were determined.

"Inside," Manny ordered.

She helped him gather up their gear, then with the trepidation of a condemned prisoner, entered the realm of the dark . . . and the unknown.

The shouts of rebel forces grew closer and louder as Manny wrapped his fingers around the stone door and pulled it shut behind them, blocking out all outside sound and light.

Blackness swallowed them whole.

———

With the flashlight guiding the way, Manny moved slowly into the temple. Beside him, Lily clung to his arm. She didn't say a word, but he knew she was spooked. She was wet, and despite the heat of the jungle, she was probably cold. The temperature inside the temple ruin had dropped by a good twenty degrees.

The cooler temperature helped him clear his head of any lingering wooziness from the knock he'd taken, but it still throbbed like a bitch.

"Amazing," Lily said as the slim beam of light bounced off the interior walls.

Other than their breathing, only a steady, heavy drip of water into water broke a silence as hollow and thick as the dark.

Manny shined the flashlight around every corner and

finally found the source of the sound. It was a small pool—maybe four feet around—in the center of the stone floor. Shining the light upward, he found the source of the drip. A tiny pinpoint of light shined down from outside. A hole in the earth that formed a natural dome around the abandoned temple.

"I wonder how old this place is." Lily's voice was hushed as their footsteps made hollow, echoing sounds in the cavernous room.

"Very," he said finally, sizing up the room as approximately ten by twenty feet wide. "According to the guidebooks, there are abandoned ruins all over the area. This one's evidently been forgotten for a while."

"It's in the middle of a jungle," she pointed out. "I'm not surprised. It's also pretty spooky.

"Those paintings." She nodded toward the ceiling, shivered again, and Manny suspected it wasn't just from a bad case of the creeps. "They're, um . . . quite graphic."

He agreed and added "explicit" to the depiction of couples in various sex acts.

"This must be where they sent the bad monks," she said after they'd both studied the truly remarkable drawings. "The ones who couldn't toe the line."

Manny couldn't help it. He grinned. "And their punishment was to paint what they were missing?"

"I'm thinking graffiti—idle minds and all that," she said, and he heard, rather than saw, the tremulous smile in her voice. "Of course, that's just a theory."

This woman was strong. She was also cold. He heard the slight chatter of her teeth.

"We've got to get you out of those wet clothes and into something dry."

"We will. But first I need to take care of your head.
No debate," she said, bristling when he opened his
mouth to argue. "It needs attention. If something happens to you, it's not going to matter if I'm warm and dry,
so sit, be quiet, and take your medicine."

Since it was obvious she wasn't budging, he chose not
to argue. Shining the light around the room, he found a
blocky wooden chair next to what was probably a bed
frame—also solid wood and blocky.

He dragged the heavy chair away from the wall. The
legs screeched like jungle monkeys as it slid across the
stone. Chances were good that he was going to be doing
some screeching, too, before she was through with him.

"Okay, Doc. Get it the hell over with."

Manny sat, then gritted his teeth to silence a yelp when
she started cleaning the wound.

"Christ," he hissed through a strained breath.

"Sorry. It's the alcohol," she explained as she dabbed
at the cut with a piece of gauze she'd soaked in liquid fire.

"What other instruments of torture have you been
carrying around in that bag?" he grumbled when she set
the medical kit on his lap.

"All kinds of fun things." She rifled around and found
an instant ice pack, smacked it to activate it, and laid
it against the cut. "This will numb it a little, take the
swelling down."

She cast him a concerned frown. "You know that you
need stitches."

He heaved a thick breath. Yeah. He'd figured.

"I didn't have access to any lidocaine. It's gonna hurt like hell."

He'd figured that, too. "Just do it."

She raised one of his hands to the ice pack. "Hold this tight against it." Then she directed the flashlight he held in his other hand. "Right here . . . yeah, there," she said as she prepared a suture kit.

When she was ready, she drew in a bracing breath, frowned again. "I'm not going to be able to see."

"I can hold the light. Just tell me where to point it."

She looked skeptical, but in the end, there was little choice. She cupped his hand in hers and positioned the light.

"Ready?"

He gave her a clipped nod, removed the ice pack— then swore a litany in his head as she dug right in and worked the needle through his scalp.

"I'm sorry. I'm so sorry," she whispered, and drove the needle into his scalp again.

"María santo, la madre de Dios," he gritted out as blinding poker-hot pain had him seeing stars and lightning bolts and clenching his teeth so hard he swore he heard one crack.

"Okay. I'm done," she said, sounding breathless and relieved. She repositioned the ice pack on top of the stitches. "It's not pretty, but it will stem the bleeding."

Beneath his wet shirt, he'd broken out in a cold sweat. He hung his head, waited for the pain to subside.

"Take these."

He looked up. She held four capsules in her hand.

"Antibiotic and ibuprofen. One will cut the pain, the other stave off infection—which is the last thing you need."

It was only then, as he took the medication from her hand, that he realized how badly she was shaking.

"Okay, Doc," he said, "now it's your turn. Get into some dry clothes."

She shook her head. "I need to check you over first. Take off your shirt."

He opened his mouth to protest.

"You took the brunt of the fall. I need to see if you've got any more open wounds. You don't take chances in a jungle, where infection breeds faster than mosquitoes."

Resigned, he started working the buttons. "Were you always this bossy or is this something new?"

"With age comes attitude. Believe me, I've earned it."

Just like she'd earned his respect. Manny undid the last button, peeled the sodden shirt off his shoulders, and tossed it to the floor.

It landed with a soggy slap.

"I need the . . . um . . . flashlight." Her voice sounded a little breathy and not nearly as bossy as it had a moment ago. "And put that pack back on your head."

He handed her the light. Would have wondered at the cause of her sudden tension—if he hadn't looked up and into her eyes just then. In the translucent light of their underground sanctuary, he read her reaction as clearly as if it had been daylight.

Awareness. Sexual and stark.

She swallowed thickly as her gaze trailed over his bare chest. He felt an answering awareness, the same one that had incited an instant hard-on when he'd come to under the blanket and her lush body had been intimately pressed over his.

And it was happening again. The throbbing in his groin suddenly outdistanced the throbbing in his head as she reached out a hand—cold with wet and shock—and touched his shoulder. His own skin was damp and chilled, yet where she touched him it heated by degrees.

"Bruised," she said, her voice husky, the sound of it trailing over his senses like a velvet fog. "Does this . . . does this hurt?" She probed the round of his shoulder, her fingers expert but gentle, warming his skin to fire.

He shook his head. Clenched his jaw. No. It didn't hurt. But something else did. Christ, he wanted to be inside her.

Not the time. Not the place.

He stared straight ahead, tried to think about rebel forces and big goddamn guns and how they were going to get out of this.

But then she moved in front of him, touching him with those soft, cool hands that somehow managed to leave a path of fire in their wake. She explored his upper arm, lingered over the scar Poveda's men had ripped through his arm.

The memory sobered him . . . until she drifted her hands over his ribs, tested another bruise, then moved behind him.

And the slow, delicious torture began again.

"Here?" She leaned in close to apply pressure at the base of his spine. "Does it hurt here?"

Her breath feathered across his back, just below his shoulder blade, inciting a riot of sensual images that outdistanced the pain from any injuries he might have. All he could think about was stripping off his pants and letting her take this little physical exam way, way south of the border.

He was beyond gone when she pronounced him fit.

As if. He was far from fit. And that ended right here.

It may not be the best time, it may not be the perfect

place, but he was finished with the wanting and the waiting and the dancing around the need.

She may be done with him . . . but he hadn't even started on her.

"Your turn," he said, hearing everything dark and carnal in his voice and knowing she heard it, too.

A heartbeat passed. Then two.

In the shadowed temple, her eyes burned like a night fire. "My . . . turn?"

He set her medical kit on the floor. Tossed the ice pack and reached for her hand. He drew her around in front of him until she was standing between his spread legs. He didn't pretend he was on a wound-finding mission when he started to work on the buttons on her shirt.

Neither, thank God, did she.

His hands were shaking now. And she was the one whose breath was fractured as if she were getting stitches.

"Fuck it," he swore when his fumbling fingers and the wet cloth made unbuttoning her shirt impossible. He knotted either side of the hem in each hand and ripped. Buttons flew. She gasped.

And then there was nothing between his hands and his mouth and the flesh he wanted to touch but a white cotton bra.

He gripped her waist. Pulled her close. Pressed his forehead against her midriff and breathed her in. Her essence. Her warm, wet woman scent. Everything that was Lily. Everything he remembered and missed and had dreamed of on those endless nights when he'd hated her. On the infinite nights when he'd loved her.

She was his. She'd always been his.

And he was going to have her again. Right now. Right here.

He turned his face into her flesh. Opened his mouth wide over her skin and fed.

"Mina." *Mine*, he whispered as she sucked in a sharp breath and cupped his face in her hands.

"Sus senos." *Your breasts*, he growled, covering her with his palms, brushing his thumbs over wet cotton, and feeling her nipples harden. "Mina.

"Su cueropo." *Your body*. He lifted his face, drew her breast into his mouth, and tasted her through her bra. "Mina."

She groaned and pressed into him as he skimmed his hands up and over her shoulders, knotted his hands in her wet hair.

"Su boca." *Your mouth*, he murmured, claiming her lips with a wet, opened-mouth invasion that possessed and destroyed and tasted like life and passion and everything he'd been missing for so damn long. "Mina."

With one hand tangled in her hair, he skimmed the other down her back and worked the clasp of her bra. When he couldn't get it undone, she reached behind her back, undid it for him.

"Manolo." She guided his mouth to her breast. "Manolo."

His name eddied out on a sigh as she moved closer, caressed his jaw as he suckled her, giving herself over to anything he wanted. Anything he desired.

Her acquiescence fueled the flame . . . in his loins, in his memory. She'd always been like this. Giving. Yet greedy in it. It drove him crazy.

"Mi mujer." *My woman*, he whispered urgently, and found the snap on her trousers.

She helped him strip them down her hips along with her panties. He filled his hands with her bare ass, then caressed her thighs, urging them open, and wedged his knee between them.

"Mi mujer," he repeated on a serrated breath as she straddled his lap and he found her center with his fingers.

She cried out when he touched her, stiffened when he stroked her, then, bracing her hands on his shoulders, melted around him like butter. His cock swelled and twitched at the liquid heat of her, the scent of aroused woman, the need to be inside her.

Somehow, he managed to one-hand his belt, open his fly, and free himself. She lifted, moved over him like silk, and, gripping him in her hand, guided him to her slick, wet opening.

"Dios. Cristo Dios." He sucked in his breath on a rush as, banding his hands around her slim waist, he lowered her onto him and buried himself deep.

She cried out again, dug her fingers into his shoulders, and let her head fall back, the picture of total abandon. The flashlight had fallen to the floor long ago. It had landed at an angle that caromed light off the walls and onto her incredible body.

Her lush breasts quivered as she drew in tremulous breaths; her black hair trailed down her back like wet ribbon. And the sounds she made, God, the sounds she made.

They called to his soul. Called to his heart as he rocked his hips into hers, lifting her, then plunging her down on top of him again and again, cloaking himself deep inside her giving warmth.

She came with a strangled cry, a series of breathless little hitches that bowed her back and thrust her naked breasts up to his waiting mouth. He buried his face between them, drove into her once, twice . . . three times more and shot into her like a cannon.

"Mi corazón. Mi alma. Son tuyos." *My heart. My soul. They are yours*, he whispered against the generous curve of her breast as a million sensations, all of them hot, all of them rich, all of them straddling the razor-sharp edge of pain, ripped through his loins like a flash fire and stripped him of everything but consciousness.

"Tuyo. Todo que tengo es tuyo." *Yours. Everything I have is yours.*

CHAPTER 19

The chair was hard. The wooden bed was even harder, though Manny had made a makeshift mattress out of his extra clothes and hers.

Even so, Lily had never felt so relaxed. Her body had taken on the consistency of that stuff kids liked to play with. *Silly Putty*, she thought, and nestled closer to Manny's side. No form. No bones. Just pliable flesh and blood that warmed in his hands and molded into anything he wanted her to become.

She was in the moment now. Wanted to stay there. Loved. Loving. Wasted on amazing sex and the drugging power of pheromones.

So she let herself. Just for a few more moments, she let herself languish in the cocoon of safety where nothing and no one existed outside of these stone walls. Just a few moments longer . . .

But then Manny's voice, soft, deep, and drifting on the downside of the love they'd made, ended the illusion with one long-anticipated question.

"What's he like? Our son."

Our son.

Lily resisted the urge to read any more into Manny's quiet question than curiosity, at least where the two of them were concerned. But his hesitance told her much about his own uncertainty. And his longing.

She ached for him. For Adam. And yes, even for herself and all the years she and Manny had missed.

"He's amazing," she said, her eyes filling with the tears she sometimes couldn't control when she thought of her son. "Smart. Even a little musically inclined. I'm not sure where he gets that from. But he has a guitar. Acoustic—so far he hasn't asked for electric, something I thank God for every day," she said around the lump that had lodged in her throat.

She felt more tears form at the thought of never standing in his open doorway again and watching as he painstakingly practiced a difficult chord. With a bracing breath, she fought them back. She would see him again. She would hold him again. His life was too precious, too vital, to be lost before he made his mark on the world.

Beside her, Manny's silence spoke for him. He wanted to know more.

"He loves soccer," she continued. "And the girls— well, the phone rings a lot. A lot," she repeated with a soft smile. "He doesn't have much time for them, though. At least not yet.

"His smile," she began, then swallowed back another thick lump, "it lights rooms. Dazzles." *Just like his father's,* she thought, and sent a plea to the powers that be that Manny would get to see for himself.

"And he's strong. Mentally. Emotionally. Physically, too, although right now he's got more angles and elbows than muscle groups. God, he's growing up so fast."

"Does he know about me?"

Manny's question came out of a silence in which they'd both absorbed and clung to thoughts about their son.

"Yes. He knows who you are. What you believe in. What you fought for. What I thought you'd . . . died for." Her throat ached from the strain of holding back tears.

And even though his hard, warm body didn't stiffen, didn't pull away, she knew what he was thinking.

"I couldn't tell him you were alive, Manny. When I found out . . . I couldn't risk it. Not until I faced you," she continued, taking heart from the fact that he hadn't pushed her away. "Not until I knew if you wanted to know him. I couldn't give him his father if you didn't want to be a part of his life."

"You think I would turn my back on my own flesh and blood?"

His voice was neutral, but his breathing had quickened ever so slightly.

Lily pushed up on an elbow. The flashlight power had wound down long ago. Its light was faint, a pale bluish white beam that cast more shadows than light. She could barely make out his face in the dark, but the hard set of his jaw was unmistakable.

She lifted her hand from his bare chest, pressed her fingers to his cheek, and turned his head to face her.

"Manny, you weren't the only one who struggled with the idea of betrayal. For seventeen years, I thought you were dead. Then eight months ago . . . when I saw you in that Special Forces documentary . . . well. I was . . . stunned. And so gloriously happy that you were alive. But then . . . then I wondered. Had you faked your death? Had you done it because you wanted to leave me?"

"Leave you?" He uttered the words on a disbelieving breath. "I loved you."

I loved you.

It was impossible to ignore the past tense of the word.

Just as it was impossible to ignore the irony.

And the sadness both brought to her heart.

"So," she said after a long moment, "we both made wrong conclusions."

He said nothing. Did nothing. Not for a very long time.

Her heart beat with anticipation when he reached for her hand, brought it to his mouth, and lingeringly kissed her palm.

"We are a pair, eh, Liliana?"

She smiled, slow and sad. "Yes. We are a pair."

He lowered her hand to his chest. She felt his heart beat steady and hard, felt his body tense as, with his hand still covering hers, he guided it slowly down his body. Over his ribs, across the rock-hard muscles of his abdomen, and lower to his penis, erect and hot and pulsing with need.

"We must go soon," he whispered, arching his hips against her hand as she boldly caressed him.

"Soon," she agreed with barely a sound, and rose above him. Watching his eyes over her shoulder, she swung her leg over his hips until her knees were planted on either side of his ribs, her bare toes tucked under his armpits.

He groaned and caressed her buttocks as she lowered her weight to her forearms and took him into her mouth.

All of him. The pulsing and hot length of him. The hard and yearning core of him. Lily closed her eyes, wanting to give. Needing to give. Aching to give. Yearning to connect, to mend, to bridge chasms and erase years of loss.

His labored breaths told her she was taking him deep into sensation, desperately into desire. And right now, it was enough. Giving him this, after all he'd lost, was everything she needed—until he gripped her hips and lowered her to his mouth.

She gasped and arched into his hot, wet seduction. Her breath caught, her heart shattered, as he held her firm against his tongue, laving and stroking and drinking her in like he lived for the taste and the swollen lushness of her body.

Her orgasm ripped through her. A rich, wild rush of white-hot pleasure. A head-spinning rocket of a ride that destroyed her. The sensations were so intense and strong they possessed her. Lasted so long they consumed her.

"Manny," she wept his name, and collapsed on top of him, pressing his jutting erection between her cheek and his abdomen. "Manny," she murmured again, and rode the current of pleasure and delicious pain that hurt . . . so good.

He held her at the peak forever . . . and not nearly long enough. She half-laughed, half-cried, when he kissed her there, one last time, then urged her to turn around.

"Inside you, *querida*." His whisper was as coarse as her breathing when he positioned her above him, then drove deep. "I need to be inside you."

And then sensation began again as she braced her palms on his chest and he took her for another wild, reckless ride.

"Liliana," he sighed her name, and, clutching her hips in his hands, pumped one last time. "Lili-ana."

He came with a high arch of his hips and a groan that could have been anguish or ecstasy. His chest rose and fell with his erratic breath as he dragged her down against him, wrapped her so tightly in his arms it felt like he wanted to absorb her into his body.

Panting, deliriously wasted, she liquefied against him, damp with sweat, limp with languor.

"Mina," he whispered, and, knotting a hand in her

hair, tipped her head back and kissed her fiercely. "Sleep now," he said against her mouth. "You need to sleep."

She should argue. But she couldn't. She was physically exhausted, emotionally drained. During the past few days she'd run the gauntlet from the height of anxiety to the depth of despair. Making love with Manny had been inevitable. She accepted that. The desire that had been building between them was the only emotion with a viable outlet.

As she drifted off, she had no choice but to face the truth. She was still in love with him. And though he desired her, though he would protect her with his life, the one thing he could not give her was his trust. And without trust, love would never be enough.

———

"Lily. Wake up, *querida*. We need to go now."

Manny had rewound the flashlight and propped it on a rock shelf built into the wall. It cast a blue-white glow over the temple room.

He watched from a distance as Lily slowly roused herself. She stretched like a sleek cat waking. And it was all he could do not to go to her, to reach out and pet her. To run his hands over her beautiful breasts, slide between her slim thighs, and awaken her with the glide of his fingers in her slick, wet heat.

From the moment he'd seen her that fateful night in Nicaragua, she'd been an obsession. Nothing had changed. He'd loved her. Hated her. Craved her. But he'd never forgotten her.

He never would. And he didn't honestly know where that left them.

"You're dressed," she said, and he realized she'd opened her eyes and was watching him.

"Time to go," he repeated.

She yawned, sat up, and stretched, and he had to tear his gaze away from the sensual picture she made, naked and abandoned, her hair streaming down her back.

"How long did I sleep?"

"Not long. You need more rest, but we must go."

She dragged her hands over her face, pulled the hair back out of her eyes, and blinked up at him. He saw the moment the guilt hit her. Knew exactly what she was thinking.

"Do not second-guess, Lily. What we did here, it was meant to happen."

"We made love while . . . while Adam—"

"No," he cut her off. "Don't even think it. We needed rest. We needed release. We couldn't leave before now anyway. Not with the rebels out in force. We haven't placed him at more risk, Lily. I wouldn't let that happen. I would never let that happen."

She lowered her head, not looking at all convinced.

"Only an hour has passed. It was an hour we needed. Even now, it will be a risk to leave here. They have to know we are hiding somewhere near."

She reached for her backpack, drew out dry panties and a white T-shirt. "You think they're still searching for us?"

"They have to be," he said, hating that he had to break the news. "They can't let us report to anyone about the gun."

Face grim, she stood, shimmied into her panties, and looked around for her bra. He picked it up from the floor beside him, handed it to her. Then watched with hungry eyes while she put it on, then stepped into her pants.

"I'm ready," she said after slipping into her damp shoes.

"Eat first," he said. "Rehydrate." He handed her a Power-Bar and a bottle of water.

"What about you?"

"I already ate."

"And your head?"

"Fine." It hurt like hell, but he'd deal with it. He'd deal with it and the rebel soldiers.

As soon as they left the temple and cleared the ravine, he'd try to reach Ethan on the SAT phone again. He needed to fill Ethan in about the company of soldiers. The howitzer. None of which added up.

Something was way off here. And Manny had a sick feeling in his gut that there was much more going on than met the eye.

"Ready?" he said after checking outside and grabbing his rifle and his ALICE pack.

Lily had hurriedly worked a brush through her hair, plaited it into another thick braid that hung down the center of her back. She nodded, shouldered her backpack. "Ready."

Yeah. She was ready, he thought. He only hoped she was ready to deal with what they might encounter when they finally found Adam.

"Head down. Follow me. Quiet as a mouse, *querida*. I suspect there are many big cats still lurking in the jungle."

———

They'd made it a quarter of a mile through undergrowth as thick as sludge and had cleared another ridge before

Manny had felt it was safe enough to call Ethan. His sat phone rang before he got the chance.

Lily startled at the sound that cut through yet another eerie silence that had set them both on edge with concern that the Tiger soldiers were still in the area and would hear it.

As was the norm this time of year in the Sri Lankan rain forest, the storm that had deluged them had long since moved out. Sun filtered down through the canopy trees, casting long, flickering fingers of hazy, laser-type beams through the thick vegetation as Manny dug into his ALICE pack.

"Ortega." He picked up on the second ring, silencing it.

"Where the hell have you been, man?"

It was Ethan. And he was as agitated as Manny had ever heard him.

"Out of range. Long story. What's happening?"

In concise sentences Ethan filled him in on the video and the midnight deadline that was now less than nine hours away.

Manny glanced at Lily. Her lips were swollen from his kisses, her cheeks red from his beard. A surge of lust punched him gut deep just looking at her. Dread quickly replaced it. He hated the thought of telling her about the deadline as he fought with his own reaction to the news. Nine hours. Nine fucking hours and they still didn't have a clue where Adam was.

"Here's the thing," Ethan added as Manny handed Lily a bottle of water and motioned for her to drink. "Dallas made it to the Tiger headquarters. General Ramanathan's adamant that he knows nothing about the abduction."

"Dallas buys it?"

"Yeah. He does. Ramanathan's big goddamn issue right now is finding a misplaced howitzer."

"Howitzer?" Manny glanced at Lily. "What's it worth to him if I can tell him where it is?"

Dead silence. Then a disbelieving, "You're fuckin' shittin' me."

"Wish I was, but my ears are still ringing from the blast. I can lead you to the gun and a full company of Tiger soldiers."

"Holy . . . wait. Wait, wait, wait. This doesn't add up."

Manny could visualize the frown darkening his friend's face. "A lot of that going around," he agreed.

"Ramanathan is royally pissed because someone stole his cannon, so it can't be Tigers who fired at you. And another thing. The Tiger leader says he pulled all of his troops out of the area a week ago."

Manny thought back to the rebel camp. "Something . . . I can't put my finger on it, but something's been bugging me since we spotted the gun and the shooters.

"Fuck," he swore when it came to him. "I should have picked up on it sooner. The soldiers—they spoke Hindi. *Hindi*," he repeated for emphasis. "Not Tamil."

Manny didn't know much Tamil, but he'd picked up some Hindi when he'd been deployed briefly in India several years ago—and it just occurred to him that he'd understood some of what they'd been saying when he and Lily had been hiding at the opening to the temple.

"You're saying they were Indian?"

"So it seems. Damn. What would a group of Indian soldiers be doing in the thick of the Sri Lankan jungle with a Tamil rebel gun? And wearing Tamil uniforms?"

"Thicker and thicker," Ethan said, and Manny could

almost see him dragging his hand across his jaw. "Where did you spot the gun?"

Manny gave him the coordinates.

"Exactly where Darcy's covert contact said the Tamil camp would be," Ethan said.

"So if Ramanathan's being straight with Dallas," Manny speculated aloud, "that means the new boys are squatting on the old Tiger campsite with Ramanathan's big gun and we're back to square one with Adam."

"Or not," Ethan said with a thoughtful pause. "It's a long shot, but who's to say there isn't a connection here somewhere?"

Yeah, who's to say there wasn't a connection? Manny agreed, and glanced at Lily, who sat silently on a tree stump, waiting with an expectant urgency for him to fill her in.

"Okay, look," Ethan said. "I'm going to call Dallas back, run it all past him to present to Ramanathan. See what he has to say. In the meantime, where are you?"

"Hold on." Manny dragged their map out of his pack and with Lily's help got a fix on their location. "Best as I can figure, we're about three hours from Elkaduwa. We're on foot and we need to find transportation."

"What happened to the jeep?"

Manny grunted. "Starts with an *h* and ends with a boom." He tucked the map into his hip pocket.

"Jesus," Ethan swore when understanding dawned.

"Yeah. He was there, too, or we wouldn't be here to tell the tale. Look, we're in some pretty rough terrain and we need to make tracks. I'm not so certain we don't still have some bad guys on our tail . . . which makes me think we stumbled into the thick of something big or they'd have given up searching for us long ago."

"Roger that. Keep your heads down. I'll be back in touch after I talk with Dallas."

"What?" Lily asked when Manny disconnected.

He didn't have a chance to tell her.

A soldier appeared out of nowhere. Rifle butt locked against his shoulder, finger tight on the trigger.

"Easy," Manny warned Lily as he stood and raised his hands above his head. "Just take it easy and follow my lead."

———

"Faint," Manny whispered as, hands above their heads, he and Lily marched at gunpoint back the way they'd come.

Lily didn't need a second cue. She folded like an accordion and dropped to the ground.

The young soldier was so shocked, he stumbled. Before he could recover, Manny was on him like spice on curry. The rifle discharged into the air as Manny wrestled him to his back and clamped a hand over his mouth.

Beside him, as he drew his knife out of its sheath, Manny could see Lily scramble for the soldier's weapon.

"Get Adam's photograph," Manny said, and set the side of his blade against the boy's throat. "Show it to him."

Eyes wild, the young soldier shook his head.

"Why do I not buy that?" Manny said, then accused in Hindi, "You are not Tamil."

The boy shook his head again.

"Indian?"

He hesitated, then gave a jerky nod.

"Where did you get the big gun?"

The boy swallowed, Manny's blade pressing against his Adam's apple.

"Where?" Manny demanded. "Talk or I'll slice off your left ear. Then your right. And then I'll start on your fingers. You'll die slowly and in pain—and for what?"

He pressed the blade deeper against the boy's neck, drawing blood.

"Lily . . . show him the picture again," Manny ordered when he was certain the boy was convinced he meant business. "Have you seen him?"

This time the boy gave a reluctant nod.

Manny heard Lily's indrawn breath.

"Where? Where?" Manny repeated when the boy shook his head again.

"Bulutota Rakwana," he finally confessed.

"Lily, get the map," Manny said, never taking his blade from the boy's throat.

"It's northwest of here . . . near Embilipitiya."

Manny heard paper rustle as she studied the map.

"Found it. It's maybe . . . oh God, maybe five or six hours on foot."

"If you lied you just died," Manny promised the boy.

"Truth. I speak truth."

"How many troops guard them?"

The young boy closed his eyes, heaved a shaky breath.

Manny pressed the knife deeper. Blood trickled down the soldier's neck. "How many!"

"Twenty. No more."

"Who is your leader?"

Something in the young soldier's eyes told Manny he'd been pushed as far as he would go. The boy was finished talking.

Manny pinched the boy's neck right at the juncture of his shoulder. His body went limp.

"Is he—"

"Dead?" Manny stood, sheathed his knife. "No. Just unconscious."

There were tears in Lily's eyes when Manny looked at her. He understood. They were tears of hope in a situation that had grown more and more hopeless. This was their first solid lead on Adam. "Don't fall apart on me now, Liliana. We're almost there."

She drew back her shoulders, managed a tight smile. "Let's go get him. I want my baby back."

"We'll get him back. That's a promise." He reached for his SAT phone. "I need to raise Ethan and let him know we've got a location on Adam."

Before he could dial, the staccato rap of automatic weapon fire ripped through the air around them and he dropped the phone in a puddle of water at his feet. A squad of soldiers cleared the rise and started running their way.

"Shit," Manny swore, picked up the phone, grabbed Lily's hand, and took off at a dead run.

CHAPTER 20

Fifteen minutes later, they were winded and soaking wet with sweat. They'd run for their lives . . . and they'd just run out of real estate.

"Whoa!" Manny skidded to a stop. He grabbed Lily, catching her before she ran straight off the edge of a cliff and into nowhere.

The jungle just stopped, right at the edge of a deeply gouged riverbank. And to really make it fun, the bank fell at a 180-degree angle to a wide, swollen river, running wild with white water as it careened over rocks and rills a good fifty feet below.

Was nothing ever easy?

"It always fucking comes down to heights and water," Manny grumbled as he glanced across the divide to the other side some thirty feet away.

He found a thick, woody vine and grabbed it. He tested it for strength and length and draped the tail of it over the side of the bank.

He looked at Lily. She glanced from him, to the vine, to the thirty-foot chasm in front of them. "You're not serious."

He pulled a compartment from his ALICE pack and

stuffed it with everything from rations, to water, to a pair of NVGs, to several magazines full of ammo.

"Trust me. If there was any other way," he said as the not so distant shouts from the forest caught up with them. "Grab what you can carry. We'll have to leave the rest. Hurry."

While she scrounged for portable medical supplies, he reached inside his shirt. He pulled his St. Christopher's medal over his head and kissed it. Then he draped it over Lily's neck, hauled her up against him, and kissed her until he felt her knees buckle.

"This is the part where you get to say, 'Geronimo.'" He shot her a game smile to shore her up. "You can do this, Liliana."

He physically took her hands in his and wrapped her stiff fingers around the vine. "Just hang on. That's all you have to do. It's going to be a helluva ride. When you see ground beneath you, let go, tuck, and roll. Got it?"

She closed her eyes, nodded, and tightened her grip on the vine. Then he pulled her back, like he would pull a child back in a swing, gave her a hard push, and she was airborne.

Heart in his throat, he watched her sail across the ravine like Jane of the Jungle.

"Go, Lily." More prayer than plea, he held his breath.

It seemed like forever before she reached the far bank. When she finally did, he started shouting, "Let go! Let go!"

Then he breathed a sigh of relief when her feet touched the ground and she rolled like a pro. He didn't have time to whoop and holler over her amazing feat. He waited for the vine and snagged it when it sailed back past him. Then he tucked the SAT phone in his pocket and slung his rifle and small pack over his shoulder.

Rounds from an AK-47 whizzed by his head as he pushed off.

"Christ," he muttered, swung out over the wide expanse of bottomless air, and prayed the vine would hold. Add his body weight to his rifle, ammo, and gear, and he figured he had more than a hundred pounds on Lily.

The vine snapped just as he reached the other side. He hit the embankment waist high. Felt himself slipping backward into the abyss—and then felt Lily's hand clasp his.

He looked up and into her eyes. Sunlight slanted down through the trees and haloed her hair as she lay on her belly on the bank, his very own angel, pulling for all she was worth. He dug and clawed and finally, with her help, managed to haul his hips up and over onto solid ground.

Panting, he rolled to his back, heaved a deep breath, and looked at her. She was still on all fours, panting just as heavily as he, the medal hanging around her neck like a talisman.

Her hair was wild around her face, her cheeks red from exertion. She had mud on her chin, grass in her hair.

He thought she was the single most beautiful sight he'd ever seen. Because they were alive, because by all rights they shouldn't be, he grinned at her. Then he laughed, because it was just too wild not to. "Do I know how to give a good date or what?"

He thought he saw a smile just before a hail of gunfire broke into his relief at having survived yet another brush with heights and water.

"Head down. Let's move it," he barked, and together

they belly-crawled into the thicket and out of the line of fire.

Out of breath and feeling the monkey off their back for the first time since the jeep had been destroyed, Manny dropped and leaned back against a Palu tree. Lily slumped against a tree opposite him.

"Just a quick breather," he said on a panting breath, and reached into his pack for a bottle of water. "I'll get ahold of Ethan."

He cranked off the lid of the bottle and handed it to Lily.

She gulped greedily as he rifled around in his pocket for the SAT phone and dialed.

"Not working," he said when she shot him a questioning look. Frowning, he tapped the phone on his knee. "Wet," he muttered when a drop of water shook out. He laid the phone on his lap and took the bottle of water when she held it out to him. "Maybe when it dries out . . . I'll try it again after a while."

"We have company," Lily whispered.

He tensed and reached for his rifle.

"No. It's okay. Look."

Since she was grinning as she looked behind his left shoulder, Manny relaxed. He turned slowly to see a toque macaque monkey sitting on his haunches not four feet away, stroking his long tail and watching them with huge, humanlike eyes.

The brightly colored macaque was about the size of a big house cat. He screeched and, pushing off with the knuckles of his front legs, scooted over to Manny's side.

"Trusting little dude," Manny said. "We'd love to sit and chat, but—hey!"

The macaque snatched the SAT phone off Manny's

lap and took off like a bat out of hell, screaming and scrambling high up into the trees.

"God damn it! Come back here with that!"

Manny pushed to his feet, but all he could do was watch as the monkey and his SAT phone disappeared in the treetops. "Fuck." Hands on hips, he turned to Lily.

She was all round eyed and worried. "Now what?"

God, he'd seen that look on her face too often to count in the past few days. And there wasn't a damn thing he could do to make it go away. "Now we look for a phone in addition to transportation when we get to Elkaduwa.

"Come on." He held out a hand, helped her to her feet. "Let's move."

He glanced at his watch, felt his gut knot. There was no point in telling her about the deadline. No point in telling her that if they didn't get to Adam and the Muhandira-malas, they would be executed in less than eight hours.

———

Kandy

Ethan glanced at Darcy as he spoke with Dallas on the SAT phone. "Ramanathan wants to do what? . . .

"Holy shit." He shook his head when Dallas finished. "Yeah. . . . Yeah. I can arrange a call. Give me," he checked his watch, "fifteen minutes. I'll be back in touch."

"What?" Darcy asked when Ethan had hung up.

"Ramanathan wants to join his military forces with the Sinhalese military and take out the boys who stole his howitzer."

Darcy blinked. "Say what?"

"I know." Ethan scratched his jaw. "We came here

worried about starting up the civil war again and it looks like we might have actually backed into a way to put the Tigers and the Sinhalese on the same side of a fight."

"Why would Ramanathan want to do that?"

"Simple. He wants his gun back. And Dallas honestly thinks the rebel leader is tired of the fighting. Maybe he was looking for an excuse to end it and this dropped into his lap."

Ethan shook his head again. "Get Griffin on the phone, babe. We're about to make history."

"And Adam? The Muhandiramalas?" Her worried look echoed his thoughts. "Where do they all fit into this?"

He pulled her to him, wrapped his arms around her, and kissed the top of her head. "I wish I knew. All we can do now is hope we can get this thing off the ground in the next few hours and beat the deadline. If we have any chance of finding them, my money's on it being tied to the boys who stole the big gun."

He checked his watch. They were down to a little less than seven hours until time ran out. "Go ahead. Call Griff. Then I'll try to reach Manny again."

And in the meantime, Ethan would do a lot of praying that this new development worked for them instead of against them.

———

On the road to Elkaduwa

"I don't need to be coddled," Lily snapped, a little too sharply, when Manny suggested they stop again and take five.

She regretted her waspish tongue immediately. But

she didn't want to stop. She wanted to walk. Hell, she wanted to run. To her son. Away from the soldiers who were bound to be trailing them.

Away from the reality that when the smoke cleared and she put their situation in perspective, she was a health-care professional and, for the second time in her life, she'd had unprotected sex with a man she barely knew. That it had been the same man both times was little consolation. That it had been mind-bending, perception-altering sex was no longer at issue. That he'd wanted her with the same uncontrollable craving as she'd wanted him didn't hold much sway, either.

Neither did his total lack of comment about what had happened in the aftermath of the storm they'd literally ridden out in that abandoned temple.

And what *had* happened? Other than the two of them connecting with a physical release that had been inevitable given their level of tension and forced confinement.

Step after step, as they'd slogged through the jungle, her mind had been spinning in directions she didn't want it to go. Back to the feel of his hands on her skin. The electric sensation of his mouth. The weight of him heavy and deep inside her.

The feel of his medal between her breasts.

It had been seventeen years since she'd felt the magical give and flow between their bodies. She'd thought, over the years, that she'd remembered big. Like remembering a special place from her childhood as being huge, then going back as an adult and finding it small. The truth was, her memory hadn't been large enough to accommodate the feelings—acute, consuming, incredible—that she'd felt when Manny made love to her again.

Just like she hadn't remembered the depth of her feelings for him.

So no, she didn't want to stop. No, she didn't want to rest. And she'd been pushing herself to the limit since they'd stumbled onto a road thirty minutes ago.

At least it was a road of sorts. They'd been dodging muddy potholes and crawling over trees that a recent windstorm had toppled.

She started climbing over another downed tree that blocked their way. Manny's hand caught her arm and stopped her. She snapped her gaze to his.

"Easy," he said after a quiet moment. "Just ease up a bit, okay? No good is going to come of you dropping from exhaustion in this heat."

She opened her mouth to argue, but it caught up with her then. The humidity. The suffocating furnace of the sun. The realization that he was right. She needed a break. She needed to rehydrate. And by the looks of him, he did, too.

She nodded. Sank down on a stump and dug into her pack for another dose of antibiotics and some pain medication. "How's your head?"

"Don't worry about my head."

"Yeah, well, it's easier than worrying about whether or not we're lost."

"We're not lost."

She unscrewed the cap on a water bottle and handed it to him.

He shook his head.

Fine. She'd drink first.

Only when she had drunk her fill did he accept the bottle and take the meds.

"If we're not lost, then what are we?" She ignored his

wince when she applied topical antibiotic ointment to his cut and checked the stitches. "And don't say we're fine, because we aren't. We've got no transportation, no way to communicate with Ethan or Dallas, no clear idea of how to get to Adam, and no way of knowing if we *can* get to him before something happens to him."

Manny scrubbed a hand over his dark, stubbled jaw and gauged the angle of the sun. "But we are having fun, right?"

She didn't want to smile at his deadpan delivery. She didn't even know he had a deadpan delivery. Mostly he did brooding. At least, Manny the man did brooding. Manny the boy had been full of the devil, quick with a grin, easy with a laugh. Deadpan hadn't been on his list of character traits, either.

Which was probably why she gave it up and smiled for him. Then apologized.

"I'm sorry I'm being so bitchy. It's just—"

"It's just that you're worried about Adam."

She looked down at her hands. Nodded.

"And you're wondering," he said in such a reflective tone her head came up, "about what happened back there. In the temple. About what it meant. What it means."

She held his deep, dark gaze. Yeah. She'd been wondering. As understatements went, it was one for the record books.

"Me, too," he said, then touched a hand to her face, caressed her jaw. "When this is over, we'll sort it out, okay?"

She closed her eyes, nodded again, and damn, she was sick of blinking back tears.

"Come here, *querida*," he whispered, and drew her into his arms.

And held her. Beneath a sun that beat down as relentlessly as her fear for Adam's life.

She leaned into Manny, embraced his promise as much as the sheltering strength of his body.

We'll sort it out.

A sigh let go inside of her that felt bigger than she was.

Yes. They'd sort it out.

In the meantime, they *would* find Adam.

Manny squeezed her hard, let her go. "No less than five, no more than twenty," he said, reminding her that less than five minutes of rest did no good, but more than twenty could cause muscles to tighten. Reminding her that he was more bruised and battered than she was.

Sweat and dirt stained his shirt, and other than his lack of sunburn, he looked every bit as beat as she felt. And so outrageously gorgeous it was tempting to hit him just on general principles. She had to look like the wreck of the *Hesperus*.

"I'm ready," she said instead, then turned her face to his to see him watching her with a look that spoke of longing and encouragement and even, she thought, a little bit of pride.

"Mother bear," he said approvingly. "Adam is fortunate to be your cub."

Then, with his thumb lightly caressing her cheek, he kissed her. It wasn't sexual. It wasn't even tinged with heat. What it was, was necessary. The look on his face said so. He'd just needed to kiss her. To connect. To affirm. To assure her that all would be well. To encourage her to trust him to know what to do. To sort things out. But more important, at the moment, to find their son.

"Let's go." Manny twisted around to pick up his rifle and pack.

That's when Lily saw it. And her heart rate picked up to a flat-out gallop.

"Is that what I think it is?"

He stopped short when she latched on to his arm. He glanced ahead on the road—probably figuring the bad guys had found a bridge by now and come looking for them.

But it wasn't a bad guy or a tree blocking the road.

"Depends," he said, moving in front of her like a protective shield. "I'm thinking elephant. Are we close?"

"A little too close," Lily said, peeking around his broad shoulder.

Even at a zoo, she'd never been this close to approximately six tons and ten feet of bull elephant. And she knew it was a bull because of his size and massive tusks.

"What do we do?" she asked, then breathed a sigh of relief when a young man walked out from behind the elephant and lifted a hand in greeting.

He wasn't any more than five feet tall. His skin was dark, his teeth blazing white. He wore the traditional baggy white mahout garb. In contrast, below thin calves and bony ankles he wore a pair of Air Jordans that were almost as big as he was.

"Su-bhah dhah-hah-vah-lahk." *Good afternoon*, he said, approaching them with a grin. A grin that grew even broader when he walked close enough to see them clearly.

"You speak English?" he asked as the elephant stopped directly behind him, the massive trunk snuffling around in his pockets.

"Nah-vah-thin-nu." *Stop*, he scolded the pestering pachyderm, and absently shoved the wandering trunk away.

"English. Yes," Manny said with a watchful eye on the elephant as a toque macaque swung down from a tree and landed in the middle of the elephant's back.

"I don't like that sucker on general principle," Manny said under his breath, eyeing the monkey as he screeched and scratched his armpit and stared Manny straight in the eye.

"American?" the mahout asked, sounding hopeful.

Lily nodded. "Yes. We're Americans."

The young man almost jumped for joy. His grin split his face and he clapped his hands. "I love America!! 'Go ahead; make my day,' " he said in heavily accented English. "Clint Eastwood, yes? *Sudden Impact.* I love American movie."

He spouted off several more movie quotes before Manny could quiet him down.

"Look. We're in a bind. We need to get to Elkaduwa." He pulled out the map and pointed to their destination.

Another broad grin. " 'That's thirty minutes away. I'll be there in ten.' Harvey Keitel, yes? *Pulp Fiction.* What a movie. I am good, yes?"

"Yeah. Yeah, you're great." Manny tapped the map again. "We're here, right? How long before we get there?"

The mahout studied the map. "Walking? Four hours. Maybe five. Or maybe running?" he speculated, taking in Manny's head wound, their ripped clothes, and the rifle slung over Manny's shoulder. "You have problems, friend?"

Manny made an "if you only knew" sound. "And once we get there . . . if we can get a vehicle, how long to get to Bulutota Rakwana?"

The mahout scrunched up his face. "Long time from Elkaduwa. Maybe three more hours? But . . . is not long time from here. I, Kavith, the poet, can take you. On Rajah, we can be to Elkaduwa in five hours. You good man. Good woman. Rajah and Kavith, we can tell. You have trouble?" he asked again.

About that time they heard the whine of gears and looked down the long expanse of road ahead of them.

A military jeep barreled down the road toward them.

"We have trouble," Manny said on a growl.

"You go. Hide there." Kavith pointed to the jungle to the side of the road. "Rajah and Kavith. We will fix. Go. Go."

It wasn't like they had a choice. Manny grabbed Lily's hand and they sprinted for the undergrowth. Crouching low and out of sight, they waited for the jeep to stop. Manny drew his rifle to his shoulder and sighted down the barrel. Lily understood that one threatening move the mahout's way and Manny would take those guys out before they could cock a trigger.

After much head nodding and grinning and pointing, Kavith managed to convince the jeepful of soldiers to turn around and head the other way.

They shifted gears with a grind and a jerk and tore off back down the road the way they'd come.

Kavith watched them go, then beckoned with a wave when the jeep was out of sight. "All clear. Come," he said quickly while the monkey jumped up and down on the elephant's back and screeched, like he was laughing at the joke Kavith had played on the soldiers. "We must hurry. They will come back. We must not be here."

Lily scrambled out of the brush, looked the elephant up and down, then looked at Manny.

He looked dubious.

"Here's the way I see it. I've been shot at, I've hidden

in a cave, and I've played Jane on a vine swinging across a raging river. I'd just as well make the jungle experience complete and ride an elephant. And if it will get us to Adam faster, I say we go for it."

Manny studied Kavith, the poet who herded elephants and wore Air Jordans, through narrowed eyes. "And what's in it for you?"

Again Kavith grinned and shook his head. "No. No. You mistake what you are thinking. Make wrong notion. I, Kavith, am not what you Americans call a . . . a . . . tout, is it? No. I am apprentice. No, that's wrong. Student. Yes. At university. This day I am on holiday—visiting my grandfather. Rajah, he is my grandfather's beast. I am uninterested—no. Again. Wrong word. I am bored . . . yes, bored today. Nothing to do. So I consider, today I take Rajah for a walk. And look. I find you." His white teeth flashed again. "Not bored anymore."

"You're getting into some heavy stuff here, Kavith," Manny warned.

"Yes. Yes. Much heavy. Much fun. And with you I can perform my English. Make better."

He looked at Manny, his eyes full of hope. " 'Well, what do you say, Reverend? You think a prayer's in order?' Clint Eastwood, *Space Cowboys*, yes?"

More than a prayer was in order, Lily thought, and gave Manny a nod when he looked at her for a yea or a nay.

CHAPTER 21

Jaffna Peninsula

Dallas sprinted across the tarmac beside a huffing Ramanathan. They ducked beneath the rotor blades of a hulking Cobra that was revved and rocking and vibrating the cracked asphalt beneath their feet.

Dallas still couldn't believe this dual assault was going to come off. But it was happening. The Sri Lankan prime minister and Ramanathan had spoken, agreed that there was a common threat, and mobilized a joint task force in a grand total of two hours. No bickering. No jockeying for position.

No fucking way, is what Dallas would have thought had he not heard Ramanathan agree to let the Sri Lankan military call the shots. There were already two units of special operations infantry in place twenty miles to the north of the previously held Tiger camp, and three more were closing in from the south. Ramanathan had mobilized two units of his Tigers stationed on the coast in Batticaloa. The Sri Lankan army general had agreed to wait for the rebel forces to get in position before launching the assault.

Done deal. Everyone was playing nice with everyone else. Dallas checked his watch as he swung up and into the chopper. If all went as planned, in a few hours it would be all over but the shouting.

Ramanathan would have his big gun back. The Sri Lankan military would have rousted an unknown insurgency, and for the first time in history Tamils would be fighting someone other than their countrymen.

An hour or so ago Ethan had connected with Manny. They still didn't have a fix on the boy.

"Friend," Dallas said to Ramanathan when they'd donned headsets and he could be heard above the rotor noise. "Don't forget. I get your gun back, you owe me a favor."

"Your life is your favor," the general said as they lifted off. Then he smiled and shrugged. "But perhaps I am feeling generous. Maybe I will grant you two. Because of those balls of yours," he added, then looked toward the south as the snake ate up the knots and headed for the battle.

———

Bulutota Rakwana range, northwest of Embilipitiya

Adam glanced across the cave at Minrada. Silence. It scared him. So did the fact that they'd been moved again. Shortly after they'd filmed the video this morning, they'd been blindfolded, herded onto a truck bed, and off they'd gone. He didn't know how far they'd traveled or how much time had passed. Several miles. Several hours. Adam had no clue where they were. North, he'd guess, and that was only because the new cave was colder.

It was also full of bats. He could hear the muffled flutter of their wings above. Their high-pitched squeals. Somewhere from the dark recesses of the cavern he could also hear the sound of water. Underground rivers? Pools? He didn't know. Wasn't sure it mattered.

What mattered was that this time the four of them were together.

Adam thought about the video. "Will your government meet the rebel terms?" he asked Amithnal, who sat, exhausted, on the damp stone floor beside him.

Amithnal's hushed voice confirmed what Adam had already decided. "No. They will never give in to such outrageous demands."

Another silence stretched out as the implications of their fate dug deep.

"The rebels know that," Amithnal said. "They know it is an impossible request."

"Then why did they even ask?" Adam's voice barely carried in the dark.

"This I do not know, Adam. It makes no sense to me. Unless . . ."

"Unless?" Adam prompted.

"Unless," Amithnal continued with reluctance, "killing us has been their intent all along."

Sathi's quiet weeping prompted soothing sounds from Amithnal.

"Then why haven't they done it?" Adam mused aloud. "Why didn't they kill us right away? Why make the video? What was the point?"

"That, my young friend, is a question I have been asking myself from the beginning."

"There's something else going on here," Adam finally whispered.

"Yes. I have thought that as well. Today . . . I heard the guards talking in Hindi."

"Hindi?"

"The language of India. I am no longer sure they are Tamils."

"They're Indian?"

"I am thinking so, yes."

"What would Indian soldiers want with us? And why would they pass themselves off as Tamil rebels?"

Amithnal was silent for a long moment. When he finally spoke, his words were flat with defeat. "This we may never know. There can't be much time left."

Amithnal had given up, Adam realized. He'd resigned himself to dying here.

"We have to fight them," Adam whispered vehemently.

Amithnal's breath was heavy with resignation. "They are twenty. We are only two."

"Three," Minrada's whisper came out of the dark. A renewed resolve filled her voice and made Adam's heart swell.

Adam reached for her hand, squeezed.

"Four."

Sathi. She had gained strength from her daughter. "There are four," she said, determination making her voice stronger.

"Yes, we are four," Adam agreed, and as he sat there, head pounding, body and pride battered and bruised, a seed of a plan took root.

Kandy

"Ethan, please. Quit pacing. We're stuck here." Darcy sat at a computer in the mayor's office where they were being detained as "guests" of the city. "There's nothing you can do about it."

Griff had managed to move heaven—the joint operation was a go—but not earth. They'd begged, threatened, and cajoled, but Ethan and Darcy hadn't been granted clearance to accompany the military to the Wahala-purha temple ruin site where a staging area was being assembled. As they spoke, the Sinhalese military supported by the Tiger rebels would soon confront the company of foreign insurgents.

Ethan was using their "forced" stay to bring his blood to a slow rolling boil. Darcy had decided to make better use of her time. She'd been searching the Web for militant Indian groups. She was desperate to come up with something to tie the Hindi-speaking fighters Manny had told them about and the suspected insurgency to what was happening with Adam.

"This is bullshit," Ethan sputtered for the tenth time in as many minutes. "We need to be there when the dust settles. Something tells me the bad guys will give up the goods on where they're holding Adam and the Muhandi-ramalas." He glanced at his watch. "Fuck. Less than six hours."

"Oh my God." Oblivious to his ranting, Darcy felt shock stiffen her spine ramrod straight. "Ethan. Come look at this."

Ethan walked up behind her, read the computer screen over her shoulder. "Holy shit."

"That's one way to put it."

The information she'd just uncovered on a militant blog site might be the key to this entire ugly business.

"Ethan . . . we've got to get out of here. If what's happening is what I think is happening, somehow we have to convince the powers that be to hold off on the assault. If they engage the insurgents before Manny and Lily find Adam, we can kiss the midnight deadline good-bye."

Ethan snapped up his SAT phone and dialed. She knew he was trying to reach Manny.

"Still no signal," Ethan said grimly, and Darcy could see he had to physically resist the urge to throw the phone across the room.

"Okay, babe. It's now or never," he said with a dark look. "We're getting out of here." He walked over to the door and stood behind it. "Use your best decoy ploy."

"My best?" She gave him a sharp look.

"Okay. Not your best. Save that one for me. Just get the guard in here. I'll take care of the rest."

"He's not dead, is he?" Darcy asked a few minutes after the hapless guard came running at her hysterical scream for help.

"No, but he's going to wish he was when he wakes up and finds himself tied to that chair. Help me." Ethan handed her a piece of the man's shirt that he'd ripped into lengths to make bindings and a gag. Together he and Darcy tied up the guard.

"Let's go." Taking her hand, Ethan headed toward the door at a run. "Adam and the Muhandiramalas are running out of time. And we're late for a war."

———

Within two hours of Elkaduwa

"I can't fricking believe this." Manny stood by the water's edge. Hands on his hips, he glared at Rajah. The elephant wallowed in the shallows of a backwater tributary, trumpeting in ecstasy and spraying water from his trunk in a cascading shower over his head.

Kavith, his Air Jordans high and dry on the bank, stood knee-deep in water, scrubbing the elephant. He smiled his usual smile. It was getting goddamn grating.

"Many, many sorrys," Kavith apologized for the hundredth time. "But is necessary. Rajah is a working elephant. He wait for—thinks he is *entitled* to—bath. Top to toe. Every day. Must do. Critical—one elephant my grandfather own try one day to kill him when dirty. Not so upset when clean. Elephant very clean animal. Rajah go faster when done."

Beside them on the bank, the monkey—Tito, they had learned—sat like an old man leaning against Manny's leg, plucking at his pants and inspecting the hem.

Manny glared from the elephant to the monkey and back to Kavith.

God save me.

"How much longer?"

Kavith grinned. Shrugged. "When Rajah is ready."

"Kavith."

Manny turned when Lily spoke.

"Please. We must hurry."

For the first time since they'd met him, the boy's smile unfolded. He stared at Lily. Concern furrowed his brow as he waded from the water and stood in front of her.

Kavith had a serious case on her. Manny understood. In spades.

"New friend, Lily." Kavith patted her shoulder. "Not to cry. We will find your Adam."

A single tear leaked down Lily's cheek. She was banged up, scratched up, sunburned, and sweaty. Not once had she complained. Manny felt his gut clench for her. For the tear she would shed for her son but not for herself.

"We're running out of time." She hugged her arms around herself and turned away.

"What can we do?" Kavith looked miserable.

"You could convince that elephant he's squeaky clean," Manny grumbled. "And as long as you're at it, you could conjure up a cell phone. That'd be a helluva start."

A grin so huge it closed his eyes broke out over Kavith's face. He dug into his baggy pants pocket, fished around forever, and finally pulled out a phone.

A SAT phone.

"That's my fucking phone!" Manny roared.

Tito screeched and jumped up and down.

"Tito has been a bad thief." Kavith made tsking sounds at the monkey. "My apology. Kavith did not know it belonged to you."

Swearing under his breath, Manny snatched the phone, turned it on, and dialed, hoping it had dried out enough to make a connection.

He heaved a breath of relief when he heard a ring tone followed by Ethan's clipped hello. Lily rushed to his side, her face animated with the first ray of hope they'd had in a very long while.

"It's me," Manny said. "I've got a location on Adam."

"Jesus. Where in the hell have you been? Never mind. Just listen. We may be fighting a new deadline."

Manny stiffened, reacting to the urgency in Ethan's voice. "What's happening?"

"We're pretty certain that Darcy discovered a link between Adam's abduction and the group that captured Ramanathan's big gun."

A lump lodged in Manny's throat as he listened. Ethan quickly filled him in on the soon-to-be-launched joint Sri Lankan–Tamil assault on the camp at the Wahala-purha temple ruins.

Manny pinched the bridge of his nose. Fuck. This was all they needed. If Darcy's speculation was accurate, Manny had to reach Adam and the Muhandiramalas before the group of radicals who held them got wind of the joint attack staged for Wahala-purha. If the attack was launched first, someone in the insurgent camp was certain to contact the abductors holding Adam. If that happened, Manny had no doubt that the midnight deadline would go out the window. They'd kill Adam on the spot—if they hadn't killed him already.

Manny checked his watch. Four hours to the deadline. "Okay, look. We're less than two hours from Adam." He gave Ethan the coordinates. "What are the chances you can stall the assault and meet us there?"

Slim and none, Manny figured, those were the chances.

But this was Ethan Garrett he was dealing with. A man who'd had Manny's back in more dicey situations than he could count—and vice versa.

"I'll be back in touch," Ethan said. "I've got to reach Dallas. We'll figure something out. And we'll get there. Count on it."

———

Wahala-purha temple ruins

Dallas hung up the phone, swore roundly, then headed across the staging area where Ramanathan and the Sin-

halese field general, Kalukapuge, had their heads together over strategy.

Dallas was one man. And Ethan had just charged him
with stalling an army.

Make that two armies.

Piece of fucking cake.

Low-level floodlights illuminated the makeshift
encampment that had been set up out of sight and
sound range, a quarter of a mile from the insurgent
campsite. Jeeps, trucks, armored vehicles, and even a
few bicycles—it was, after all, Sri Lanka—littered the
nightscape where the Sinhalese elite Special Forces
and Tamil rebels readied for battle. Fifty men, prepared
to take on twice that many. Fifty well-trained, seasoned
warriors who they were betting were better equipped
and more experienced than the company of insurgents
who were blissfully bedded down for the night.

The soldiers were chomping at the bit. Testosterone
and the promise of glory elevated heart rates and made
even these hardened and tested soldiers restless.

The Sri Lanka Special Forces—rapid mobilization
units—had arrived ahead of Ramanathan's teams and
were prepared to flank the insurgent camp to both the
north and the south. Under cover of darkness and the jungle, Ramanathan's equivalent specialized teams were in
place to move in from the west and east.

It had been an hour since Ramanathan's Cobra had sat
down. It had been flying under a full moon and blackout
conditions and trusting the prevailing winds to carry away
the chopper noise. The Sinhalese spotters on the ground
had waved them in with more low-wattage portable lights
set up well out of sight range of the insurgent camp.

With Sri Lankan field general Kalukapuge calling the

shots, the two military leaders and their joint task force were about to make history. With a little luck, Dallas was about to stop it—or at least slow it down a bit.

Both Ramanathan and Kalukapuge glared at him when he approached. "There's another bird coming in," he said, and two pairs of eyes looked skyward.

"He's flying blackout. I need permission to talk him in."

"A friend of yours?" Ramanathan asked sourly.

"My brother. And he has information that could affect the outcome of the confrontation."

"You press your luck, Garrett." Ramanathan held Dallas's gaze for several long moments before turning to Kalukapuge. The field general shrugged.

With a reluctant nod, Ramanathan relented.

"Bro," Dallas said when he reached Ethan on the radio. "What's your ETA?"

"You should be able to spot me."

Just then a dim beam from the tail section of a low-flying chopper came into view. Shortly after, Dallas heard the muffled *whoop, whoop, whoop* of rotor blades; then the shadowy hulk of a bird popped up over a rise and made a beeline for the center of the staging area.

"Got a visual," Dallas said, and proceeded to talk Ethan toward the LZ.

It was a civilian chopper, Dallas realized when the bird fell into the arc of the spotlights. One he remembered seeing at the Kandy airport and had passed on when he'd gotten a look at the motor. The sucker had to have three thousand hours of airtime since its last overhaul, and he didn't fly in birds in need of maintenance.

Dallas held his breath as the chopper sputtered, spat, stalled, then finally caught. Ethan set her down with a none-too-gentle bounce.

Wasting no time, Ethan jumped out of the cockpit, ducked under the rotor blades, and ran toward Dallas.

"Jesus," Dallas sputtered with a nod toward the bird. "Did you get stupid or decide it was time to fulfill a death wish?"

"Missed you, too," Ethan said.

"Where's Darcy?"

"Guess you could say she's a little . . . tied up back in Kandy and most likely working on ripping me a new ass."

"You didn't."

"I did. Sent her for water while I revved up the bird, then took off without her."

"Extreme, bro. Even for you."

"I lost her once. No way was I going to take a chance on losing her again. I don't want her anywhere near us when the fat hits the fire. She can get over pissed. She can't get over dead. Now what's happening?"

"They agreed to wait for you—because *you* have information that could affect the outcome of the battle."

They jogged toward the waiting generals. "Why did I know you were going to pass the buck to me?"

"That's what big brothers are for. Make it good. These guys are locked and loaded."

Ethan put on his politician's hat and geared up to negotiate.

Five minutes later, they'd bought an hour. It wasn't much, but it was better than a kick in the ass. When the insurgent leader found his balls against the wall, there wasn't any question that he'd put in a call to the abduction team. And midnight deadline or not, it would be over for Adam and the Muhandiramalas.

Dallas grabbed Ethan's arm and stopped him when he

ran toward the civilian chopper. "Fuck that. I'm not going up in that piece of shit."

"Like we have a choice?" Ethan barked back.

"Yeah—like we do." He hitched his chin in the direction of Ramanathan's Cobra.

Ethan did a double take when he saw the snake. "Ramanathan will kill you—"

"He's gotta catch me first. Get in the snake. I've got to grab something and I'll be right with you."

Thirty seconds later, Dallas jumped up into the Cobra. "Let's move. Time's wastin'."

CHAPTER 22

Bulutota Rakwana, 10:45 P.M.

Bellied down on a ridge with his NVGs, Manny strained to get the lay of the land in the dark. The sun set late this time of year in Sri Lanka, but darkness had descended about an hour ago. The moon hung like a great white lightbulb, bathing the area like a strobe. Still, except for some chatter around a campfire and the occasional movement of a torch, he couldn't see much activity. Not without getting closer. And he would. Just as soon as the cavalry arrived.

It better, by God, be soon. He'd counted twenty soldiers just as the sun had pulled a disappearing act. And he'd gotten a good glimpse of the cliff wall that housed the cave. Things didn't look good for the good guys. The camp was a fucking fortress.

"Where are they?" Lily whispered, her voice sounding strained.

She could have been asking about Adam and the Muhandiramalas. Could have been asking about Ethan and Dallas. Either way, Manny shared her anxiety. They were down to a little more than an hour before the insurgent deadline, a half hour before the joint military assault back at Wahala-purha. If they pulled this off under the wire it would be a miracle.

He'd counted on miracles more than once. Prayed he hadn't used up his quota, because one way or another they had to get Adam and the Muhandiramalas out of this mess.

Failing wasn't an option.

"Tell me more about the cave," Manny prompted Kavith, who lay on his belly beside him, thoroughly enjoying playing soldier, even though Manny had strongly suggested he take Rajah and head for the hills.

The elephant was happily grazing in a field of grass behind them. About the fifth time Manny had caught Tito trying to filch the phone again, he'd threatened to cut his tail off. Tito had screeched and scooted off into the trees.

"The cave of Rakwana," Kavith said quietly, "is cut into a rock wall that runs one hundred yards high and fifty wide. See how it rises? Like a giant out of the jungle floor, yes?"

Yeah. That pretty much summed it up.

"You've been inside?"

"Oh yes. As a boy. I explored here often."

"How many caves are there?"

"Only one—but many fingers spread out from the hand."

Manny exhaled a heavy breath. Adam could be held in any one of those fingers.

" 'Now remember, when things look bad and it looks like you're not gonna make it, then you gotta get mean. I mean plumb, mad-dog mean. 'Cause if you lose your head and you give up, then you neither live nor win. That's just the way it is.' "

"What the hell is he talking about?" Lily asked, her tension level about maxed out.

Manny slanted Kavith a look. "Eastwood?"

In the dark, the mahout's teeth gleamed white. "*Outlaw Josey Wales.*"

Manny grunted, knowing he needed to somehow get rid of Kavith and keep him out of the line of fire, yet oddly glad to have this strange little person around to ease the tension while they waited. He lifted the NVGs again. "I take it you like Eastwood."

"And Bruce Willis," Kavith said, his enthusiasm hitching up a notch. " 'Yippee-ki-yay, motherfucker!' "

Jesus.

"*Die Hard,*" Kavith added proudly.

"About the cave . . ."

In his sometimes convoluted English, Kavith gave Manny a picture of what they were up against. The rest Manny could see for himself. A natural footpath cut into the cliff face and led in a series of switchbacks to the mouth of the cave. The path was narrow and steep, only a foot or so wide, and elevated at a twenty-degree incline to about forty feet off the floor. Fuck—it *had* to be high, didn't it? Best guess, it was about fifty yards long—which placed whoever scaled the cliff face firmly in the sitting-duck category if they were made by the bad guys.

Inside the cave it got even trickier.

"Many caverns," Kavith said. "Many rivers and holes to fall into. Many, many bats," he added on a shiver.

Speaking of bats, when the unmistakable sound of a Cobra spooked Rajah, Kavith took off like a bat out of hell to catch and calm him. It was too late. The elephant ran hell-bent for election toward the cover of the jungle, Kavith hot on his heels.

"Come on," Manny said, figuring that was the last

they'd see of the mahout. "Let's give Ethan a target to shoot for."

Manny pulled Lily to her feet and they ran down the bluff away from the cave. He dragged out his flashlight and shot a beam of light skyward. A short, answering flash of light—no longer than an instant—told him that Ethan had made his signal. Counting on the wind to carry away the sound of the chopper, he watched the bird set down on a grassy plateau.

"Where the hell did you get the snake?" Manny shouted as the rotor wash wound down and Ethan and Dallas jumped out of the bird.

Dallas grinned. "Little gift from Ramanathan. I must be growing on him. Either that or he's getting mellow in his old age. He didn't even shoot at me when I lifted his chopper. Of course the stack of bills I tossed his way earlier today might have made a difference.

"For you, Rambo," Dallas added, reaching back into the Cobra, then tossing Manny a rifle. "Merry Christmas."

Shit. Manny lifted the Russian Dragonov SVD sniper rifle to his shoulder. Sighted down the night-vision scope, then sliced a glance at Dallas.

"And Happy New Year to me," Manny said with a tight grin.

The Dragonov wasn't anywhere near the quality or as state-of-the-art as the Barrett that Dallas had "acquired" for him on the Jolo op, but it would do. It would do a helluva lot better than the Kalashnikov that had been dragged through enough mud and muck during the course of the day.

"So what's the story?" Manny asked Ethan. "Who are we facing up there?"

"Long or short version?"

"Make it short and sweet."

"Once upon a time," Ethan began in deference to the request for sweet, "Sri Lanka was under the governance of India. According to the Web site Darcy found, there are those who feel it should be again.

"SASL," Ethan continued, "Society for the Annexation of Sri Lanka."

"Let me guess," Manny interrupted. "They're an extremist militant organization. Militant enough to infiltrate Sri Lanka, pose as Tamil fighters, and steal Ramanathan's howitzer."

"Why would they pretend to be Tamil fighters?" Lily asked, shocked, yet seeing the logic.

"If I were a small but zealous group and had lofty hopes of carrying out a takeover," Manny said, thinking aloud, "and knew I didn't have a prayer of building enough firepower or popular support to overthrow a nation, how would I go about it?"

"By misdirection," Lily concluded with a nod as understanding dawned.

"You both get an A plus," Ethan said. "They stage something so violent and repugnant and have the Tamil rebels take the blame; the Sinhalese have no choice but to retaliate."

"So," Manny said, seeing it all now, "the plan was to let the two military forces in Sri Lanka duke it out until they either obliterated each other or diminished their military arsenal and personnel to the point where they were no longer effective."

"And open the door for India to step in, restore law and order, and establish a temporary government under their control," Dallas added. "Most likely with the sanction of the international community."

Manny applied face paint, then handed it to Ethan. "A temporary government which would eventually become permanently controlled by India."

"And Amithnal Muhandiramala," Ethan added, building on the theory, "was the key Sinhalese government official whose execution couldn't be ignored. They'd have to retaliate—especially if the SASL turned the howitzer loose on a city in the Central Province."

"Which we figure is exactly what they planned to do," Dallas added. "Then, as added incentive to incite, they'd produce Muhandiramala's body—along with the rest of the family and Adam, who were all incidental to their plan—to ensure the Sinhalese military would launch attacks on Tamil territories for committing the atrocity."

"The incidental hostage." Lily looked sick. "People as pawns."

"It's a war game as old as time," Dallas said grimly.

"And yet it's still hard to believe anyone would be capable of bartering with human life."

"Or human death," Ethan added darkly, "which in this case, suits their cause much better."

"Okay. Let's move." Manny turned to tell Lily to stay back. She was busy shoving rounds into an extra magazine. His heart dropped to his balls when he realized she intended to go with them.

"Someone has to wait with the chopper," he said, making it clear he wanted that someone to be her.

"The chopper isn't going anywhere." She met his gaze in the dark. Dared him to deny her the right to help find her son.

Manny's gut told him to haul her over his shoulder and lock her in the bird. But his heart told him she was entitled. After all she'd been through, all she'd endured, she was entitled.

He glanced at Ethan as if seeking guidance.

"Don't look at me. I've already pissed off one woman tonight. This is your call."

Dallas tapped his watch. "Ten minutes before they launch the assault at Wahala-purha."

Manny glared at Lily. Bit the bullet. And he'd never forgive himself if something happened to her. "You do exactly what I say, exactly when I say it. Got it?"

She gave him a clipped nod.

"So help me God, if something happens to you—"

"Let's just do this," Lily interrupted, and, chin high, pistol on full cock, marched toward the ridge and the waiting cave like an avenging angel.

———

"Are you ready?" Adam whispered. He couldn't see their faces in the dark, but he could hear Minrada and her parents' hushed, "Ready."

They were all as scared as Adam was.

Push through the fear. He knew that's what he had to do. He'd read about guys who faced danger every day. They all said they pushed through the fear. That to not feel fear was stupid. And the best way to get killed.

He was going to die anyway if he didn't do something. So he'd made a plan. With Minrada standing guard, he'd spent the day exploring the cave, mapping out a route to a hiding place, and planning.

It was time to implement it.

"Now," he said, and hunkered back in an elbow of the cave entrance, a softball-sized rock gripped between his bound hands.

"Hurry! Please hurry!" Sathi cried.

It took a few minutes for the guard to respond—more out of annoyance than concern.

He held his rifle in one hand, a torch made out of co-conut husk in the other. The fire bathed his features in an orange-yellow glow as he stepped inside the cave and barked orders for Sathi to be quiet.

As planned, Sathi, Amithnal, and Minrada had wedged themselves as far back in the cave as possible, out of sight.

The guard stepped farther into the cave when he couldn't see them—that's when Adam moved. He brought the rock down hard on the back of the guard's neck.

It made a sickening sound—like bones breaking—and the guard dropped like a bag of cement.

Making himself look past the fact that he might have just killed someone, Adam stepped over the downed soldier.

"Hurry," Adam whispered as the other three scuttled forward, grabbed the guard by his feet, and dragged him back into the dark. "Minrada, get his knife."

Adam snagged the rifle from the floor, then stomped out the flame from the torch, sending them back into to-tal darkness. He'd never shot a rifle. But he'd seen pic-tures on the Web, read articles. He'd been curious about his father, about the Contra movement, and about the weapons they'd used.

Minrada came to Adam, cut the rope binding his wrists.

Fire ripped through his broken skin when the rope that had embedded itself into his flesh peeled away. He bit back a cry. Breathed through the nausea.

"Let's go." He tucked the rifle against his side and the four of them followed the wall deeper into the bowels of the cave. "There'll be another guard coming soon to check on this one."

This time, Adam was armed with more than a rock. He'd kill if he had to. To save Minrada. To save her parents. To save himself.

In the meantime, if their captors wanted to kill them, they had to find them first.

They'd just felt their way around the first ninety-degree turn when Adam heard shouts from the other guards.

"Hurry," he whispered. "They'll be looking for him and we can't be here."

———

Single file, low to the ground, Manny leading the way, they moved to the base of the enemy camp. With a hand signal, he sent Ethan left, Dallas right, and staged Lily well out of the line of fire behind a beat-up van where she could guard their flank.

Manny didn't plan on it getting to that stage. They were going to take these bastards out before they ever knew what hit them.

Laughter broke out among the men lounging around the campfire. Manny caught bits of their conversation. They'd raised their voices, taunting one of the guards who had apparently gone into the cave to check on the captives and hadn't returned.

The sexual references made Manny's blood boil.

He signaled Ethan again, then Dallas, designating which of the targets they were responsible for taking out. Manny was about to give the go signal when he heard it. The unmistakable sound of a trumpeting elephant.

"Sweet Jesus Christ," he muttered when Rajah's massive silhouette came charging into the middle of the camp, running full bore.

Mounted behind Rajah's great head, Kavith lobbed coconuts to a war cry of, "Go ahead; make my day!" as the pachyderm trampled through the campfire, sending the soldiers scattering and swearing and grabbing their guns.

"Go!" Manny shouted, knowing they had to break into the melee before it got out of control and Kavith got hurt.

Manny fired on the first guard to lift a rifle, saw him spin and go down. He took aim at a second, then a third, taking each of them out with a single shot. Behind him, he heard the pop of Ethan's AK-47; then Dallas fired off a burst and mowed down another contingent of the bad guys.

Rifle still at his shoulder, Manny moved in on the downed guards, kicked their rifles out of range of their bodies, then lifted his hand to Dallas and Ethan in a signal to stand down.

"Friend of yours?" Ethan asked as Kavith and Rajah came thundering back into the center of the camp.

"What in the fucking hell did you think you were doing?" Manny yelled up at Kavith.

"Yippee-ki-yay, motherfucker!" Kavith grinned, flying on a combat high. With coconuts, no less. "We did it, friend Manny!"

"*We* damned near got *you* killed," Manny pointed out, then spun around when shots from the ledge leading to the opening of the cave strafed the ground at his feet.

He returned fire, aiming for the fire flashes from the automatic weapon, then lunged for the cover of a boulder. "Kavith, get back!"

But it was too late. The boy took a hit. He slumped over onto Rajah's great back, then slowly slid to the side. Dallas caught Kavith before he hit the ground, then dragged him back behind a jeep.

"How bad?" Manny yelled as Ethan belly-crawled to Manny's side, both of them too busy returning fire to turn around and check.

"Hit to the arm," Dallas said, suddenly bellied down beside them in the dirt. "Lily's got it."

Manny rolled to his back with an oath, looked over his boot tops, and saw her. She'd run into the thick of things and was busy working over Kavith.

"Goddamn it, I told her to stay back!" Manny ground out, rolling to his belly again and joining the Garrett boys, who continued to hold down the shooters in the cave.

"Yeah, well, spank her later," Dallas said. "How many are we up against?"

"Based on the count down here, gotta be four—no more than five—left."

"So what's the new plan, Stan?" Ethan glanced at Manny.

"Cover me."

Manny pushed to his feet and, running hunched over in a zigzag pattern, headed straight for the cave.

CHAPTER 23

Heart in her throat, Lily glanced toward the men as she knelt over Kavith and secured a pressure bandage on his upper arm. The round had hit him clean. The bullet had only nicked him and passed on through. As close as she could figure, it was the sight of his own blood that had made him pass out. He'd be sore, but he'd be fine.

She didn't feel that confident about Manny. She searched the dark, then sucked in a breath when she saw him. "What's he doing?"

Her reply was several short bursts of gunfire as Ethan and Dallas unloaded on the opening to the cave where she'd seen the fire flashes from the barrels of the gunmen's weapons.

Manny was a dark silhouette against the tan cliff face. He was crouched low, hugging the wall of rock as he swiftly made his way up the steep, narrow slope while Ethan and Dallas laid down cover.

She held her breath when Manny stopped within five feet of the cave entrance and signaled for Ethan and Dallas to hold their fire. Then Manny shouted something in what she assumed was Hindi.

Lily ducked over Kavith, who was coming around when Manny's answer was a burst of gunfire and shouts.

Panicked for Manny, she appealed to Ethan and Dallas. "What's going on?"

"He told them to throw down their weapons." Ethan never took his eye off his rifle sight. "Let them know that their buddies were dead or wounded and their commander and his troops at Wahala-purha have been defeated. At least they should be by now," Ethan added, checking his watch. "He told them they have no cause left worth dying for."

"What did they say?" She shushed Kavith, who was trying to sit up.

"They warned him that they'd kill all four hostages if he came any closer."

Four hostages. Oh God. Terror and joy. Lily didn't know she could feel two such raging emotions simultaneously, but both rolled over her like a freight train. Adam wasn't dead. Joy leaped in her heart. For a brief second, it bypassed her terror for him.

Adam was alive. He was still alive.

The relief was overwhelming. All this time, in the back of her mind she'd fought, scrapped, and brawled to beat back the notion that he was already gone.

But he was alive. And in the midst of the gunfire and the lingering threat, a calm settled over her.

They hadn't gotten this far to lose Adam now. And she hadn't come this far without complete trust that the man who would lose as much as she did if these killing bastards won was going to see to it that their son stayed alive.

———

"Kill them and I guarantee your death," Manny shouted when the gunfire stopped. "It will be slow and it will be painful. This I promise. Now put down your weapons and walk out. Hands up."

Manny waited for his words to settle. Gave them time to consider their chances. Weigh the consequences.

While he considered his options if they balked.

He had to assume that Adam and the Muhandiramalas were in there somewhere. It only made sense for the bad guys to head for their hostages. Hostages whose life spans grew more precarious with each passing moment. And each moment that passed now was one too many.

"You have thirty seconds," Manny shouted, then without waiting the span of a heartbeat, charged the opening.

He had the element of surprise on his side, the rock at his back as he dropped and rolled. Rifle shouldered, he aimed in the direction of the fire flash from an automatic weapon.

He heard a shout of pain, the thud of a body hitting the ground, then a frantic, "Surrender! I surrender!"

"Out where I can see you!" he ordered, and rose to one knee.

Two men, hands above their heads, took tentative steps out of the mouth of the cave.

"The others!" he demanded. "Where are the others?"

"Dead," the younger soldier said, and glanced back over his shoulder.

"Got 'em," Dallas said, and Manny realized he and Ethan were suddenly beside him, flex-cuffing the Hindi soldiers.

Peripherally aware that Ethan led them away at gunpoint, Manny stepped into the cave, the stock of the Dragonov pressed flush against his shoulder, still sighting down the barrel.

Inside, he spotted one downed soldier. The other was

nowhere to be seen. Call him crazy, but he wasn't convinced that the other guard was dead.

"Come out, come out, wherever you are," Manny said in a low, lethal voice, then tightened his finger on the trigger when he saw a slight flicker of light emerge from deep in the cave. The light grew brighter and a shadowy figure appeared.

It was the fourth soldier. Not dead. Possibly wishing that he were, though, as he walked slowly, holding his hands high above his head. Behind him, wild-eyed and beat all to hell, was a young man wielding an AK-47 from his hip.

The boy's expression stalled somewhere between fierce determination and stark terror.

And Manny knew—bone deep, blood thick—that for the first time in his life, he was standing face-to-face with his son.

"Drop the gun," Adam ordered shakily, his gaze tracking wildly from the surrendered soldier to Manny, whom he clearly regarded as hostile.

"Whoa, Adam," Manny said, as calmly as he could manage, around the lump that had lodged in his throat. "Easy on the trigger there, bud. It's okay. I'm one of the good guys. We've come to take you home."

"I said drop it!" Adam shouted jerkily as a young woman, her eyes as wild and as determined as Adam's, joined him, a knife in her hand and blood in her eyes.

"Minrada?" Manny ventured, keeping his tone calm. "Are your mother and father with you?"

"Drop the fucking gun!" Adam roared, and jerked the rifle to his cheek. "I swear to God I'll shoot you."

Lily came out of nowhere, rushed past Manny and into the line of fire. "Adam. Oh God. Adam."

"M . . . Mom?"

Tears of joy and relief and days of terror filled her voice as Adam lowered the rifle and Lily ran toward him.

Too late for Manny to stop her.

The Hindi soldier grabbed her. He jerked her up against him and turned so she was directly in the line of fire. Before Manny could act, the soldier pulled a knife and held it to her throat.

"Mom!" Adam cried, and wilted with panic.

"Okay. Easy. Easy now," Manny said in his best impression of a man in total control. Then he repeated the words in Hindi.

"Let her go," he ordered softly. "You are one against many."

The guard drew Lily closer against him and pressed the knife to her throat.

Manny sensed more than heard Dallas ease up behind him. He wasn't sure what Dallas had in mind, but he was ready. When he heard a rock whiz past his ear, he understood.

The rock hit the ceiling of the cave, startling the sleeping bats. They screamed and screeched, and wings flapping against rock and one another, thousands of the flying rats rushed out of the cave in a great swooping swarm.

The guard, startled, ducked.

It was the opening Manny needed.

"Go!" He moved in high and grabbed the guard's knife hand while Dallas dropped, rolled, and kicked both Lily's and the guard's feet out from beneath them.

The soldier screamed, then dropped to his knees, doubled over in pain when Manny snapped his wrist. Manny caught Lily against him for a brief second. Long enough to make certain she was okay. Long enough to let his hammering heart adjust. Long enough to know she needed to hold her son.

With a soft cry she ran to Adam, wrapped him in her arms, and, oblivious to the frenzied bats evacuating the cave, whispered his name over and over again.

———

Peradeniya General Hospital, Kandy, 3:00 A.M.

Lily couldn't stop touching Adam. Couldn't stop smiling. Couldn't stop fussing. Couldn't stop—didn't *want* to stop—the flood of joy and relief. A consuming sense of wonder filled her to bursting as she watched this lean, bruised, and brave young man sleep on the pristine white sheets of the hospital bed.

"Don't you think you ought to try to get a little rest?"

Lily glanced over her shoulder at Darcy, who'd met them at the airport two hours ago after Ethan had called her. With the assistance of the local city leaders, Darcy had arranged to have an ambulance waiting for the Cobra when it landed.

"I'm not letting him out of my sight."

"And I can't seem to get that man of mine cornered long enough to get him *in* my sights," Darcy sputtered, but there was a smile in her voice, so Lily knew she wasn't as angry as she let on.

"They were amazing," Lily said softly, and with the slightest of touches ran her fingertip over the back of Adam's hand. He'd needed stitches over his eye. He had a cracked rib. A bone in his elbow was chipped, and his arm was now in a cast. He was dehydrated, half-starved.

He was alive.

She wouldn't think about what they'd done to him now. She couldn't or she'd break down.

"They are amazing," Darcy agreed.

And she should know, Lily thought. The three of them had stormed a terrorist stronghold in a remote jungle in the Philippines and brought Darcy home.

"Who *are* those guys?"

Lily snapped her gaze to Adam, just then realizing he was awake and watching her.

Tears filled her eyes. She stood, leaned over him and brushed the hair back from his forehead.

"Friends," she said in a hushed voice. "Very good friends. Sleep now, baby. We'll talk about it when you're stronger."

"Minrada?" Adam's voice was dry and brittle as his eyes drifted closed again. Lily heard the concern . . . and maybe something else in that one raspy word.

"She's fine, sweetie. So are Amithnal and Sathi. Everyone's fine. Everyone's safe."

"He's a brave kid," Darcy said quietly when it was apparent that Adam had fallen asleep again.

Lily wiped a tear from her eye. "Yeah. But God, I wish . . . I wish he'd never had to be."

It caught up with her then. The grief boiled up like a storm that had been building for a season. She started shaking; the tears brimmed and burned her eyes. After days of containing them she could no longer hold them back.

She spun away from the bed, shoving her fist to her mouth to quell the sound of her grief—and was caught up by two strong arms.

"Let it go. It's okay. Let it go."

She didn't know when Manny had come into the

room. Didn't care. Knew only that she needed him.
Every bit as much as she needed Adam to be safe, she
needed Manny to make *her* feel safe. To let her be weak.
To tell her that everything really was okay.

"I'll stay with Adam." Darcy touched a hand to her
shoulder as Lily let Manny walk her out the door. "You
rest now. I'll take care of him."

———

When Lily woke up, she was stretched out on a cot in
a sparsely furnished waiting area. She closed her eyes
again, rolled to her back, and stifled a groan when her
stiff muscles complained. Blinking sleep from her heavy
lids, she forced herself awake—and smelled coffee.

She must have sniffed and moaned again, because
someone chuckled.

"Yes," Darcy said, "it's really coffee."

Lily sat up, worked out the kinks, and reached out
blindly.

Darcy laughed again and placed the cup in Lily's out-
stretched hands. "Savor it. It came at a premium and it's
the only cup you get. Now tea—I could have gotten you
all kinds of tea."

Lily sipped, savored as ordered, and let go of an ap-
preciative, "Ahhh. You're my new best friend."

"I could work with that."

The warmth in Darcy's voice brought Lily's head up.
Darcy was smiling at her. A friend, smiling at a friend.

"Thanks," Lily said. "Thanks for that.

"And the same goes for me," she added after a moment, not sure exactly why she felt a little self-conscious
about admitting she considered Darcy a friend.

Old habits, Lily decided. She wasn't used to unqualified acceptance. Hadn't gotten it from her parents, that's for certain. Had always felt she'd had to work to prove her worth.

But not with Darcy. And that fact felt special and new and real.

"Who's with Adam?"

"Relax, Mom. Manny's got it covered."

Whether it was the caffeine or the nerves that started tap dancing through her abdomen, Lily was suddenly wide awake.

She shot off the cot.

"It's okay," Darcy said gently. "He hasn't told him."

Relief—or maybe it was disappointment—partnered up with the nerves and sped up the pace of Lily's pulse again.

On one hand, it was probably best if Lily broke the news to Adam about Manny. On the other, well, if Manny had taken care of it, she wouldn't have to.

"I'd better go in there." She wiped damp palms on her pants—only then realized she was wearing a set of green hospital scrubs.

"So it wasn't a dream. I *did* take a shower and wash my hair."

"And you were almost awake when you did it." Darcy handed her a hairbrush. "Better do something with that."

Lily touched a hand to her hair. Felt the snarls.

"You were out before we had a chance to get a brush through it."

"We?" Lily asked with a heart-tripping trepidation.

"Me and your Latin bodyguard," Darcy said with a grin. "He's a little protective of you."

It would have been easy to smile at that thought. And

Lily might have if she weren't so anxious to get back to Adam.

She hurriedly dragged the brush through her hair. "Better? I don't want to scare him."

"Scare? Sweetie, if I didn't like you so much, it'd be real easy to get bitchy. You should look like death warmed over after all you've been through, but look at you—you look amazing. When the guys dragged me off Jolo, I couldn't bear to look at myself in a mirror for a week. Not fair," she singsonged with a grin.

Lily felt herself choke up, and before she knew it, she pulled Darcy against her for a hard hug. "Thank you," she whispered hoarsely. "Thank you for being so ... wonderful."

And then she rushed away to see her son before she got all watery.

Heart in her throat, Lily paused outside Adam's hospital room door. Manny's voice, deep and low and more animated than she had ever heard it, spilled into the hall. The amazing, miraculous, beautiful sound of her son's laughter was like a song.

And tears—God, would the tears ever stop?—threatened again. The joy she felt at having Adam back was consuming. The idea of the two—father and son—laughing together after all these years was as huge and whole as the Sri Lankan sun. It washed over her in radiant waves as Manny's soft chuckle joined with Adam's. In joy's wake, regret drifted like flotsam. They'd all lost so much. So much time. So many memories.

For a moment, she considered leaving them alone.

Didn't want to intrude on what was a special moment between them. More special for Manny than Adam could possibly know.

A nurse walked by just then and gave Lily a curious look, so she pasted on her best mom smile and entered the room.

"So, here they come," Manny was saying, oblivious to Lily behind him, "Rajah trumpeting like a corps of buglers, Kavith spouting Bruce Willis lines. The coconuts are flying, men are flying, and Dallas and Ethan and I are bug-eyed with shock."

"Mom," Adam's grin broadened when he saw her, "Manny was just telling me about the big rescue."

"So I hear." She smiled from Adam to Manny, who looked gorgeous and a little nervous suddenly. He stood when he realized she'd entered the room.

"Got to admit," Manny said, looking a little hesitant, "they made a helluvan entrance."

Lily saw all kinds of emotions in Manny's eyes. Happiness. Hesitation. Questions.

Was it okay? Is it okay for me to spend time with him?

"Yeah," she agreed, letting Manny know it was more than okay. "It was something else, all right."

She walked to Adam's side, aware of Manny's gaze on her. "How you doing today, sweetie?" She leaned down and kissed his brow.

Embarrassing him, she realized, in front of this warrior who had saved his life.

"I'm fine, Mom. You can quit fussing."

She pushed out a snort. "Yeah, that's going to happen."

Adam rolled his eyes, but he was smiling as she smoothed the hair back from his forehead, relieved to find it cool.

"Well, I'll be leaving you two alone."

Lily turned to see Manny backing toward the door, looking uncomfortable—like he felt he was intruding.

And for that she felt more regret over all the years he'd lost with Adam.

"Just . . . just give us a few minutes," she said with a meaningful look. "Don't go far, okay?"

He swallowed hard and when his eyes met hers she could see he understood. She was going to tell Adam. With a clipped nod and a long look, Manny turned and walked out of the room.

Lily pulled a chair up by the bed. Took Adam's hand. Squeezed. "Sweetie . . . there's something I need to tell you."

CHAPTER 24

Manny scrubbed a palm over his jaw. He should have shaved. Should have—hell, he didn't know. Should have done something. Something to make himself look like a man a boy would want to have for a father.

Would it come to that? Would it come down to Adam deciding if, after sixteen years on his own, he'd want Manny in his life? As a father? Hell, after meeting the kid, he'd settle for being a friend.

Or not.

Not.

He wanted it all, he realized as he paced outside the door. After meeting this amazing young man who had every reason to be traumatized and cowering after what he'd been through but was, instead, strong and adjusted and . . . and damn, he was something.

And he was his.

Or might be.

Shit. Manny felt like he was waiting for Lily to give birth. Worried. Happy.

Mostly worried.

He kept moving. Tried his damnedest not to overhear any of the conversation. Was half-scared that he'd hear Adam's response and it wouldn't be good.

How had this happened? How had it happened that Manny had been drifting along through life, content alone, and now the thought of losing Adam damn near ripped his heart out?

Hell. He'd been fine. Alone. On his own. No one to answer to. No one but himself to be responsible for.

He'd been just fine.

Hadn't missed the hassles of parenthood. Hadn't missed the headaches. Hadn't wanted any of it.

And now he wanted it all. And he wanted Lily, too. But that was another issue. One he'd tackle when the time was right.

He let out a breath through puffed cheeks. Paced some more.

Forever passed.

Then an eternity.

What was taking so damn long?

His back was to the door when he heard Lily call his name.

And he suddenly wished he had more time. Time to prepare for the worst. Time to prepare for the best.

He made himself turn around . . . couldn't make himself look at her. Couldn't bear to see sorrow or, worse, pity or regret.

He tucked his hands in the hip pockets of his pants. Slowly entered the room.

And on a heavy breath, sought his son's eyes.

Oh God.

Adam's eyes were red—like he'd been crying.

Oh God. Oh God.

Manny hated knowing that he was the cause for the boy's tears.

Manny didn't know what to say. Wasn't aware of

anything going on around him. Saw only his son on the bed. Saw only Adam's tentative and hesitant gaze searching his own.

"So," Adam finally said, his voice rough, his chin a little wobbly. He was trying his damnedest to be cool, but Manny could see the kid was every bit as wired as he was.

"So," Manny said, and damn, all he could do was wait.

"You're . . . you're my dad, huh?"

Manny compressed his lips.

Nodded.

Watched.

Waited.

Adam's eyes filled up and Manny realized his own were burning, too.

"Cool," Adam said after another eternity had passed.

A lump the size of Ramanathan's stolen howitzer lodged in Manny's throat. Along with a relief so huge it crammed his chest to bursting.

"Yeah," he managed, and smiled at his son. "Very cool."

Two days later

"Come on, Mom. Don't go all taz on me."

Lily swallowed back the urge to scream. She was not supposed to *go all taz*?

"But why, Adam? Why, after all that's happened, would you want to stay here?"

Adam had been released from the hospital yesterday. Lily had booked them a room at Mahaweli Reach on the banks of the Mahaweli River, just outside Kandy.

It seemed like the perfect place to rest and regroup after Adam's ordeal and before they caught their flight home tomorrow. They were sitting under the shade of a colorful poolside umbrella—Lily and Adam, Manny, the Garretts, and Darcy—surrounded by trailing vines and flowers, sipping sweet fruit drinks and rehashing some of the events of the past few days, filling in the blanks for Adam.

What he'd been through—what the Muhandiramalas had endured—made Lily's stomach clench with horror. And now Adam was telling her he wanted to stay here.

She turned to Manny, looking in support in what was sizing up to be a major argument. He and the Garretts had also decided to stay an extra day while they tied up a seaman's chest full of loose ends concerning their role in both Adam's rescue and the successful joint assault on the larger force of insurgents at Wahala-purha.

Their conclusions about the SASL had been right on the money. Had Manny and Lily not found the howitzer, had Dallas not risked his life seeking out Ramanathan, and had Darcy and Ethan not found the information on the militant group online and pieced it all together, there would have been a full-fledged war raging between the Tamils and the Sinhalese that would have been devastating.

There had been mention of national recognition for the part they had all played not only in the Muhandiramalas' rescue, but also in uncovering the intended coup. Even Kavith was to be honored. And the joint Tamil/Sinhalese military op was being hailed as the most encouraging sign of putting the civil war to bed in the history of Sri Lanka.

"Did you know about this?" Lily asked when Manny didn't join her in her argument. "Did you know he intends to stay?"

When Manny gave her a blank look, then cut a glance at Adam, Lily had her answer.

"I can't believe you sanction this."

Unable to sit still, Lily rose, walked toward the courtyard rail. Far below, the rain forest and the snaking path of the Mahaweli flowed—a thin blue ribbon amid a lush sea of green.

"I signed on to do a job, Mom. I want to finish it."

Adam's voice was strong. Determined.

And Lily knew she was fighting a losing battle. That didn't keep her from trying to lob one more argument.

"Adam—"

Manny's hand on her arm stopped her. She'd been so focused on Adam, she hadn't realized Manny had moved in beside her.

"Let's take a walk." With a firm but gentle nudge, he guided her toward the far end of the courtyard.

"I can't let him stay." Realizing it sounded like a plea, she reined herself in. She was frustrated and scared— yes, scared. "I came so close to losing him."

"*We*," Manny said with emphasis. "*We* came so close to losing him."

She swallowed, nodded. "And yet, you seem to be on his side on this."

She tried not to make it sound accusatory, but she heard the accusation just the same. So did he. Along with a hint of something else.

"Look. I'm sorry if I sound irritated. Maybe even a little . . . God, this is hard to admit . . . possessive of him."

She dragged a hand through her hair as the south wind picked it up and licked it around her face. "I've . . . well, it's just always been him and me, you know? I've never had to share him before. Never had to consult with anyone on decisions about his welfare."

Manny said nothing. He simply waited.

She shook her head. "Manny, I'm thrilled the two of you are bonding. I am. I look at Adam when he looks at you and . . . the joy I feel in his joy . . ." She felt those damn tears well up again and blinked them back. "It's a wonderful thing to watch."

"But the transition from single parent to one of a pair— that's not so easy," he concluded, leaning a hip against the concrete rail and crossing his arms over his chest.

She gave him a tight smile. "No. Not so easy."

"What do you want me to do, Lily? Do you want me to tell him I think he should go back to the States with you?"

She squinted against the sun, then met his eyes. Dark eyes. Beautiful eyes. Earnest and truly seeking.

"I want you to tell me what you think he should do," she admitted, drawing her gaze away from his because she had so many questions that had nothing to do with Adam. Questions about the two of them. About what happened next. *If* anything happened next.

"He has something to prove, Lily. To himself. To you . . . even to me."

"He more than proved himself these past few days."

"Agreed. But he has to put a period on the end of that sentence. He thinks that if he leaves, he's running."

She tucked a handful of hair away from her face. "He told you that?"

He shook his head. "He doesn't have to."

She breathed deep of floral-scented air. Looked out over the valley again. "I don't know. . . ."

"There's something else at play here. Have you noticed how he reacts when Minrada's name comes up?

The way he looked at her the day she visited him in the hospital?"

Lily snapped her gaze to Manny. "Minrada? He's got a thing for Minrada?" She shook her head. "She's lovely and all, but . . . my God, she must be five, six years older than he is."

One corner of Manny's mouth tightened. A smile of sorts. Of satisfaction. Maybe even pride.

"You find that amusing?"

"Yes, *querida*. Amusing and satisfying to know that my blood runs strong in his veins. Adam, too, appreciates the allure of an older woman."

She could happily dwell on the implication of that declaration if she let herself. And she would. Later. When they weren't talking about her child.

"He's just a boy."

"Who survived with a man's wit, a man's cunning. A man's bravery. Not a boy, Lily. He is not a boy any longer. I know. I have been where he has been."

As a sixteen-year-old soldier/spy for the Contras. *Yes,* Lily realized. Manny knew exactly where Adam had been.

"Maybe . . . maybe that's what's bothering me the most," she confessed after a long moment. She wanted her little boy back. But Manny was right. After all Adam had been through, all he'd survived, he would never be a boy again.

"I'd give anything . . . *anything,* if he hadn't had to lose his innocence this way."

"He's strong, Lily. He'll be fine. He'll be fine because you've done an amazing job raising him."

She took some small comfort in Manny's approval. And yet . . .

"I'm staying with him," Manny said quietly.

When she searched his face she saw that he'd given it a lot of thought.

"I want . . . hell. I've lost so much of him. I want to get to know him better. And since he's determined to stay, it'll make me feel a helluva lot better to be here with him.

"Yeah," he added sheepishly when she wrinkled her brow. "I talk a good line, but you aren't the only one with reservations about him staying on by himself."

Lily supposed she ought to breathe a sigh of relief over Manny's news. He was staying behind with Adam. Manny would make certain their son stayed safe.

And she was relieved. And disturbed, yet again, by the reality of this new shared parentage. What Manny said, what he did, mattered. Held weight.

"Lily? It's only six more weeks."

She gathered herself, met Manny's concerned eyes. "Okay," she said, and accepted that she may have gotten her son back, but that nothing would ever be the same between them again.

She forced a smile, hoped it didn't look as pained as it felt. "Okay. He can stay."

Manny held her gaze for a long moment. A moment in which she sensed he wanted to say something more. Or maybe that was just wishful thinking on her part, because he finally nodded.

"He'll be all right. Come on. Let's go let the poor kid off the hook. He's probably thinking we're about to arm wrestle to settle this."

Like she could possibly win in a test of strength.

Or a test of will.

She smiled because that's what Manny wanted her to do, and walked with him to tell Adam the news. On the one hand, it wasn't right to leave him hanging.

On the other hand, it looked like Lily was going to dangle in the wind for a while yet where Manny was concerned.

Now that Adam was safe she'd had a lot of time to think about Manny. About Manny and her.

His words came back on a regular basis.

You're wondering about what happened back there. In the temple. About what it meant. What it means.

When this is over, we'll sort it out, okay?

Well, it was over.

And so far, nothing.

Yeah, she'd caught him watching her sometimes. His brows knit, his expression thoughtful, like he was wrestling with some deep, dark dilemma.

Was it really that hard? she wanted to ask him. Was it really that hard to think about a future that involved him and her together—and not just as parents who shared a child?

She was still wondering the next day when a limo, courtesy of the Sri Lankan government, drove the lot of them to the airport where Lily and the Garretts and Darcy would catch a plane to return to the States. Lily was wondering right up to the time when she gave Adam a hard, teary hug and begged him to be careful.

"Take care of him," she told Manny, who had watched the exchange with soft eyes.

"Count on it."

She nodded, gave Adam one last, lingering look, and headed toward the departure gate.

"Lily."

Manny's voice stopped her. She didn't turn around. Couldn't turn around. Couldn't lift her head and look him in the eye when he walked around in front of her.

A curled finger under her chin brought her head up.

His dark eyes were intent on her face. Warm. Thrilling. "Take care of yourself, Liliana," he said softly. Then he leaned down and kissed her.

The sound she made could have been relief or longing or even regret that she was leaving both of these amazing men. Manny answered by dragging her hard up against him, deepening the kiss, then reluctantly breaking away to search her eyes one last time.

"Travel safe, *querida.* We have much to discuss in September."

And then he turned and walked back to Adam. Over Manny's broad shoulder, she could see Adam's face. He wasn't exactly smiling. He was too much of a "son" not to be embarrassed by the public display of affection between his mother and the man he had just learned was his father.

But Adam didn't exactly look displeased, either.

———

Matara, two weeks later

Adam found Minrada alone in the empty schoolroom. She sat on the floor, her back to the wall, unwrapping her lunch. He stood in the open doorway, watching her. Because he couldn't seem to stop watching her.

Sunlight streamed in through an open window and slanted across her bare toes and the dust on her sandaled feet. A soft breeze offered a cooling respite from the heat and played with the hair at her face.

He'd been waiting for the chance to get her alone. Manny didn't exactly cling, but he never got too far away, either. Adam would never admit it, but he kind of liked it. Liked that this hard-edged warrior father of his wanted to be with him. That he was working alongside of Adam because he wanted to be with him, even though Manny had a job with those cool Garrett guys waiting for him back in the States.

Sometimes they talked—about Nicaragua, about Adam's mom. If he asked, Manny would tell him a little bit about Afghanistan. About the Contra war. He wouldn't say much and Adam didn't want to pry, had figured out that his new father wasn't much for talking about himself.

And that made Adam proud.

He had a dad. A dad he liked—might even love. It was cool. And weird sometimes. Like when Manny asked about Adam's mom. Yeah, it was common ground, but it made him wonder what it would be like if the two of them hooked up again.

Adam thought about the way Manny had kissed her at the airport. *That* had been embarrassing. And yet it was okay.

So yeah, it would be okay if they hooked up. Adam thought about the three of them together and liked that idea, too.

And he was stalling.

He'd come looking for Minrada. He'd found her. And he needed to know how she was doing.

She'd been so quiet. And each time he thought of the reason why, a swell of hatred surged up inside of him for the men who had made her this way.

On a deep breath, he cleared his throat so she'd know he was there.

She looked up, startled, then smiled tentatively when she saw it was him.

And he got all light-headed.

"Want some company?" he asked when he mustered up the courage.

She patted the floor beside her.

For a long time, they just sat there and ate their lunch in silence. It was a good quiet. Comfortable. But he hadn't sought her out just to sit here like a stump and chew and swallow.

It seemed like he'd been waiting forever to get her alone. Part of the wait had been for him to screw up his courage. Part had been to give her time to heal.

But he wanted her to smile again. Laugh again, so he would know she was going to be okay.

"I spy something beautiful," he said at long last. His heart beat like thunder as he waited for her reaction.

She was quiet for so long he thought she wasn't going to say anything. Finally, she met his eyes.

"You're beautiful, Minrada. Inside. Outside. Nothing . . . no one could ever change that."

Her eyes filled with tears and then she nodded. Smiled for him.

"Life," she said, her dark eyes as soft as the cloud of hair falling around her shoulders. "Life is beautiful."

Yeah, Adam thought, a soothing relief washing through him. Life was beautiful. And because she was brave, because she was strong, hers was going to be beautiful again.

CHAPTER 25

Boston, four weeks later

Lily was a mess. Emotionally. Physically.

Adam was coming home tomorrow.

Six long weeks she'd waited, so busy catching up at work she hadn't had a spare moment to plan a welcome home party.

Or for that matter to put her house in order.

Wearing baggy old jeans and a seen-better-days T-shirt, she'd pulled her hair into a long tail on top of her head and at six in the morning started painting his room. It was a promise she'd made when they'd first moved into the apartment. Purple was so not his color.

Scratching her nose with the back of her hand, she stepped back to admire the new sage green walls. Very clean looking. Very masculine. He'd like it and the new curtains and bedspread she'd splurged on as part of his welcome home gift.

Home.

That was *her* gift. Tomorrow he was coming home. It made her feel warm and rich all over.

Until she thought of the man who would be coming with him. Thinking of Manny had an entirely different effect on her internal temperature. She flushed hot and

cold at the same time, shivering with an electric mix of
anticipation and dread.

She was a mature, professional, independent woman,
for God's sake. Yet she felt as giddy as a teenager when
she thought about seeing him tomorrow.

Not good. Not good at all.

We have much to discuss in September.

She could still see his somber eyes when he'd said
those words. Still felt the butterflies in her stomach when
he'd drawn her flush against him and kissed her good-bye
at the airport.

Yes. They had much to discuss. They sure hadn't dis-
cussed anything during the past six weeks. As she'd
made him promise, Adam had called every other day.
But Manny had never even talked to her.

"Manny says hi."

That had been it. A polite, generic message passed
through Adam.

Manny says hi.

It hadn't been much. Who was she kidding? It had
been nothing.

Just like she knew nothing about where they were
headed in their relationship—if there even was a relationship. If there could *be* a relationship.

"Okay. Don't think about that now," she muttered under her breath.

She couldn't do anything about it anyway, and there
was still so much she *could* do before Adam and Manny
got here.

"Way too much," she echoed aloud when she caught
a glimpse of herself in the full-length mirror she'd hung
on the back of Adam's closet door. "You're a fine mess,
Campora."

She had paint on her hands, on her cheek, and even a little splotch in her hair. She needed to hit the shower, then the market. She wanted to have all of Adam's favorite dishes for dinner tomorrow night.

And Manny's favorite wine.

She reached up, touched Manny's St. Christopher medal that she still wore around her neck. A vivid, erotic, seventeen-year-old memory of him drinking deep burgundy wine from her body sent another shock wave through her system.

She breathed deep, shook it off.

"That's not helping matters," she sputtered.

When the doorbell rang, she headed for the foyer, wiping her hands on her jeans. Hoping it was the cake she'd ordered, she swung open the door . . . to see Adam and Manny standing in the hall.

"Hi, Mom. I'm home," Adam said with a grin as big as Texas.

"Oh my God!" she squealed, and caught him up against her. She hugged him hard, buried her face in the curve of his neck, and breathed in the familiar scent of him.

He was home. Safe. Sound. And . . .

She pulled back, all smiles as she studied him at arm's length. "What are you doing here? You weren't due until tomorrow," she sputtered inanely. "Oh, who cares? I'm so glad you're back. And . . . you've grown. I swear, you're half a head taller. Is that possible?"

"Considering he eats like a linebacker, I'm not surprised."

Self-conscious suddenly, Lily eased up on her hold on Adam to see Manny watching her with a soft smile on his face. The same smile that never failed to do crazy things to her stomach and melt the marrow in her bones.

"Call it a wild guess," he said after giving her a lingering once-over that sent her pulse rate off the charts, "but have you, by any chance, been painting?"

Oh God. She'd forgotten. This was so not how she'd wanted to look when she saw him again. By the time she'd left Sri Lanka she'd been bruised and battle weary, sunburned and skinned up. When she saw Manny again, she'd wanted to look like a woman, not a survivor of a war. And she sure as the world hadn't wanted to be covered in paint and wearing rejects from a thrift store.

"You guys really know how to ruin a welcome home party." She tugged the band from her hair and let it fall around her shoulders. "I was going to have everything . . . well, special."

"It is special," Manny said softly as Adam shouldered around her and into the apartment. He dropped his duffel on the floor and headed for his room, leaving them alone.

Several heartbeats passed while she tried to regulate her breathing. Wasn't going to happen.

Not with Manny looking like that. All bronze warrior and Hollywood good looks. All dark eyes that probed and assessed and didn't miss a single thing.

"You look beautiful, *querida*."

Her heart did that little kick, stutter thing it always did when his voice washed over her that way. Like a warm rain. Like a midnight caress.

Nervous. She was so nervous around him.

"So, you're into the domestic turmoil look," she said, groping for an outlet for the sudden tension. Tension that revved to a chest-tightening crush when he took a step across the threshold and stopped directly in front of her.

"I'm into the Lily Campora look." His Latin dark eyes roved over her face. His big hand touched her cheek. "I've missed you, *mi amor*."

Now would not be the time to point out that in six long weeks he hadn't called her, hadn't written, hadn't given her any indication that he was even alive, let alone missing her.

Like she'd been missing him.

Now would be the time to confess, instead.

"I . . . missed you, too."

She waited then. For the touch of those lush, mobile lips. For the end to six weeks of waiting for and hoping for a happily ever after to this story that had spanned so much of her life and that she desperately needed to end in something other than good-bye.

Ever so slowly, he lowered his head to hers. His breath on her face was warm, minty. His liquid black eyes were swimming with everything she'd ever hoped to see . . . longing, yearning . . . love.

She tipped her face to his, let her eyelids drift closed in anticipation of his kiss.

"We must talk, Lily," he whispered instead, then pressed a kiss to her forehead and backed away.

She felt herself weave a little, opened her eyes, and realized he was heading for the door.

"You're . . . leaving?"

He paused in the open doorway. "You'll want some time," he said. "With Adam. And he needs some time with you."

She just stood there, struggling not to let her disappointment show.

"I'll call you," Manny said with a last lingering look.

"Tell Adam good-bye for me. Let him know I'll be in touch, okay?"

She nodded, suddenly as mute as a post.

And then he was gone, closing the door behind him when he left.

"Hey, Mom."

She turned when Adam bounced back into the room, a whirlwind of energy and light.

"It's cool," he said, all smiles. "My room. Thanks."

One look at his happy, healthy, safe-and-sound face and she shook off her confusion over Manny's sudden departure. "Come're, you. I haven't had near enough mush time with you yet."

He rolled his eyes but let her hug him close again and shower him with kisses—at least for a little while.

"All right already," he grumbled, which made her laugh. "You're not going to be so happy about things when you see the bag full of dirty clothes I brought."

Wrong. She'd never grumble about doing his laundry again.

"Where's Dad?"

Dad.

It rolled off Adam's tongue so easily. Yet Lily sensed the wonder and pride that accompanied that small three-letter word.

"He said to tell you good-bye and he'd be in touch."

Adam's face fell. "He left?"

"Baby," she said gently when she read the emotion in those words. Panic. Uncertainty. And she understood. Adam had just found his father. He didn't want to lose him. "He's not leaving you."

Several days later, however, when neither Lily nor

Adam had heard a word from Manny, she started to worry. And to wonder if maybe she'd been wrong.

If maybe Manny had left them both.

———

One week later

Manny had trained in black ops. He'd carried out more missions behind enemy lines than he could count. He'd faced men without conscience, men without scruples or honor. Survived firefights, RPGs, and IEDs. Once, in the jungles of Nicaragua, he'd survived in a foxhole for four days, living on grass and monkey meat, tending to a wounded comrade, rather than leave him to die alone.

Manny had faced the fire. Of war. Of hell. With his nerves intact. His courage fortified and strong.

And yet the thought of facing Lily Campora, of the soft dark eyes and valiant heart, made his blood clot with fear.

Battling back the urge to turn around and run, Manny rapped his knuckles on her door, stood back, and waited.

He didn't wait long.

The door swung open and there she was. Elegant. Vibrant. Expectant. Her eyes were wary with it.

"Hi," she said, and offered a tentative smile. "I've been expecting you."

Yeah. That was his insurance that he wouldn't back out. He'd called her earlier today, asked if he could come see her tonight.

To have that talk.

The one he'd been putting off.

The one he'd been certain would reveal him for the man he was, instead of the man she needed him to be.

"You could come in," she suggested with a lift of her brows when he just stood there.

The view was fine where he was. She'd dressed up for him. Taken special care with her makeup and hair. Not that she'd needed to. She could wear a sack and he'd still think she was beautiful.

Tonight she wore black. Like her hair. Like her eyes. Black cut low against her pale ivory skin that he itched to touch. To taste. To claim . . . if she'd let him when he was finished saying his peace.

A long silver chain hung around her neck and disappeared between her breasts beneath her dress. His medal. Lying warm where he wanted to lay his head.

Suddenly the prospect of spilling his guts didn't seem nearly as necessary or smart as it had when he'd screwed up the nerve to call her.

"Manny?"

Her dark eyes questioned.

He bit the bullet and walked into her apartment—wishing, suddenly, that Adam were here for a buffer. But Manny had talked to his son earlier today. His son. Manny still felt a swell of pride and amazement every time that truth sank home.

But home was where Adam was not going to be tonight. At least not for several hours. Adam had told Manny on the phone that the team members who had spent the summer in Sri Lanka were getting together tonight at the home of one of the sponsors to share pizza and photos and experiences.

Manny was betting that Adam was going to be the hit of the night.

"Would you like some wine?"

She looked beautiful. Nervous. And he realized he was making her that way.

"Wine would be good. Thanks." He moved on into the living area when she lifted a hand, motioning him to make himself comfortable.

"I'll be right back."

He watched her walk away. Watched the sweet sway of her slim hips in that clingy dress. Watched the supple muscles of her calves beneath the floating hemline.

And felt need burning low and deep in his gut.

He pushed it back. He needed to talk to her. And if he didn't keep his head in the game, they'd end up naked and in bed before he ever had a chance to say his piece.

Not that the prospect of Lily naked and hot beneath him didn't hold an amazing amount of appeal. It did. Lord God, it did. But she needed more from him tonight. And he was determined to give it.

He hadn't gotten more than a glimpse of her apartment when he'd brought Adam home last week. Manny liked it, he decided, as he wandered slowly around the living room. Classy. Sleek. Like the woman.

"Here you go."

He turned and accepted the glass of burgundy wine she held out to him.

"Salut." She lifted her glass.

"Salut." He watched her eyes above the rim of the wineglass as he drank.

And he could see that his silence was undoing her. That was the last thing he wanted.

"Let's sit down."

She nodded, hesitated, then settled into a suede armchair.

Cautious. Yeah. He understood.

He sat opposite her on the sofa instead of beside her, so he wouldn't be tempted to touch her. Touching her would lead to loving her, and loving had never been a problem between them.

He cradled his glass between his palms and contemplated where to start.

"Jesus, Manny," she finally said, her voice breathy, her eyes beseeching when he met them. "If you came to say good-bye for good, just get it over with."

Only then did he realize how truly hard his silence was on her. "I didn't come to say good-bye, *querida,*" he said quickly. "At least I hope not."

"Then what?" Her dark eyes glistened.

He hated that he was responsible for testing her control. But he would hate it more if he made her cry.

"I'm not . . . not a man who admits his mistakes easily, *mi amor.* But I have many to admit to you."

"Starting with why you didn't call me? Why for six long weeks while I missed my son, worried about his safety . . . worried about yours . . . you couldn't have once called and talked to me? Why another week passed and not one word from you?

"Oh God. I can't believe I said that." She gave her head a little shake, looked away.

She had a right to be angry. She had a right to be hurt.

"Yeah. Starting with that."

He stared at his glass, then back to her brimming eyes. "I was being pretty self-indulgent," he admitted. "And I'm sorry if I hurt you. That was a mistake. But it wasn't a mistake to have that time with Adam."

"I don't begrudge you spending time with him."

"I know. I know that. And I needed that time, Lily.

Just him. Just me. To learn about him. To realize and appreciate what a wonderful job you've done with him. And to learn about you through him."

"Learn about me?"

"He may not tell you," Manny continued, "he is, after all, cut from the same cloth as his father . . . but he loves you, Liliana. He's very proud of you. He told me how you worked and went back to school to get your master's. He told me how your parents could have helped and didn't."

She swallowed hard.

"He knows how much you gave up for him. And now I know how you raised an amazing boy on your own to become an amazing man. A good man with his mother's values.

"I need to thank you," Manny added as her features softened and she finally let out a breath that he suspected she'd been holding since he'd shown up at her door. "For telling him about me. About how much you loved me."

At that, she looked away, then into her wine. Lifted it to her mouth with an unsteady hand.

"And you did love me, didn't you, Lily? No matter that you always denied it when I asked."

"I . . . I knew I had to leave you," she said, still avoiding his eyes and his question. "I wanted you to move on with your life. To find someone your age. Someone you could build a future with."

He understood that now. Just as he understood so much more.

"You were right about many things back then. But about that, you were wrong. I may have been a boy. But I understood love."

"I'm not so sure you were ever a boy." She looked up from her wine, a world of regret in her eyes.

Soft. Her eyes were so soft.

"I loved you, Lily. So much. So much that it was easier to believe you would betray me, easier to hate you for
that betrayal, than to deal with the prospect of losing
you. I realize that now.

"Just like I realize," he added after searching her eyes,
"that hating you became easier than loving you. Loving
you hurt too much. Hating you gave me purpose."

It had taken him the past several weeks and a lot of
soul-searching to understand all of this.

"As the years passed, it wasn't even about you anymore. It was about me. If I hated you, I didn't have to
hate myself."

"Hate yourself?"

This was the hard part. This was the part that cut closest to the bone. "For letting my country down. Letting
my family down. For the men I've killed," he added,
swallowing thickly. "The lives I've taken."

Death. He'd been a part of it. And now he had to live
with it.

"You protected, Manny. You fought for freedom. For
basic human rights. There's no guilt in that. There's only
honor. And the only regret is that you have to live with
the result of the wrong choices others made."

He closed his eyes, saw the stark, gray faces of
death—in the jungles of Nicaragua. The mountains of
Afghanistan. Even on the streets of Boston. Most recently near the caves in Sri Lanka.

They were always with him. He never slept alone.
Never woke alone.

He didn't know when Lily had stood and moved in beside him. Didn't know when he'd leaned into the comfort

of her arms around him. Pressed his face against the soft, giving warmth of her breasts.

Didn't know there were tears inside him to shed until he felt them wet and hot on his cheeks.

Embarrassed, he pulled out of her embrace. Stood with his back to her. Sucked in a bracing breath.

Jesus. He'd come here to tell her he loved her, to beg her to forgive him, and he was coming apart in front of her.

"We all have demons," she said behind him. "We all have regrets. The trick is to not let them define who we are. Decide what we do."

Yeah, he thought. That was a trick all right.

"I love you, Manny."

He stiffened. Not sure he believed what he'd just heard. After he'd just spilled his guts, exposed his deepest secrets, laid bare the ugly truth of his transgressions, and cried in her arms like a baby, she couldn't have said . . .

"I love you."

He turned to her then. Saw the tears on her cheeks. Tears for him. Love for him. Honest. Open. True.

"I love you because of where you've been," she said when he drew her into his arms. "Because of who you are. Not in spite of it. Ti amo, Manny. I have always loved you."

He touched a hand to her cheek, pressed his forehead to hers, and squeezed his eyes shut to stem the tide of emotion rising inside him.

"It's time," she whispered. "It's time we get on with our lives."

Love swelled, ripe and hot and sweet, as she tipped her face to his and kissed him.

Then she took his hand and led him to her bed.

CHAPTER 26

"It's as true now as it was then." Manny dipped his head, took her breast in his mouth, and savored. "It should be against the law for a body as beautiful as yours to be covered by clothing."

Lily stretched with pleasure under the possessive caress of Manny's mouth and the hand that trailed over her ribs to caress the curve of her waist, the flare of her hips.

She was forty-five. She knew what her body looked like. Her breasts were heavier. Her hips a bit wider. Her muscle tone not as tight. But he loved her this way.

For the past hour he'd been making certain that she knew without a shadow of a doubt that he *adored* her this way.

"Have I told you that I love it when you go all Latin lover on me?" she said with a smile.

And oh, had he gone Latin lover. She hadn't yet recovered from the sweetest, most tender, most exquisite lovemaking and he was gearing up for another round.

"You must not mock me, *querida*," he warned, both devil and desire in his voice. "The punishment will be severe if you continue to do so. In fact, I think I should give you a little taste of it now, just to keep you in line."

She loved this playful side of him. Loved that earlier

he'd spent the passion and the power of his pain pumping into her body. Loved that love did heal and that she would play no small part in his recovery.

But most of all, she loved that he loved her. Trusted her enough to let the boy in him come out and play.

She giggled, then shrieked when he pushed off the mattress, gloriously naked, 100 percent aroused. With little effort, he pinned her arms above her head and imprisoned them there with one big hand.

"Oh, please, sir." She batted her lashes—a blushing fair maiden helpless against a marauding bandito—and feigned dread. At least she tried to. No easy feat considering they were both laughing. "Show some mercy."

"I'll show you mercy," he promised, and, straddling her with his knees on either side of her hips, bent down and captured a quivering nipple in his mouth.

She sucked in her breath on a rush as sensation shot from her breast to low in her belly where it pooled between her legs like quicksilver. Hot and liquid and melting her from the inside out.

And then his hand was there. Between her legs, stroking her, teasing her, driving her over the edge of sensation.

"Sweet mercy, woman . . . the sounds you make," he murmured against her breast.

She was too caught up in pleasure to be self-conscious when he lifted his head, watched her face as his fingers finessed and pleased and had her writhing against his hand.

"Beautiful. Sexy woman. My woman," he whispered, and, releasing her hands, slid down the bed and took her in his mouth. "Come for me. Scream for me, Liliana," he demanded as he sucked and licked and drove her beyond awareness of anything but the heat of his mouth, the stroke of his tongue, and the fire he kindled and swept to flames.

"Scream for me."

She barely heard him above the roar in her ears as he drove her over the summit with a cry that made him growl deep in his throat as she dug her heels into the mattress and strained against his mouth, clinging to every last shred of sensation.

Wasted, spent, she went lax against the sheets, murmuring his name, pledging her love, as he turned her over, pulled her to her knees, and knelt behind her.

Gripping her hips, he fit himself to her swollen core and eased himself inside.

And the sensations began again.

Vital.

Intense.

Amazing.

Over and over he pounded into her, increasing the rhythm, wonderfully greedy to finally satisfy his own need and drive her wild in the process.

Just when she thought she couldn't take any more, just when she thought she would shatter from the stark, raw beauty of his total possession, he drove into her one final time. His fingers bit into her hips as he held her against him and spilled inside her.

Lost. She felt totally and irreversibly lost in him, in love with him, as, without ever leaving her body, he eased down behind her, turned her on her side, and snuggled her back against him. Beneath his sweat-drenched chest, his heart pounded heavily against her back.

Moments passed. She treasured each one. The familiar weight of him, the seductive scent of him . . . of his spent desire, his utter stillness and contentment in the aftermath of physical love.

She was responsible for that. And for that she felt

grateful. And suspended in the most amazing pocket of timeless lethargy—until his drowsy whisper shattered the moment.

"What time is Adam due back?"

Adam. Oh my God. She'd forgotten about Adam.

She shot up, checked her bedside clock, and breathed a sigh of relief.

She sank back down and snuggled into the strong arms that welcomed her. "We've got an hour."

He nuzzled her behind her ear. "Just enough time for a shower, I'm thinking."

She laughed and turned in his arms. "Shower or water sports?"

He grinned and caught her chin between his teeth. "Why don't we see what comes up?"

She knew exactly what would come up. In fact, it was already coming up and pressing prominently against her belly.

"You're going to wear me out, lover boy."

He gave her bare bottom a soft slap, then urged her out of bed. "Well, I do have that Latin lover image to uphold."

———

Forty-five minutes later, the bed was made; they were squeaky clean, dressed, and sitting on the sofa like proper, parental adults, sipping wine.

"I forgot to tell you—Kavith sends his warmest hellos."

Lily grinned. "You saw him again? How's his arm?"

Manny grunted. "His arm is fine. He's fine. Back in school and thinking of changing his major to film production. Wants to put his adventures saving the day in a movie."

"Yippee-ki-yay," she said with a grin, then sobered. "And what about Minrada? How was she doing?"

"She went through a tough time," he said, sobering, too. "But she's strong. She'll be all right. Adam really is in love with her, you know."

Yeah. She knew. Her phone bill was going to be astronomical. "Well, if it's meant to be, those feelings will still be there when Adam is old enough to know what he wants to do with the rest of his life."

Manny nodded, thoughtful. Took a sip of wine. "What will he say, do you think, when we tell him?"

Lily studied his beautiful face and dancing eyes and felt her heart dance right along with them. "Tell him what?"

"That we're getting married."

She felt her heart bump against her breastbone. Several times as his dark eyes roamed her face, serious suddenly and endearingly full of uncertainty.

"I think," she said, not mentioning the fact that he hadn't asked and she hadn't answered, "that he'll be as thrilled as I am to hear it."

He'd been holding his breath. He let it out on a long, heavy sigh. "I love you, Liliana. And more than anything in this world, I want you to be my wife."

"I know," she said simply, and snuggled back against him.

For wonderful easy moments they simply sat that way. His arm around her shoulders, his thumb absently caressing her arm.

"I thought I knew you back then," he said into the comfortable quiet. He kissed her temple. "When I wanted to believe the worst. I was so wrong. It was myself I didn't know—haven't known for all these years."

With a gentle touch, he tipped her face up to his. "I

know who I am now. Know what I want. Just like I know you now. Through the eyes of our son. Through the woman you are. I know your heart. And I know you would never have betrayed me."

He lowered his mouth and kissed her—just as the front door burst open.

"Is he still here?" Adam's voice carried into the living room, hopeful, anxious.

"I'm here," Manny said, grinning down at Lily. "And I'm going to be here for a very long time."

EPILOGUE

"You look beautiful."

"You always say that." Standing on the sidelines, Lily looped her arms around Manny's neck and swayed to the music while in the center of the dance floor Ethan and Darcy danced their first dance as husband and wife.

"That's because it's true, *mi amor.*"

Lily had to admit she felt pretty good today. Like Ethan's sister, Eve, and Darcy's sister, Della, who were also part of the wedding party, Lily wore a dress that was a deep orchid silk. The straps were thin, the hem was tea length, and there wasn't a ruffle or a flounce in sight.

A bridesmaid. Her. For a best friend.

"Here's another truth," Lily said, whispering close to his ear. "You look beautiful, too."

Hot. That's how he looked in his cutaway tux in charcoal gray. So for that matter did all of the Garrett clan, who had turned out in their finest for the eldest Garrett boy's wedding.

"Only for Ethan would I wear this monkey suit and subject myself to being called beautiful."

"Does that mean we're going to elope?"

He pulled her closer. "For you I will make another

exception. You want a big wedding, we'll have a big wedding. You want me in a tux, you got it."

It was tempting, Lily thought. But even more tempting was the thought of a quiet ceremony with only Adam and the Garretts as witnesses.

"All I want is you," she said. "And as much as I like you in that tux, Manolo, I can't wait to get you out of it."

He grinned down at her. "Who's going to wear who out?" he teased, reminding her that she'd accused him of the very same thing.

Feeling very much in love and very loved, Lily toyed with the notion of pinching herself. Sometimes it just didn't seem real. Here she was. With this amazing man who cherished her. Adam was the most incredible child a woman could ask for. She was surrounded by new friends and about to embark on yet another exciting change of career. She was going back to school. Getting her P.A. credentials. Something she'd always wanted to do—for herself, not for her parents.

"You're still okay with the move?"

She loved that Manny was so in tune with her thoughts. "I'm more than okay. And Adam is over the moon. He loves the idea of moving to West Palm Beach."

"And maybe the fact that Minrada plans to attend the U of Florida starting winter semester?"

"Umm, yah. There's that. He's growing up. Way too fast," she added, feeling melancholy all of a sudden. "Look at him over there, hanging with the big boys."

The big boys being Nolan Garrett and Jase Wilson. Jason was another key member of the E.D.E.N. team that Manny had joined in September. The three of them had their heads together by the bar in the corner of the room. Adam was eating it up with a spoon.

"And he's more than bonkers over Janey," Manny added.

"So am I," Lily admitted. Sweet Baby Jane Perkins, also known as Mrs. Jason Wilson, was one of the biggest names in the music business. "She's very nice. And she's been so generous with her time with Adam."

Everyone had been wonderful—including the Kincaids, whom Lily had finally had the chance to meet and thank for their part in financing Adam's rescue.

"And Jillian," she added, referring to Nolan's beautiful wife, the Kincaids' daughter and a local TV personality. "She's gorgeous. Nolan dotes on her and the baby. I wonder what their story is," she mused aloud.

"One for the books." Manny looked thoughtful. "Someday I'll tell you about it."

"Can I have everyone's attention please?"

Lily looked toward the center of the room where Eve—blond, beautiful, and, from all accounts, able to more than pull her weight with her brothers in the family firm—had commandeered the mike.

"What's she got in her hand?"

"Oh, boy," Manny said when he realized what Eve was holding. He grinned, shook his head. "Here it comes."

"Here what comes?"

"The challenge. Just wait."

"First," Eve said, when the room had quieted down, "on behalf of the entire family, welcome, Darcy. Welcome home."

A round of applause broke out across the room.

Eve raised her hands, signaling for silence.

"Make him happy," she said with a warm smile, "but keep him in line, okay? You can use this if you have to."

The entire room broke into laughter.

Lily strained to see. "Is that a croquet mallet?"

"Yup."

"And now, ladies and gentlemen," Eve said with a huge grin, "game on."

"They're going to play croquet?" Lily asked as they followed the bride and groom and the rest of the Garrett clan—Wes and Susan Garrett, the proud parents of the groom, included—outside onto the terrace lawn where a croquet course had been set up.

"They're going to play croquet," Manny confirmed, and snagged him and Lily each a glass of champagne from a passing waiter.

"I'm missing something, right?"

"Not for long, I'm thinking."

Manny was right. Before long, Eve, accompanied by her hunky hubby, "Mac," ferreted them out and dragged them out to join the rest of the wedding party in a game of cutthroat croquet.

Lily laughed when Nolan sent her ball sailing off the course. "Hey," she groused. "I thought this was a gentleman's game."

"Sorry, Lily." Nolan leaned down and kissed her on the cheek. "White gloves are off when the Garretts play the game. This is serious shit."

"All right, Garrett," she said in her best tough-cookie voice. "You wanna play rough? I'll show you rough."

Beside her, Manny laughed. "God, I love it when you talk butch."

"Out of my way, Rambo," she warned, retrieving her ball and lining it up opposite Manny's. "I'm about to get serious."

"I *like* her," Eve said, her eyes dancing. "The woman understands the sanctity of the mallet."

"The woman," Manny said, pulling Lily close and kissing her after she'd set his ball way, way off the course, "is pushing her luck."

"What? You going to punish me, Ortega?" she whispered against his mouth.

"Oh yeah. You're in trouble now. I've got a special kind of punishment in mind for you."

She grinned. "I can hardly wait."

"Do you suppose they'd miss us if we just sort of slipped out of here?"

She loved how his eyes grew dark. "Unfortunately, I think they would. How about we make a date for later tonight?"

"I've waited half my life for you, *mi amor* . . . I guess I can wait another few hours."

"Um . . . Excuse me. You two do know that you're holding up the game?"

Lily grinned over her shoulder to see Nolan patiently waiting for them to move out of his line of fire.

"You gonna make something of it, Garrett?" Manny's gaze never left Lily's face.

"Nope. Not me. But it looks like you are."

"Yeah," Manny said, and smiled into Lily's eyes. "I'm going to make something of it. I'm going to make you happy, *querida*. Count on it."

She did. She would. For the rest of her life.

Midnight

It had been a long, long time since he'd gotten piss-faced, pie-eyed, fall-on-his-ass drunk. Dallas had decided early on that this would be the night he'd break the fast.

What better reason to tie one on than his big brother's wedding? It was a celebration, right? *Damn straight,* Dallas told himself, lifted his glass of scotch, and found nothing but ice.

"Screw it," he muttered, and rose from the table in the far corner of the room where he'd settled in to watch the festivities in peace. He needed to get some air.

He was happy for his brother. For both of his brothers and his sister. For his brother in spirit, Manny Ortega. Hell. They were all paired up. All tied up neat and tidy to the women of their dreams. Even Wilson had found himself a girl.

Good for them, Dallas thought, and wandered outside onto the terrace. It was cool outside. The moon was high. The scent of the ocean hung like a salt bath in the air.

Yeah, good for them.

"Dallas?"

Dallas turned. Saw his old man standing there.

"You okay, bud?"

Dallas nodded. "Just getting some air."

Wes Garrett joined him under the moon. "Some party, huh?"

Dallas grunted in affirmation. Stared into the night.

"Something bothering you, son? You've been awfully quiet lately."

Dallas turned, looked at his father. "Mom send you out here on a seek-and-discover mission?"

Wes grinned. "You know your mother. She's worried about you," he said after a long moment. "Does she have a reason to be?"

Okay, Dallas had figured this was coming. He'd seen

the concerned looks on his mother's face. The gentle smiles that subtly probed.

"How'd you know that Mom was the one?"

And where in the hell had that come from? The booze, Dallas decided, and thought, *What the hell. How had he known?*

"You just know," Wes said with a shrug. "When you think about her all the time, want to be with her all the time, know you'd put your life on the line for her . . . well, you know she's the one."

Dallas nodded. His dad's answer made him want to march back inside and renew his mission of getting falling-down drunk.

"I'd better go back inside," his dad said. "You coming?"

Dallas nodded. Forced a tight smile. "You go on ahead. I'll be there in a little bit."

But another half an hour passed while he stood there . . .

Thinking of Amy Walker, like he thought of her all the time.

Wanting to be with her. Hell, it seemed like he'd been wanting her all of his life.

Knowing he'd put his life on the line for her again. Wondering if it would someday come to that.

He stared at the black canvas of sky. Amy was out there somewhere. Amy—who had the ability to mess up his neat and tidy life the way a frag grenade could mess up a helluva lot of terra firma.

He felt anger suddenly.

Where the hell was she?

Was she safe? Was she whole?

Was she missing him?

Did she have any idea that she'd messed up his life by the very fact of her absence from it?

He dragged a hand over his face. Heaved a weary breath.

And headed back inside. Where, he promised himself, he'd get with the program this time and drink himself blind.

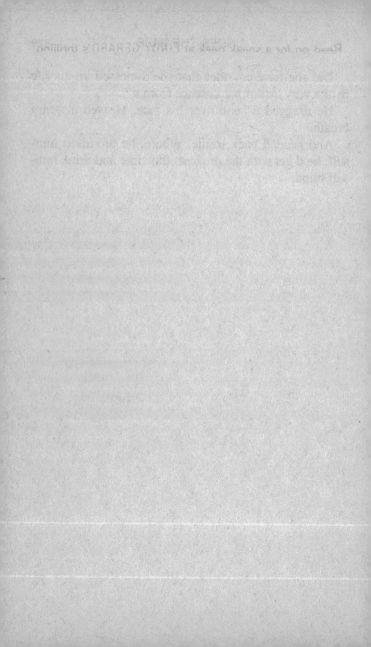

Read on for a sneak peek at CINDY GERARD's thrilling
next novel in the Bodyguards series,

INTO THE DARK

Coming June 2007 from St. Martin's Paperbacks

West Palm Beach, Florida

"So, what brought this on?"

Dallas didn't so much as glance at his brother, who stood in Dallas's open bedroom doorway, a root beer in hand, a dark scowl on his face.

"What? I'm not entitled to a vacation?" A man on a mission, Dallas continued rifling through his bureau drawer, ignoring Nolan's long-suffering breath. "E.D.E.N. can get along without me for a few days. You three over-achievers can handle things," he pointed out, referring to his siblings, who were all partners in the security firm their old man had turned over to them several years ago. "And with Jase and Manny on board now, you've got plenty of bodies to fill the holes," he added, reminding Nolan that E.D.E.N. was at full force with the addition of Jase Wilson and Manny Ortega, two ex–special ops brothers in arms who'd recently joined the company. "Perfect time for me to take a break from bullets and bad guys."

Without warning, a vivid assault of memory hit him like a gut punch.

Dead.

Ski. Gates. Rodriguez. Stover. They were all dead or dying.

He sucked in air. Stalked across the carpeted floor.

But he couldn't move fast enough to outrun the seven-year-old memories.

The stench of burning flesh seared his nostrils. The sick, sweet scent of blood and gore suffocated him. And the sounds. Jesus. Terrified cries of pain from both men and horses.

When he came to, the ground was grave cold and running with blood, rubble and snow. Dead ahead . . . aww, God. Pain throbbing through his entire body, he clawed his way to Gates's mangled corpse. The corporal's eyes were vacant, unfocused as he lay sprawled in the debris, half of his face shot off. Twenty-three years old. His mother would never see him whole again.

Dallas swallowed hard. Shook his head. Cleared his vision.

Seven years. Seven fucking years and the images he thought he'd buried with his men were once again rising up out of the mucky swamp of his memory, sucking at his soul like leeches.

Never was a good time to relive this shit. So why the hell was this happening again? Why was it happening now?

"Bro?"

Dallas straightened. Wiped a shaking hand over his face and snapped at Nolan, "What!"

Brows knit, Nolan pushed away from the doorframe where, until now, he'd been attempting to look nonchalant. "What the hell is wrong with you? You're either sniping like a great white or as silent and stoic as a monk."

Dallas grunted and tossed several pairs of socks into the duffel that lay open on his bed. His brother was spot-on right. And he was sorry about that. Just not sorry enough to muster the will to do anything about it. Except give Nolan a break and get out of his face for a while. "So I'd think you'd be glad to get rid of me."

"Talk to me." Concern knocked the edge off the ex-Ranger's command.

Talk to him? Christ. Dallas had made that mistake once already. Two weeks ago. The night their oldest brother, Ethan, had remarried Darcy Prescott.

Dallas had been shit-faced drunk—not his usual MO—and lightweight that he was, he'd spilled his candy-ass guts. Cried to Nolan about the recent recurrences of the flashbacks, the night sweats, the black holes that had become a part of his life again. Nolan had wanted to play touchy-feely ever since.

"You know, the VA has head men who specialize in—"
Fuck.

"Don't even go there." Dallas cut Nolan off with a dark look. He was a Marine. Okay, ex-Marine. For over five years now. Still, the Marine doctrine was forever ingrained in his DNA. And it was pig simple: Solve your problems, live with them, or shut the fuck up. He wasn't about to flop down on a cushy couch in some psycho-babbling little cucumber's office and puke out his inner demons. "Philosophy" battalion in the mosquito-infested swamps of South Carolina had made certain of that. The head "philosopher's"—AKA, the drill sergeant's—therapy of choice had been to apply a size-thirteen boot directly to the ass whenever the urge to whine came over a raw recruit. Effective as hell.

"Have you thought about looking for her?"
Double fuck.

He'd forgotten. He'd spilled the beans about Amy Walker that same night. Boo-hooed about the fact that he hadn't been able to stop thinking about the woman he'd helped escape from that clew of Abu Sayyaf terrorist worms with Ethan, Nolan and Manny when they'd staged an unsanctioned, civilian op to rescue Darcy from Jolo Island six months ago.

Amy had endured more degradation and torture than any human being should be expected to bear. She'd survived because of her strong spirit and guts. But she would carry the scars—both physical and emotional—for the rest of her life.

He respected her. Admired her. Cared about her. Wanted her.

Yet even though he'd suspected that she was planning to disappear from his life shortly after they'd returned to the States, he'd let her go. Because he'd known. Alone, they might have a chance. Together, their excess baggage would break an elephant's back.

"Or is that what this sudden trip is really about?" Nolan crossed the room. Dallas watched his brother set his root beer bottle on the bedside table, then lay back on the bed and get comfy, crossing his arms behind his head. "You finally going after her?"

"That's going to leave a ring." Dallas evaded the question by glaring toward the sweating bottle.

Just like he'd been evading thinking about the probability that the ground assault they'd launched getting Darcy and Amy out of the terrorist hellhole had been the catalyst for the resurgence of his PTSD. Post-Traumatic Stress Disorder. Long convoluted term. Shrinks preferred it to "fucked-up in the head." Go figure.

"Anal to the bone," Nolan grumbled after a long, silent stare and grudgingly moved the bottle onto a coaster. "Did you ever think that might be part of your problem?"

"No, but I've been thinking that *you* are. Don't you

have a wife and a baby to go home to and harass?"

"You know," Nolan said, purposely ignoring Dallas's hint to leave him the hell alone, "I remember a day, not so many moons ago, when you and Ethan invaded my inner sanctum and dragged my sorry hide out of a perfectly good drunken stupor."

"Too drunk to remember that Ethan came alone. If I'd been along—"

"Oh, right," Nolan interrupted with a tight grin. "You weren't with him. Guess I *was* drunk."

"Well, I'm not, so bugger off."

According to Ethan, Nolan had been close to the edge that day, Dallas reflected. Beyond just drunk, deep in denial and ready to piss his life down the toilet. His little brother had DX'd out of the Rangers three months earlier, was laying a lot of blame on his big bad self for a buddy's suicide, and Dallas and Ethan had decided Nolan needed something to live for.

Joining E.D.E.N., Inc., as a securities specialist and protecting TV anchorwoman Jillian Kincaid from a crazed stalker had started out as a job. A means to bring Nolan back among the functional. Who knew he'd not only straighten up and fly right, he'd end up marrying his client, the daughter of one of the fattest cats in the publishing business?

"Okay. So drinking's not your problem—or your forte," Nolan added, dragging Dallas's attention back to the immovable object currently stretched out on his bed, "but you're about a pin pull away from going off like a frag grenade."

Dallas worked his jaw. One thing about brothers. They understood things. Nolan wasn't going to let up.

"I'll handle it," he said, because he knew that Nolan

was worried about him. "I'll handle it," he repeated with a grim nod when his brother's expression relayed only skepticism. "I just need a little space, okay?"

Nolan studied him long and hard. "Give me more than crumbs here, D. You know I have to report back to the troops."

The "troops," Dallas knew, consisted of their mom and dad; Ethan and Darcy; their sister, Eve; her husband, Mac; and Nolan's wife, Jillian. And he'd already figured out that they'd sent Nolan here to get the goods on the only Garrett who had broken Army tradition and joined the Marines—a choice that had always made his sanity suspect in their eyes.

"Do *not* sic Eve on me," he warned, figuring that would be the next move.

Nolan's twin sister was five feet two inches of blond hair, blue eyes and TNT. Eve loved hard, cared hard and wouldn't think twice about pinning him to the wall if she thought she could protect him by doing so. The best thing that had ever happened to that woman was marrying Tyler "Mac" McClain. Mac gave back as good as Eve dished out, didn't take any of her lip and, Dallas was relieved to know, was crazy in love with her.

"Give me a reason not to send her over. Tell me where you're going."

That was the hell of it. Dallas didn't know. He didn't know squat—except that he needed distance. The concerned looks were wearing on him. The worry that creased his mother's brow fueled his guilt.

"Fishing," he said, making it up on the fly. "I'm going fishing, okay? With some buddies from my old unit."

He'd go to hell for lying but since odds were he was

heading there anyway, one more sin against mankind wouldn't make a difference.

"So when do you leave?" Nolan clearly wasn't taking the bait and was doing a little fishing of his own trying to catch Dallas in a lie.

"In the morning. Early flight to the gulf. I'll see you in a couple of weeks. Happy now? Good. Now get the hell out so I can finish packing."

Dragging a hand over dark hair that was badly in need of a cut, he strode out of the bedroom toward his condo's front door, swung it open and waited for his brother to follow. The sultry heat of the Florida night slogged into the room in thick, heavy drifts. A sky that had been threatening rain all day finally let go with a burst of fat drops as he stood there. Needing to be alone.

After what seemed like a decade, Nolan finally sauntered toward him. Hands tucked in his hip pockets, he stopped about a foot away. Though Nolan was the youngest of the three brothers, he stood within an inch of Dallas's six feet one inch frame, carried his weight in the same lean, rangy build, and stared at him through the same intense blue eyes.

"If your ass isn't straightened out when you get back—"

"Yeah, yeah, I know," Dallas interrupted. "You're gonna introduce it to my shoulder blades."

"Damn straight."

And then Nolan did the damnedest thing. This ex–special ops soldier who was now a full partner with Ethan, Dallas and Eve at E.D.E.N. Securities, Inc., this hard-as-steel warrior who took no prisoners and cut no slack, grabbed him in a bear hug and squeezed until Dallas's ribs cracked.

"Take care, man," Nolan said and let him go. Without a backward glance, he walked out the door and into the rain.

Thank God.

Thank Jesus God.

Because if his little brother had taken the time to look Dallas in the eyes, he would have seen they were wet. And that was one humiliation Dallas positively could not bear.

———

Dallas was dry-eyed and hard-faced when he heard the knock on his door five minutes later.

Eve, he thought with a sick knot in his gut. The little bastard had gone straight to Eve—and she'd be on him like a pit bull after a T-bone until she got some answers.

Muttering under his breath, he stomped to the door and swung it open, determined to nip this little inquisition in the bud.

Only it wasn't his sister standing there, drenched to the bone as rain came down like buckshot.

His heart cracked him sledgehammer hard, dead center in the middle of his chest as he stared into the face of a woman he'd seen for the first time six months ago in the fetid jungles of Jolo.

Amy Walker.

Soaking wet.

Sodden blond hair hanging in her face.

Cornflower blue eyes speaking to him without her uttering a word.

Sweet Jesus Christ.

He'd thought of her, dreamed of her, worried for her, even cursed her for messing with his head after she'd disappeared. But he'd never planned on seeing her again.

Too much baggage.

Too many problems.

Too much work, he'd told himself over and over again.

Told himself now.

All of that flew out the window when she took a halting step toward him and collapsed into his arms.